When All Things Were New

C. HADLEY EASLEY

CROSSBOOKS
PUBLISHING

CrossBooks™
A Division of LifeWay
1663 Liberty Drive
Bloomington, IN 47403
www.crossbooks.com
Phone: 1-866-879-0502

First published by CrossBooks 05/22/2013

ISBN: 978-1-4627-2689-9 (sc)
ISBN: 978-1-4627-2690-5 (e)

Printed in the United States of America.

This book is printed on acid-free paper.

Table of Contents

Introduction

My name is Adam. I have no last name, as they were not needed in my day. I will be relating this history with the benefit of hindsight—and I possess that in abundance. Many years after my creation, with God's guidance, Moses wrote a more-to-the-point account.

Although my present and eternal home is now in heaven, God permits me to look upon the earth and observe the activity of mankind; not that I am the only one who has this right. It is just that most souls, once they are permitted entrance and become accustomed to perfection, find it somewhat disturbing to view for any length of time the troubles and unrest at their former homes. So they take an occasional peek at the business of their children and grandchildren, and after a glimpse or two, focus back on the peace and beauty of their new life and trust in the Lord to hold things together in the life below.

Things are different with me. There is a feeling that continually clings deep inside that mans' sorrowful condition is, initially at least, due to my failure. Thankfully, forgiveness was granted to me long, long ago. Many have kindly expressed the notion that Satan would have eventually defeated someone else (add to that the fact that God already had a plan in place just for a case like mine), but that is not really comforting. So, as I observe the violence on Earth, feelings of guilt still plague me from time to time. Wonderfully so, God comforts and encourages me to forget the mortal and enjoy my citizenry in the splendid surroundings of this eternal. Still, I cannot escape the thought that my weakness caused all this unrest; so I am compelled to observe even though it makes no difference and not much sense. I look forward to the Day that will end all reproach, but until then, I want to speak to you, the reader, of the events that led to conditions as they are now.

The Creation

You probably know some general information about me, but not a solitary soul living on the earth really knows me. I am one of only two people who remember their first day of existence—and remember it in detail! My Creator molded me from the dust of the earth and breathed life into my body of clay. I was His crowning achievement, precisely fashioned in His image with all the tender touch deemed necessary for the first-born of the human race. There was no time spent in infancy or childhood; my first moment was as a strong, healthy, adult male. And I gazed in wide-eyed wonder at a brand new world, complete with sun, sky, mountains, rivers, trees, soil, plants, and a vast array of animals to serve as companions.

God was very pleased with me, and He joyfully pointed out His handiwork one masterpiece after another; the whole experience being absolutely overwhelming.

As soon as the feelings inside me began to calm, speech came forth from my lips, and question upon question using words that no one taught me flowed freely. The questions were just what one would expect, such as: Where am I? How did I get here? What is my purpose here? Who made all this? Who are You?

He patiently answered most of my queries and in such a way as to make plain the complicated. However, some questions He did not answer, telling me that it was beyond my understanding or not for me to know.

He told me that I was the most precious of all the creatures on this earth and that He formed me in His image from the dust. My reasons for existence were to worship, respect, and love Him; to enjoy the gift of life, and to tend the Garden.

But . . . before beginning any labor in this Garden, there was still some work to do concerning the sixth day of creation. God brought the animals to me for the purpose of naming them. The gift of speech that He gave me was delightfully advanced and names rolled off my tongue with ease. And my memory was such that I did not forget what I dubbed them. Thankfully, I did not have to be very specific at this time because that would have taken much too much time, especially with insects. I mean, for the most part, anything that had six legs or more and crawled on the ground was just an insect. A little more time was devoted to the four-legged creatures and birds. Later in the day, after the last title was dispensed, I was struck by the fact that the animals had many of their own kind for companions, where I had none. I was too new to really understand about feelings and emotions, but there was discomfort inside me, an emptiness that stole the peace from me.

God sensed it and caused me to sleep—a deep sleep—and while I was unaware, He used one of my ribs to form another like me. By using a part of my body, this new person would, in a sense, owe their existence to me. And the rib, being near the heart, would make for a special bond. Upon awakening, my eyes beheld a most lovely sight! She was the very last of all creation and God truly outdid Himself. In general, she was like me, but there were some major physical differences; and though these differences were beyond my understanding there was no disappointment whatsoever and I was truly convinced of God's infallibility.

She had reddish-brown hair, where mine was dark. Her skin had a softer look, lighter complexioned with some freckles on her nose and cheeks. Her eyes were the color of the sky, maybe a little darker. Her nose was somewhat long, but straight. She smiled at me evidently recognizing the approval that shone out from my eyes (telling me that it might be difficult to keep some thoughts to myself). Her figure was trim and well-rounded, much in contrast to my more angular, muscular build. There was no other person on the earth with whom to compare her, but had she been a flower surely the bees would have chosen her over all the others.

He gave the woman to me as my wife in the first marriage and commanded us to be fruitful and multiply. Then, for reasons unknown, kept us from following that command for what seemed to me a very long time. Still, we had the first "birds and bees" discussion, and later, although things were at first a little awkward, Eve and I were of the mind that if there was anything better than this, God saved it for Himself!

Responsibilities

T he land all around as far as the eye could see was called Eden, and we were placed in the Garden of Eden. It was the most beautiful scene imaginable with its lush foliage, flowers of every color, all manner of fruit trees and vegetables, and it was to be our responsibility to tend this sizable plot of perfection. Since there were no weeds at this point, the work was not only simple, it was a joy. Occasionally, we did some watering, thinning, and light pruning (much of that for our own amusement as the plants were not in dire need of it); at other times there was food to gather. Probably the most important of my duties was to make certain that the animals did not congregate for any length of time in the Garden, crushing the plants, making too much noise, and causing an unpleasant odor. God enjoyed walking in that area from time to time and I wanted to make certain that He did not step in anything.

There was one other responsibility: Neither of us was to eat the fruit from the tree of the knowledge of good and evil. In fact, God sternly warned us to avoid that area of the Garden, saying that disobedience would result in death. The concept of death was difficult to comprehend because I had never seen anything die, but I was gaining in my understanding of emotions, and there was a feeling of fear stemming from this warning.

He told me that the woman lacked my inner strength and that it was up to me to watch over her and care for her. The sense of concern in His admonition left me to wonder what He knew that I did not.

Though my wife seemed to have *some* understanding of the gravity in these words of caution, she often was distracted in our daily life, especially by pretty and colorful objects, (and there was much to see and admire) so the desire to protect her was firmly impressed upon my mind and heart.

There was one creature in the Garden that, ever-increasingly, began to be viewed in a suspicious light by God, and to the point that I was advised to be wary of the serpent. This was truly beyond my grasp since all the creatures, up to this point, were our friends. So now there were two things with which to be concerned.

The serpent appeared to prefer his own company and usually stayed far away from us. He was rather handsome in his own way, this serpent, with colorful designs that covered his body. Unlike many of the animals, he had only two legs, and walked with his head held high in a manner that seemed to say, "Do not touch me!" All the other creatures loved having their heads rubbed and ears scratched, but I sensed that this fellow wanted no part of physical contact.

This new-found uneasiness concerning one of the citizens of Eden, again, left me somewhat puzzled, but something told me to be especially watchful if the woman and the serpent had any association whatsoever. But that did not appear likely with his aura of superiority and apparent desire to remain aloof.

The Master Plan

Revelation 12:7-8: And there was war in heaven, Michael and his angels waging war with the dragon. The dragon and his angels waged war, and they were not strong enough, and there was no longer a place found for them in heaven.

The establishment of the universe and everything within it did not happen with just a spur-of-the-moment, wild notion by the Creator. There was much in the way of planning, with every possible detail worked out in advance by the Father and Those closest to Him. In the course of time, some of these plans were openly discussed with certain members of the angel hierarchy. Michael and Gabriel, who were usually supportive of God's ideas, had some slight misgivings at first, but they fully trusted God and after some explanation, were steadfastly behind it. Lucifer, on the other hand, was adamantly against it from the start, especially concerning the creation of man. He was told that there would be times when all the angels would be required to serve men in hours of need, and that included him. Lucifer had always been an angel of high rank and was well thought of by many, and quite influential.

During a lengthy meeting with God, his initial words of debate were respectful, though strained, then after a time he nearly snapped: "This business of creation . . . is it not . . . somewhat misguided? Is not our heavenly home glory enough, Your Majesty? The surroundings here are beyond description, and our life here is wonderful as it is, so why create what looks to be an inferior existence with weakling men to rule over it?"

God patiently replied, "I am a being, self-endowed with an infinite capacity to love, and it is My desire, after much thought and careful planning, to create this race of men for My own reasons."

"Such as!" spouted Lucifer in a tone that bordered on insolence.

"Though I have never had to explain my actions and decisions to you or anyone else, never the less, I will answer this time: It's from My desire to display loving kindness, and a longing to receive glory, honor, and praise—and to receive all of that from innocent, child-like beings who have little understanding of the complexities of this new world and little desire to be familiar with the methods employed to bring it about."

"This will be a mistake! You will see!"

"That is enough! You seem to have forgotten your place, Lucifer. You, also, were created for the purpose of bringing Me glory, honor, and praise—along with all the angels. I have given you considerable power, rivaled only by Michael and Gabriel; but it seems the more you receive, the less you appreciate. I will say no more to you on this occasion."

Lucifer knew when it was time to hold his tongue. He, in the past, had gotten away with minor disagreement, but this time he had crossed over into disrespect, and he knew it. Although he was aware that there was a price to be paid for impertinence, he seemed to derive a certain amount of pleasure from this latest dispute. Could it be that he no longer feared God as in times past?

The more he thought about having to serve anyone, especially men, the more that hatred and bitterness welled up inside; and those forces drove him to consider acts that should have been recognized as pure folly. He knew that God would begin this major undertaking soon, and Lucifer knew that for the first time since his creation, God would leave the kingdom of Heaven for a period of time that was described as a week. (Angels were not totally familiar with the terms "days" and "weeks" but they soon became more knowledgeable.) A plan began to take shape in the prideful, ever-increasingly demented mind of this celestial schemer.

When the Cat's Away...

It was time to embark on the project to end all projects, and even God, Who seldom displayed enthusiasm, seemed to relish the thought of constructing an entire universe designed by Him and for Him. And so it began—He was gone and Heaven was left in the capable, trustworthy hands of Michael, the arch-angel.

Lucifer wasted no time in stirring up trouble within the ranks. He lobbied and campaigned to those angels who most respected him. Never before had they considered rebellion against God, but Lucifer was more than persuasive and he seemed to gain in strength and charisma with every mutinous word. Soon, a number of angels were sold on the idea that God had made a mistake and surely had not given enough thought to this venture; and after listening to many words of negativism, especially concerning the race of men, it was decided that they would do everything within their power to foul God's plan of creation. Now, with their new king going before them, they were incited to challenge all who were in opposition, even if it meant a war with Michael and their brethren angels.

The word spread and quickly reached Michael and Gabriel. No reckless, foolhardy deed such as this had ever before been entertained, certainly not in the minds of the God-fearing inhabitants of Heaven, and they were, at first, somewhat uncertain as to what plan of action was most fitting. Michael had been put in charge and hated the thought of mutiny and open rebellion taking place on his watch. God had always been in charge and seldom was there a dispute of any kind, but now, it all fell on the second-in-command.

Dialogue and diplomacy seemed the way to go initially. After all, they were brothers and all-out war was the last resort. Lucifer and his supporters (about one-third of the population) marched forward until they were face to face with Michael and those who had elected to remain true to God.

The rebels and their leader wasted no time in attempting to pressure the majority into following or surrendering. Venomous words spewed forth from the mouth of Lucifer, making it clear that he had no thoughts of reconciliation. And with arrogance and aggressiveness unbefitting one of his position and rank, he announced his terms: "The Master has not given this matter the proper consideration. Our counsel, worth a great deal in my estimation, was not sought at length. Michael, surely you, as arch-angel in charge, can see that a change of plans is essential! Has not God created within us an ability to make thoughtful and reasoned decisions! Who even knows if God will return to our kingdom here? He has developed a love for this work of creation and may decide to make it His new kingdom, with His beloved race of men to do His bidding! I say that we claim Heaven for our very own and let God keep His newly created world and all that is in it! What say you? You are either with us or against us!"

As the followers of Lucifer cheered, Michael knew that there was no longer the possibility of diplomacy or any sound reasoning. One-third of his brethren had thrown in their lot with a created being—powerful yes, but infinitely weaker than the Creator. Sensing their mindset and knowing that, as the one put in charge, he needed to straightway display strength, he exhorted those still true to God: "Do not even consider such a foolish notion! Were we to unite in a force thousands of times the size of this one, we would stand absolutely no chance against God's power and wrath! But more importantly, He has always been a kind and wise ruler, Whose every decision has proven perfect in the past and will be proven the same in the future. How could we possibly give thought to rebellion against He who has given us such flawless guidance and boundless favor! Give no further heed to Lucifer's folly!"

Michael's words were persuasive and just what was needed to return stability and common sense to the majority. Seeing that he was outnumbered two to one, Lucifer, blinded with rage and arrogance, was still of the mind that his power alone was enough to overcome the arch-angel and the remainder of God's Holy angels. He shouted, "Then you are against us! Prepare yourselves for war!"

The battle began and it was unlike anything ever before witnessed in Heaven. The magnitude of power that was unleashed in the form of lightning bolts was on a level similar to God's creation of a new mountain, with tremors that caused Heavenly ground to quake. There was such a display that God saw and heard from the newly-created earth. Certainly this was a concern, but possessing the quality of omniscience, He fully trusted in Michael and remained focused on the task at hand.

The battle up above continued for some time and hand to hand combat eventually replaced all other forms of warfare. The conflict was fierce beyond imagination with tremendous expenditures of force and energy. It was amazing that even angelic bodies could absorb such violence. Angels, being immortal, cannot destroy one another, but the stronger can subdue and imprison the weaker, as would soon be the case here.

Finally, Lucifer and his angels were overpowered and captured. Lucifer was the last to be overcome and Michael delivered the finishing blow. There appeared to be no suitable place to hold them for any length of time, so the victors debated on the best course of action. All were in agreement that there was no longer a place in Heaven for these traitors. They could not be trusted, so a decision was made (before the enemy could regain their strength) to hurl them all down to the earth and let God do whatever seemed best to Him. The Precipice of Limitless Descent was the only site in all of Heaven where such an action could take place.

The Purging and New Surroundings

Revelation 12:9 And the great dragon was thrown down, the serpent of old who is called the devil and Satan, who deceives the whole world; he was thrown down to the earth, and his angels were thrown down with him.

Lucifer was the first to be forever banished and although he was weary from battle, he did not go without a struggle; but Michael, with all the angelic power he could muster, cast his former colleague towards the earth. The force necessary for this act left a trail of bright light from the Precipice to the earth. It took much time and effort by the faithful, but eventually all those who rebelled were cast down with their leader. Heaven was once again a place of purity, but woe to the earth.

God knew what had happened and was present at their materialization in Eden. He warned these unwelcome guests that punishment would be a certainty at a later time; but for now, the work of creation was still ongoing. At this point God departed, leaving the fallen angels to brood over their present and dread their future.

Regret was not totally absent from this band of mutineers, but Lucifer quickly reasserted himself as their superior and made certain that they surrendered any notions of seeking mercy on bended knee. He lectured: "Some of you, having had time to reflect, are now having second thoughts—this will never do. Do not grovel at the feet of God! If He forgave you at all, remember that you would forever be the lowest of servants—and to the race of men! Better to suffer punishment as warriors than to escape it and exist in a world where our former prestige will never again be mentioned or even remembered. And have you forgotten that our one-time brothers turned on us without as much as a moment of proper discussion about our wishes? No, we will not return only to have the likes of them wield authority over us. Let us take our chances here—though it is a place unworthy of our presence."

Lucifer's little speech had the desired effect. His followers were further hardened, and their minds became more comfortable with the thought of continued rebellion.

God was in the middle of the all-important sixth day when His monumental and painstaking task was interrupted; later in the day, He finished with the making of the man and all the details surrounding that event, then, lastly, He created woman. That now completed, it was time for a conference with the disobedient. They were very much afraid—though they tried to veil it—at the appearance of their true King; even Lucifer felt a lack of confidence as he wondered about his punishment. But he had hardened himself to the point that his respect for and fear of God was not as in the past. Still, even though his prideful mind was now somewhat removed from sound reason, he knew that there was no place for them to hide and no way of escape. How sad to think that this being once had feelings of deep respect and admiration for the Creator.

Understand that . . . none of the angels were what one might describe as ugly, but Lucifer was given finely-carved facial features and muscular wings and arms. He was quite probably the most handsome of the lot, and this made for feelings of pride as though he was responsible for his appearance. And later, after receiving much in the way of power, authority, and prestige, a gradual spiritual decline began to lead to intensifying feelings of greed and jealousy. Only Michael and Gabriel were equal to him in rank and power, but he wanted to be above all of them. He wanted to rule at God's right hand, but his great ambition had caused him to overreach and now he would pay the price.

God approached them, and His gaze was enough to cause trembling and make weak even their strongest member. His voice thundered: "I want to hear it from your own lips! What did you do?" Under the severity of the situation their thinking became muddled and they began to make excuses. Many of them lied for the first time in their existence and God was not slow to point out each falsehood. He knew that, at first, Lucifer had led them astray, but ultimately each was responsible for his own disobedience—initially rebellion, and now, deceit and outright lying.

God decided to allow more time before rendering a decision concerning the future of this great body of unfaithful servants. He knew what had happened, but Michael and Gabriel needed to be heard on the matter. His wrath somewhat restrained for the moment, He announced: "You will remain here on Earth for a while . . . until I have ruled on your fate. I would strongly advise against displeasuring Me further. Stay away from the Garden—and especially the man and woman! Maybe it will be good for you to spend some time in reflection concerning your grievous wrongs." God returned to Heaven at this point, leaving the fallen to stew for a good while.

"Well now, that was not so terrible . . . was it?" said Lucifer with a regained coolness that sprang from his ever-darkening soul. Though the others had been filled with terror, they seemed to take courage in the charisma that emanated from every fiber of his being. And so they were led even further astray—perilously close to the point of no return.

These new surroundings were definitely not streets of gold, but there was a splendor that could not be denied. Crystal-clear streams, flowers, distant mountains—even Lucifer grudgingly agreed to some magnificence in this new world. The thought of reigning over this land, especially the Garden and all who were in it, began to form in his mind; but how would it be possible? Even he, blinded by ambition, still knew that God was all-powerful . . . but maybe he could win the minds and hearts of the man and woman and thereby defile God's crowning achievement. It would be a defeat of sorts, possibly forcing Him to hand over Eden and the two humans as a concession. So, if this jewel was to lose its luster, God might be willing to relinquish it as an act of adversarial fairness. Hmmm . . . only a few moments after God's sternest of warnings, the mental wheels began to turn and Lucifer pondered ways to claim Earth for his very own.

Patience and Planning

The days passed and the fallen ones roamed over their current setting, bitterly accepting this comparatively dull existence. As warned, they avoided the Garden and its inhabitants, that is, all but their self-appointed captain; of course, they were all privy to his latest act of disobedience and wholeheartedly supported him in it.

Exercising one of his most vital strengths, patience, Lucifer daily drew closer and closer to the Garden. He was quite cautious at first, not wanting to be seen by God or man, but growing bolder by the day he finally reached the perimeter, where he caught his first glimpse of the ones "responsible" for his sufferings. "It would have to be at a time when the Creator was there," he thought to himself as he peered through some thick vegetation.

God, not by chance, walked in the Garden and visited with Eve and me on this particular day. Lucifer remained hidden (or so he thought) at all times, not wanting to risk being seen. The ensuing days saw him reach vantage points of close proximity, where he diligently observed human activity and locked into his mind anything that might be considered a deficiency or flaw, other than our obvious physical limitations. He noticed that I held great affection for the woman; and she was attracted to the pretty colors of flowers and such. He saw that I was the stronger and thereby Eve's protector, but he took notice of my weakness concerning her desires. Little things that did not seem like much to the untrained eye, presented Lucifer with a future stockpile of information.

After much surveillance and gathering of minor details, he finally witnessed what looked to be a major breakthrough. The creature known as the serpent, seemed to exhibit an intelligence (and arrogance) far surpassing all other animals. Lucifer was particularly charmed by its evident disdain of man. It was brightly colored and Eve was quite attracted to it, but I was careful to keep her from this creature. Later on, as the daily observations continued, Lucifer saw that my attention to duty began to wane, reaching a point where the woman slowly but steadily, came to have some slight contact with the serpent.

A plan began to take shape and soon was ready for use, but the timing would be so very important. Then, one day, the woman wandered a good distance from me; further than at any other time. I was busy herding some animals out of our jungle paradise and lost track of her. She presently sighted the serpent and thinking that her husband was entirely too protective, walked up to the creature to admire him and perhaps make friends as with other animals. They were near the middle of the Garden, where was located the tree of the knowledge of good and evil. Lucifer wasted no time in employing his unique angelic power and entered into the serpent. As with other animals Eve spoke pleasantly to the serpent, telling him how pretty he was and such, but what a surprise when the serpent spoke back to her!

They began to converse and Lucifer was delighted with all the information the woman freely provided. She was innocent and naïve—an easy mark when compared to even the lowest of angels. She told all about the forbidden fruit on the tree in the middle of the Garden and how the only demand that God made was to abstain from eating it.

"Why would God warn you about such a thing? Surely He was not serious? It seems too pretty a fruit to just stay on the tree untouched by human hands—and I happen to know that the flavor is the finest in the entire Garden. I think that God knows, were you to eat of it, that you would gain in knowledge and understanding and be just like Him! Then you would no longer need Him, and you would control your own lives. That would be wonderful for both you and your man!"

At this point I saw my wife with the serpent and jogged towards them. The serpent (actually Lucifer) saw my approach and hoped that the scheme would still be successful, though he was somewhat concerned that my presence might ruin everything; so he quickly engaged in more deception.

Eve, with some misgivings said, "The Creator told us that we would die if we ate or even touched the fruit."

The serpent scoffed, "You will not die! Remember what I *told* you!"

Upon my arrival I sternly took them both to task: "You are not to have anything to do with this animal! God has made it plain to both of us that we are to forever be as strangers to this . . ."

I was cut off in mid-sentence by the serpent's feigned objection to being hurt by the rebuke: "Why all this needless anger? Surely we can grow to be friends. All the other creatures are your friends."

I was greatly taken back at hearing speech from an animal, and the serpent seized that moment to shake my confidence. Using his superior intellect and reasoning he said, "Now look, your wife and I have already discussed this at length. You need not have any fear of me. Why God dislikes me is as much a mystery to me as it is to you—I mean . . . has He given you a good reason for this misguided disdain?"

I became even more uncertain and awkwardly replied, "Well, He . . . just does not trust you and . . ."

"Why? What have I ever done to Him? Tell me. Please tell me, so that I can rectify any misunderstandings!"

By now, I was feeling completely inept and every instruction that God gave to me had seemingly vanished from my memory. The serpent then presented the very same temptations to me that were put before the woman, and within a short time found myself also desiring that which was forbidden.

Finally, my wife reached out and took hold of the fruit. It was such a deep, shiny red, and after peeling away some of the skin she saw that the flesh was firm. It even gave off a pleasant aroma—and of course, there was that talk of gaining wisdom. The serpent rejoiced inwardly seeing that there was now no turning back for us, and he continued to rouse our desire: "Why torture yourselves further? The fruit is the most beautiful in this new world with a heavenly scent and delectable taste . . . and we have already discussed the importance of knowledge and wisdom."

With no more hesitation Eve ate, then offered some to me, and I so willingly did likewise. Immediately our eyes were opened, and somehow nakedness, which had never before been a concern, now caused us great anxiety. She bemoaned, "The animals have fur for a covering, but here we are, of much more worth than they, and we have nothing to hide those parts that distinguish us, and nothing to protect our beautiful skin!"

I answered, "The need to be covered is in my mind also, but I am somewhat unclear as to why, since it has never before been an issue, and we are the only people on the earth; and it is certain that the animals care nothing about nakedness. Scarcely had those words escaped my lips when my legs weakened and I dropped to my knees. With quivering voice I lamented, "Of much more importance than nakedness is the fact that we broke God's most solemn command! Worry has taken hold of my innermost parts and my hands are shaking! All strength has deserted me and my insides are churning. What will happen to us?"

With my reaction adding to her own, Eve, for the first time in her life experienced fear and she spoke in hushed voice, "Those same feelings fill me also, my husband! Remember what He said about eating the forbidden fruit? He said that we would die. What does that mean?"

"He told me of it, but I am in doubt as to the meaning. I was so sure that we would never have this issue to face. Now that it is upon us, I . . . Oh, why did I not guard you more diligently! Let us make some coverings from these fig leaves, perhaps that will grant us some momentary peace of mind and then we will hide ourselves from God.

We had no more than finished lacing the fig leaves together when we heard the sound of God walking in the Garden, in the cool of the day. That startled us and we hid ourselves among some trees. God, already knowing what had happened, called my name to test me, "Where are you, Adam? Come out from those trees."

With composure rapidly deserting me, clear thinking vanished and I unwittingly divulged all that God needed to hear: "I heard the sound of You in the Garden, and I was afraid because I was naked, so I hid myself!"

God, restraining His disappointment and anger uttered, "Who told you that you were naked? Have you eaten from the tree of which I commanded you not to eat?"

It was at this point that I failed the test miserably and blurted out, "The woman! The one that *You* gave to be with me . . . she offered the fruit from the tree, and I did eat!"

Then God, still restraining His anger, said to the woman, "What is this you have done?"

The woman, with fear and trembling, spoke truth mixed with an alibi and said, "The serpent deceived me, and I ate."

Lucifer had long since departed the poor serpent, leaving the creature a bit bewildered as to what had taken place. But it knew that trouble was imminent and its once-proud expression had disappeared. Arrogance and a lack of respect for man facilitated the bodily possession, so God was not unjust in bringing punishment. He restrained His anger no longer and cursed the serpent by redesigning its body without limbs, forcing it to crawl on the ground for the rest of his existence. No longer would baseless pride play a part in his nature; and the children of both man and serpent would be enemies from this day forward.

God then turned to the woman and avowed, "I will greatly multiply your pain in childbirth; in pain you will bring forth children. Your desire will be for your husband, and though you may, on occasion resist it, he will rule over you."

Then, as my entire being cringed He said, "I am deeply disappointed, Adam. If only you could have resisted on this occasion—this one time of testing—I would have seen to it that no temptation would ever again come before you. As it is, because you did not keep My commandment concerning the tree in the middle of the Garden, cursed is the ground because of you; in toil you will eat of it all the days of your life. By the sweat of your brow you shall work the land to get food, and it will produce thorns and thistles. You shall work the ground until you return to it. You were made from dust and to dust you shall return."

God, speaking to Those closest to Him said, "The man is now like one of Us, knowing good and evil. I cannot allow him to eat from the tree of life and live forever." God drove the two of us out of the Garden of Eden, to work the ground. He stationed cherubim (warrior angels) and the flaming sword which turned every direction, to guard the way to the tree of life. Now, at last, it was time to deal with he who was most to blame.

Divine Justice

Lucifer left the serpent at the moment my wife and I gave in to temptation. Upon rejoining his angel comrades, he related the story of this ultimate deception to their itching ears: "It was effortless beyond belief! A novice among the cherubim could easily outwit them; the tiniest of seraphim could destroy them in an instant! And God was *so delighted* with them! I have now challenged Him, and He will be hard-pressed to . . ."

Right in the middle of all the angelic backslapping and general glee, God appeared . . . and all fell to their knees in abject fear, including Lucifer, who sensed that God's wrath had reached a level never before witnessed by any of them.

"Lucifer! Since you are so proud of your skill in the art of deception, Satan will be your name from now throughout eternity. All of you . . . after having had time to consider your transgressions have displayed absolutely no remorse. Your ways are more corrupt now than at the beginning of this ordeal. If ever I thought to show you any mercy . . . that time is forever gone; therefore, know that you shall never again set foot in Heaven.

Furthermore, I want you to know that during the six days of creation, I constructed a place with you in mind. My hope was that it would never be used, but you have chosen it through all manner of rebellion. There will be no escape from it and no comfort in it. I am sending some of you there now, the rest will be allowed to roam the Earth for a time, but in the end, all of you, along with the men whom you ensnare, will be imprisoned in this place of darkness and fire known as Hell.

"Some words for you, Satan: I saw you hiding in the trees of the Garden and knew that you would attempt to corrupt the lives of man. In My desire to test them, I allowed you to practice your art. Despite reservations, I earnestly wanted to see if they could stand against your guile. You prevailed. You captured their hearts, so to speak. You have introduced sin into their natures and it will remain there until I decide to bring an end to this world. Because of this sinful nature, especially the pride that is central in it, you will keep many captive in your kingdom. But once again, I made preparations for this very possibility, so that man may be provided an escape from you and be welcomed back into My presence. You will hold countless followers—but I will win back the hearts of many. Your power over man, for the most part, will be confined to deceit, since that seems to be your weapon of choice. You will not be permitted to harm him physically, unless I allow it. You are the only one of the fallen angels that will ever again be permitted to converse with Me until a final judgment. For now, this world is your dwelling place and many men will be your subjects. Knowing how you despise them, they are to be pitied."

God departed, leaving Satan to glory in this victory, but at the same time to ponder whether it was all worth it, as many of his band vanished into an abyss never to see the outside world again. Maybe, when the time came, he would be able to scheme his way around this punishment. But for now, he and his remaining demon followers would begin to formulate plans on how best to deceive men and women, and the children soon to come.

Return to Adam

There you have it. The foundation of this story has been laid. You now gather a clear picture as to why God warned me about the serpent and why He wanted me to watch over Eve so closely.

We were driven from our paradise home, out into a world of toil and discomfort; but God did not totally abandon us. He continued to display His love for us by furnishing animal skins for warmth; and we found a rather large cave that served well as a shelter. He also sent angels from time to time to teach us how best to survive in the rugged surroundings outside the Garden. I am most appreciative for one who educated us in the different methods of starting a fire. That proved to be a difficult task, but it was such a blessing. We were not familiar with the cold and early on, that was our toughest test. He gave us seeds to plant for food and just as promised, we fought thorns, thistles, and other weeds. There was no end to them! Until the crop was ready to harvest, He provided some wild fruit and vegetables. Of course, they were somewhat scattered and it took a great deal of searching to find enough to fill our stomachs. Later, we harvested some of our own vegetables; not a huge crop, but enough to satisfy us on most days. When some of the planted seed grew to maturity there was no fruit as I thought of fruit, just seed heads. An angel called it wheat and we were shown how to use rocks to crush the seeds into flour and bake the flour into bread. We drank water from a nearby stream, but it was not as cold, clear, or pure as the water we had known.

The friendship of the animals was not as in days past. They sometimes growled as we approached to rub their heads and they seemed to dislike one another at times, especially where territory was involved. This was just the beginning of violence in the animal world. Also, insects troubled us by eating our plants and biting our skin. We had never before had this problem with them. We continued to keep our distance from the serpents. There was just something eerie about them now that they crawled on the ground.

One of the first commands that God gave us was to fill the earth with people, but He restrained our desires while in the Garden. Once removed from our precious place of origin in Eden, we exercised our spousal prerogatives and Eve soon became pregnant; and we so longed for God's assistance in the birthing process. We had witnessed the animals give birth and so had some idea of what to expect, but God's helping hand would have been greatly appreciated. Although He was not with us in any tangible form, a messenger angel gently instructed us and we learned what steps to take; so once again, He did not abandon us in a time of need.

Since our banishment, we had seen some animals die in giving birth, and we began to understand about this thing called death. As Eve suffered through her first birth, I silently wondered what would become of me if she should die. How could I go on living with no other human being for company and comfort, and with the added punishment of God's diminished involvement in my daily life? Then, despite the pain and uncertainty, the birth soon came to be and we found ourselves the joyful parents of a boy child whom we named, Cain. Eve was especially happy for her part in this process and surprisingly was soon ready to discuss the possibility of another child—after a time of healing, that is. I was now a father and could appreciate what God felt when He created me. In those early moments after the delivery, my mind gave no thought to the miracle of birth and all that was involved in it; later on, when it was evening and time for sleep, I laid on the ground and pondered the whole notion of it: How could two people becoming one flesh, physically speaking, create life?

Taking care of a baby was more work than either of us expected and there was much to learn, such as nakedness being a blessing for babies. It was a total waste of time using fig leaves and animal skins to clothe one at this stage of life. Also, with Eve temporarily in a weakened condition and much of her time devoted to the care and feeding of Cain, my workload greatly increased. Part of Eve's purpose was to be my helper, and I took that help for granted; now that changes had been brought about, I saw just how precious her aid had been. From sunrise to sunset and then some, I worked the ground pulling up the weeds, picking off the bugs, harvesting enough to get by, and all of this under the hot sun. Night, and the rest that came with it, soon became my favorite part of existence.

Cain was one of the few real joys in our lives. Work, which had almost seemed like play in the Garden, had become more like drudgery. Many hours each day were devoted to the endless cycle of tending the ground for enough food to give us the strength necessary to repeat the same actions day after day. But now that we had a child, life was more than just tolerable. Cain received much in the way of attention and he truly enjoyed being the object considered more precious than the sweetest of fruit—our only treat prior to his birth.

Time passed and Eve became pregnant again. The whole process was not quite as scary or painful this time around and Eve gave birth to another son. We called him Abel. He was the new addition and quickly became the focus of our attention. Cain, young as he was, recognized that things were now different and that he had to share our affection. He displayed no small amount of jealousy for a little one and it was here that I witnessed an open display of his sinful nature; but at this time I gave it only a passing thought.

As parents, we sensed that it was wrong to favor one child over another, but there were times that Abel captured our hearts with a certain charm seasoned with warmth and sincerity; not that Cain was totally lacking in positive qualities. We deeply loved them both, but Cain had a jealous way that led him, at times, to try too hard to please us which seemed to have the opposite effect. It tended to be irritating instead of pleasing.

It was at this time in life that our relationship with the Almighty took a turn for the better and life became more tolerable.

The boys gradually grew in size and knowledge. Eve and I were somewhat amazed at the concept of physical growth, since we were both full-grown at the beginning; but we were quite familiar with learning, as we were taught by the Best, and we passed on as much understanding as possible to the boys. The timely lessons in life that God began to offer at this point were truly welcome.

It was so rewarding and satisfying to see the boys reach the stage where they were able to help with working the ground instead of all that constant play. Not that we resented their play, but they began to eat almost as much as some of the larger animals, so staying ahead of their appetites had forced long, hard hours on the two of us.

The timeliness of their maturity was put to the test as Eve bore two more children, both girls, and the boys began to see firsthand that work had to come first, and then play—when they had the energy. They were, for the most part, adequate workers and made it possible for their mother to put all of her efforts into caring for the young ones. And we soon had more children requiring more food and more toil.

Though Abel was a little younger than Cain, he held his own against his older brother in just about every field of endeavor. As the boys reached an age approaching manhood, wrestling became the ever-increasing, recreational activity of choice, and both took part with enthusiasm. Cain being the larger and stronger of the two usually came out on top, but on occasion Abel's skill and quickness offset that size and led to victory. It was during these times that Cain flew into fits of rage and used his fists (especially when I was not nearby). Abel's speed and agility made it interesting, but usually Cain would land a blow and end the skirmish. And he was seldom satisfied with the victory itself as he often rubbed Abel's face in the dirt or at least heaped verbal abuse upon him.

Something told me that there was more than just rivalry between these two. Hatred was beginning to take root, more from Cain's side. In Abel's heart there was not so much hatred as there was a competitive spirit bringing with it the desire to get even.

A Day of Reckoning

Though Abel often suffered pain, he still enjoyed the challenge of fighting with his big brother, but after a time of healing from the latest fit of rage he was rethinking some strategy. One day, while working in the field, he hatched a great plan. It would take some effort, but if successful the memories would last forever. Of course, he had to do his daily work first; that finished, he then walked down by the river to a secluded spot and began to dig. That first day, using his hands and a flat piece of wood, he dug a hole about knee deep and as wide and long as he was tall, all the while throwing the dirt into the water to hide his trickery. The next evening, after a particularly hard day under the sun, it was back to the river for more dirt work, making for an exhausting and challenging time in his young life. Challenging, yes, but his heart was filled with hope that the early-evening labor at the river's edge would also bear fruit.

As he labored away this second evening, darkness closed in on him suddenly and he saw that this job would require a little more than could be finished at this time, so he hastened to the family shelter. We were eating when Abel finally arrived home and I asked him where he had been.

He replied, "Just down by the river, resting and enjoying the sight of it."

That seemed likely, as all of us enjoyed the river for cooling off after a hard day. We drank its water, swam in it, and sometimes just sat at the shore.

The next evening, Abel returned to that same site and dug down deeper still. The digging became easier after getting through the gravel and rock on the surface, and the soil was quite moist beginning at the knee-deep point. After reaching a depth equal to his height the digging was mere child's play. All at once he heard a noise upstream and he peeked over the rim of the hole only to see his brother walking down to the river to cool off for a bit. Abel thought, "Why did he have to show up now, possibly causing me to be late again?" His mind shouted, "Do not come this way!"

Cain waded for awhile, looked around as though he sensed something, but seeing nothing, climbed back on the bank to rest. By the time he left, it was getting close to sunset and some of the big cats were beginning to growl. That caused Abel some uneasiness, but now it was time for the fun part. He threw thistles, thorn branches, nettles, and other choice irritants into the hole, then grabbed a nearby tree limb, stout and straight, and laid it across the middle of the hole, right where only he would know. He then took swamp grass and covered the pit.

Darkness had settled over the land and Eve and I being very concerned began to call Abel's name. He arrived shortly and I took him to task for worrying us: "Son, what have you been doing? You know very well that some of the animals have become vicious, and in fact, I have seen them not only kill, but they are now eating one another! You might be the next creature to fill some lion's belly. You were late last night! What is your excuse this night?"

Everyone was listening and Abel, knowing that he had lied previously, decided to risk it again. He did not relish the idea of lying, but he had put so much work and ingenuity into this venture that he could not bear the thought of it being spoiled now.

"Father, I worked very hard today and when I stopped by the river to rest, fatigue caused me to sleep . . . and more than just a nap. It was fortunate that I awoke when I did!"

Cain snorted, "You call that working hard! I did half again as much as you did! And I was down by the river for awhile and saw no trace of you."

"Well, I was downriver from you."

"If you were asleep, how did you know where I was?"

Abel thought to himself, "Oh no! How could my ignorant brother trap me like this?" His pulse quickened as he searched the air for an apt reply, "You always go to the same spot, so I reasoned that I had to be downriver from you."

Though suspicious, his older brother, not overly blessed with quick wittedness, dropped the subject and would never know how close he came to glorious victory. But as his father I was not quite satisfied, so I took Abel off to one side and asked him what he was planning, and he continued to assure me that all was well. I was not wholly at peace, but after a stern warning about staying too long at the river we all went to sleep. Abel's conscience bothered him, but he had made up his mind to see this thing through to the end and suffer the consequences if need be.

The next day was bright and beautiful and it made for a successful time of gathering food and working the fields for the coming crop. With the work finished the boys headed for the river at a run and I loudly repeated the warning about staying too late. They waved as if to say there was no worry about that. I started to walk home to my wife and little ones, but decided that a time at the river would do me good, also.

Abel could hardly contain his glee as the river came into view, but he managed to keep a straight face as they approached the place that would be dear to his heart from this day forward. But upon getting within a stone's throw of it, Cain decided to rest on the bank. Abel hollered, "Come on, I have something to show you!"

"I worked harder than you did today, as usual, so let me rest a bit."

Abel, not wanting to risk another tardy arrival at home persisted, "I discovered some shiny rocks yesterday; unlike any you have ever seen. Right over here!"

"Let me rest. Rocks are of no interest to me."

Abel grew impatient and decided to force the issue in a way that he knew would succeed every time: "You talk a lot about all the hard work you do—I could be puking sick and get more done than you on your best day!"

That touched a nerve and Cain was very close to calling a halt to his much deserved respite, yet he continued to relax on the bank as he plotted Abel's punishment.

Abel was becoming irritated and although one more insult would probably bring about the desired result he instead grabbed a big, juicy, glob of mud and crept close enough to his big brother to be confident of his aim, yet far enough away to avoid snap reflexes.

Cain's eyes were closed as he was still thinking about the slur to his work ethic, but he was also thinking about how nice it was to rest before administering a good thrashing, at which point he was struck full in the face by a glob of mud heavy enough to bring the instant blood-boiling and pain that Abel desired. Cain leaped to his feet, half-blind from fury and the muck, but not fully certain of what had happened. Then he cleared the substance from his face and saw his younger brother laughing hysterically. He was enraged more than at any other time in his life (and he had been enraged before) and he mindlessly chased after Abel, his only thought to inflict a severe beating. Abel had a good lead on him and quickly reached the small log that lay across the hole. He carefully felt his way along confident of keeping his balance, yet having some anxiety at the sight of the slobbering, red-faced giant bearing down on him. He reached the log's other end and solid footing just as Cain was a stride away. As chance would have it, Cain's first step was right on the log and for a moment Abel worried and wondered whether his brother had knowledge of the prank. But it was just chance, and when the second foot found nothing but air the first one slipped off and down went Cain, straddle the log. The intense pain in the young man's groin and the jolt to his body nearly caused him to black out; and the log, which was not particularly large in diameter, had some give to it which caused Cain to bounce into the air. He instinctively put his hands down to barely avoid further damage to the same area of his body managing to land on his right buttock where he immediately flipped over, head-first into the pit. Pain wracked his body as the dazed young man plunged into a cool, wet, unknown world of darkness. His lower extremities hurt so badly that he barely noticed the thorny branches that now cut and penetrated his head and shoulders.

Abel, who at first was delighted beyond measure with the unforeseen degree of his plan's success, recognized that the seriousness of the situation had abruptly escalated. He was still grinning, but was also concerned (if that was possible). Unknown to him, the river water had seeped into the hole overnight and there was enough muck and mire to bury a man in Cain's position clear to the chest.

I came over the river bank in time to see the fall. When I saw Cain's feet sticking above the hole, but not moving, I ran as hard as possible to rescue him. Thankfully, Abel had already begun the process of helping his brother and between the two of us, we lifted him out of the hole and saved him from suffocating. He was slightly delirious and quite weak, but still aware enough to mutter threats against his younger brother's life. He looked terrible! A coating of slime covered the upper half of his body, and there were enough cuts and welts to remind me of the time I fell from a tree into some thorn bushes. (Abel later confided that he got the idea from that.) And, of course, there was discoloration and swelling elsewhere. I looked at Abel with a glare that, at least temporarily, wiped that half-grin from his face. We carried Cain back to our cave where Eve and the two oldest girls cleaned him up and cared for him.

My temper had cooled by this time and I said, "You probably know, Abel, that there will be a payment for this, first by my hand. Why did you go to such . . . how could you devise such evil for your brother?"

"Father, it was not my intention for him to land on the log. The thought of that did not enter my mind. My plan was for him to fall feet-first, scratch up his legs a little, and just confound him for a while. And the water seeping into the hole overnight was not in my thinking either. And I understand that punishment has to be administered so I am prepared for it, but you know that Cain has inflicted pain on me many times. So whatever method you choose, there will be no sorrow, except for the lies that became part of it all."

I certainly knew of the bitter rivalry between them and that Cain probably deserved most of what he received, and had that been the only issue I might have gone easy on my young son. But lying and deceit had to be dealt with, especially since they had been weaknesses of mine . . . and ones that caused me to anger God and dislike myself. A message, clear and true, had to be conveyed to his young spirit, but how best to do it. Cain was a reasonably good worker, so it would do no good, by a severe whipping, to cause Abel to be less than his absolute best for who knows how long. Maybe there was another way to settle this without physical chastisement; something that might hurt my younger son's pride.

Abel was walking toward the whipping tree, the tree where many a lash had been doled out to Cain and a few to Abel, when I called him back: "Abel, your punishment will be to apologize to your brother and to tend to some of his needs in the morning before we go to the field, and then to tend to his every need in the evening, until he is well."

The initial expression on his face told me that he was nigh to total rebellion, but after a few moments of seething resistance he accepted the sentence without a word of argument. He was a good son and I hoped he would be obedient to my decision.

Upon our appearance at the cave, I explained to Cain the basics of the decision. He was at first quite loathe to have anything to do with his brother, but after a bit the idea of seeing Abel humiliated began to grow on him, and pretty soon he was very much in favor of it, his mind already conjuring up acts of service to request . . . or demand.

Cain was a quick healer and after only two days he could have gone back to light work, but he so enjoyed the role of a ruler that he decided to play it up for a third day. Abel hated his every step as Cain's servant and after two days was certain that enough healing had taken place, so he was more than a little suspicious on the next day when Cain took a backset.

"Have you not yet grown tired of keeping company with the women? By now you surely have become quite skilled in the art of preparing a meal and keeping the cooking fire ablaze . . . and taking care of babies! What you need is a good day of work in the field!"

"After you nearly brought about my death at the river!? I will be fortunate to ever walk again! The time for work will be slow in coming. Please bring me some water and a little more of that leaf salve for my sores, Baby Brother."

Abel hated to be called that by anyone, especially Cain, and he stormed outside, away from the family to calm himself. Eve, later, told me that Cain had been doing very well and was becoming impatient with inactivity. That was good to hear because our work in the field was a terrible burden without him, but I decided to give him one more day, just to be certain. I stepped outside and assured Abel that tonight would be his last night of punishment, and that seemed to lift a load from his shoulders.

Cain did go back to work the next day and did well. No words were exchanged between my sons throughout the day and their relationship further deteriorated. It seemed to me that Abel might be willing to forgive and forget old hurts if Cain would meet him part way, but Cain held bitterness in his heart and like a wound it festered.

Boys to Men

When they were younger, fights usually ceased as soon as Cain gained the upper hand and added an insult or two, but as they grew into manhood, the elder brother's temper became such that he felt a need to inflict undue pain, especially when Abel used his increasing skill to make Cain look awkward. Cain would become furious and during these times I felt fortunate to be close by to separate them. Finally, I warned, "If defeat is that devastating to the both of you, perhaps you should concentrate on work and put all that energy toward it!" So they did—but even in the act of labor there was competition between the two.

Cain grew skilled in working the ground; the younger brother also, but his interest was more in the care and feeding of livestock, especially sheep. God, for some reason, allowed for certain animals to be domesticated. (At this point in human history, animals were not yet used for meat, but wool made for warm clothing and soft bedding. We had some goats and got milk from them. And also, though the idea was at first confusing, the Lord began to educate us on the reasons behind sacrifice and the necessity of giving part of the fruits of our labor to Him. He hinted that sheep would fill this requirement very neatly.)

Time passed and the boys became full-fledged men. The two oldest daughters, Naomi and Rachel, matured to the point that noticeable changes took place and they blossomed into young women. Naomi was the eldest daughter, wise, outgoing, and a good worker; Rachel was quite pretty (I am not certain how we arrived at a conclusion concerning outward beauty; just instinct I suppose) but not given to lively conversation. And it took a little persuasion to entice her to work, but once enticed she held her own. Both sons, being the forerunners of the typical male, had their eyes on Rachel.

Abel argued, "Naomi is the oldest and you are the oldest! It stands to reason that she should become your wife!"

Cain snapped, "You are quite right my brother, when you say that I am the oldest! As the oldest, and the biggest, I will take whatever I want!"

Abel held his temper in check and said, "Let our father make this decision."

Cain, unwilling to chance his father's favor went to his strength: "Leave our father out of this! Let this be between the two of us and we will settle this as men. Long has it been since we have battled."

Eve and I thought that this day could soon be upon us as we observed the behavioral changes in our sons over the course of these latter days. Until recently, the girls were just two extra mouths to feed. Our sons complained for the longest time about having to do the majority of the work and that Naomi and Rachel were not worth the time it took to protect and care for them. Now, it seemed, things had taken on a different look and the girls were prized.

I overheard the challenge that Cain proposed. Knowing that his physical power, along with his unbridled temper could lead to tragedy, I walked from out of the trees and put a stop to the conflict. Abel had gained strength of late and would fare well against his brother, but he lacked the near-killer mentality necessary to inflict such an injury that Cain would concede defeat and forever avoid another confrontation. My presence ended the argument . . . for the time being. Later, after tempers had cooled, I tried to reason with them and warned that violence was not the way for family members to settle differences, but as usual, the younger was the only one willing to listen.

Ambition—Satan's Way

Satan lamented, "Life on this ball of mud and rock is such a waste! Were it not for Cain's willingness to be swayed by my late-night whisperings, there would be absolutely nothing of interest here. But . . . even though I hate these beings, I truly look forward to the day when there will be many more of them to deceive; many men and women to lead to ruin; many children to nurture in the ways of rebellion."

Baal, the right-hand of Satan, voiced his opinion, "What keeps us from crushing these few whose very existence is a constant irritation? We could destroy them with so little effort, and then never have to put forth all this effort in deception."

Satan answered, "Are you in such a hurry to be cast into the darkness? Is your memory so short that you fail to recall how easily and totally God intimidated us all; and how you trembled with fear when last we met with Him? And He has built a hedge around these beings so we cannot physically harm them . . . at this point. Besides, our only entertainment comes from watching our fellow earth inhabitants deal with the various forms of temptation that we set before them. Cain is so predictable with his fits of rage fueled by jealousy and greed. I could almost grow to like him, but feelings of "like" and "love" are not what I consider desirable traits. But . . . somewhere along the way he may play a part in the building of my kingdom."

"Unfortunately, Abel has much the same outlook on this life as does Adam. They both are somewhat adept at avoiding my little snares, but

Abel has some weaknesses and can be provoked into occasional lapses of judgment. If I cannot defeat him one way, another way will do. Who knows? There may even be a way to kill him; then Adam will be the only male-source of Godly influence on this new home that has been forced upon us."

Baal said, "I look forward to seeing the day when Abel might cease to exist, but what about Adam, the females, and the little males? Do you also have plans for them? I mean, who knows how long they will live . . . and Adam could still have enough time left on this earth to take part in making many more of his kind."

Satan mused, "We will labor on Adam and the others . . . at a later date. After all, we have deceived them on several occasions, and that was before we had such an understanding of the human nature."

"Now, let us return to this Abel. He has, so far, managed to side-step the major evils which are laid in front of him, but we have had more time to study the ways of man, or more to the point, man's weaknesses. I doubt his ability to continue resistance . . . as I also doubt the resistance of the others. Maybe something as minor as his attitude can be used against him. Again though, so much depends on God's willingness to provide them Divine protection. But if He ever lifts the barriers that now frustrate our desires . . . oh what a time of celebration!"

The Inevitable

Our family continued to grow as we were blessed with two more children, twin boys, which increased to twelve Earth's human residents. Pregnancy and childbirth were still not a stroll through the Garden, but Eve's body had reached a point of resilience that made the whole process at least tolerable. And each new birth did nothing to diminish the desire to fulfill her role as earth's first mother.

By now, several of the children could do a day's work and do it well. Life was no longer as harsh as in the earlier times. Strange, but we thought at first that more mouths to feed would bring incredible hardship, but how wonderful to find that more mouths also meant more hands, and we have made the most of their availability.

Cain, Abel, Naomi, and Rachel, were now educated in all our ways of life and more than up to the task of providing food and shelter. They truly were a blessing to our fledgling family, but just when life outside the Garden appeared to be approaching tolerable . . .

God had hinted, shortly after our creation and on into those first days after our fall from grace that sacrifices would soon be required in order to properly worship Him and atone for our misdeeds. We started small, just enough fruit and vegetables from each of us to amount to a good meal. A little later, Cain brought baskets of produce from his field, and Abel brought some of his sheep to God. As time passed, Abel continued to bring the very best of his flock, but Cain began to tire of this activity and soon brought less than his best, even reaching a point when he brought stunted vegetables and wormy fruit. One day, from the heavens, God spoke to them and praised Abel for his offering, but He had no praise for Cain's offering. Cain now knew intense humiliation, all the way to the core of his being, and anger seethed within his heart. He was angry with God, with Abel, and with himself, but of those three, Abel was the one most at the center of all vengeful thoughts.

God, knowing Cain's heart said, "Why is your expression dejected? You have not given your best and deep down inside, you know it; but I sense that your pride will not allow you to see it from that perspective. Resist the sin that so eagerly waits at your door, much like a crouching lion. You still have a chance to do well in this life that you have been given!"

Cain was silent at supper that evening and he mentioned nothing of God's rebuke. We knew that something troubled him, but seldom was he ever in a pleasant frame of mind so we paid scant attention to his mood. Abel chose the moment to glory in the praise that God gave him: "This makes three straight times that God has spoken well of my offering!" Then with a faint smile he cuttingly asked, "What did He have to say about your offering, my brother?"

Surprisingly, Cain slowly got to his feet and with a calmness that belied the rage within his soul responded, "He rejected my offering." At that point he walked to his bed as though he was quite ready for sleep.

We all looked at each other in disbelief; never had a wounding comment from Abel met with so little reaction. Generally, harsh words were exchanged, followed by some act of violence, and I would have to separate the two. With hope in our hearts we quietly spoke of the possibility that he was a changed man.

That night, Cain slept well enough, considering the anger that was bubbling up just beneath the surface. The brooding thoughts that often plagued his sleep were offset by the peace of mind that comes to a man who has made a decision, one that he arrived at all on his own . . . or so he thought. As he slept, Satan, like a master with his apprentice, whispered suggestions and instructions.

When the sun arose, the men woke and got ready for the usual hard day of work. As they walked to the field, Cain put his hand on

Abel's shoulder and said, "Let us work side by side this day, brother. Too long we have fought each other and labored in the field on opposite ends."

Abel was at first somewhat startled by the touch of his brother's hand, as the touch of that hand was often the beginning of a battle, but there was a look of sincerity in Cain's eyes that Abel had never before seen. Could it be that after all these years his big brother would become a friend? They talked back and forth as they walked, about their work, about getting married and starting their own families. Cain even agreed to take Naomi and let Abel have Rachel. It was at that point that Abel was totally convinced of his brother's conversion.

They reached the field and began working the dirt with wooden-handled stone tools that they had fashioned. Abel squatted down on one knee, and as he often did, displayed a genuine appreciation as he crumbled the soil in his hand and let it run through his fingers. Then, oblivious to all else, he thanked God, saying, "God has truly blessed this field with a deep, rich soil."

With Abel in an unguarded moment, Cain saw a chance to make last night's dream a reality, but the tools were lying next to Abel, so he searched the ground for a weapon. Somehow, in a field that had been neatly cleared for some time, there appeared a nearby rock about twice the size of a man's fist. Its shape was such that it looked as though it was made for the very purpose that Cain had in mind. His right hand firmly grasped a place on the smaller end. He came up behind Abel who was still on one knee, and with all of his might brought that rock down on the younger brother's skull. There was a noise like that of a tree limb snapping and at the same instant like that same rock dropped into the mud at the river's edge; then Abel fell face-first onto the ground with blood pouring from the wound. As Cain looked at his younger brother's lifeless body, he had no more feeling for him than the carcass of a wild animal out in the woods; then with an incredible coldness said, "This *deep, rich* soil will make a fine place to hide your worthless remains. I will always remember you each time I plant this field and watch my crops as they grow over the spot of our final reunion.

There was one witness to this act, and he glowed with the pride of a father watching his son take that first step. Satan quickly met up with his followers to boast of another coup in his battle against God and man. "If only all of you could have been witnesses to it! I found a way through the hedge that God used to protect these humans!"

Cheers went up at the delivery of this news and Satan was highly esteemed. His place as their king was now firmly established, and he was never to be unseated while they dwelt on the earth.

No Escaping Judgment

Cain, after throwing his brother into a hole so shallow that the body was barely covered tried to carry on with his usual work in the field, but found it difficult to keep his mind focused. He loved working the soil and took great pride in growing crops, but at this moment his evil deed began to eat at his hard heart and kept him from taking the usual pleasure in his labor. His conscience had caused him little trouble since childhood, and even then he ignored it to the point that he became insensitive to its leading, but this time it was different. He had not only witnessed the first human death, but had brought it about by a cold-blooded violent act. Satan had abandoned his pupil and was nowhere near to whisper words of comfort—if he was so inclined—and time did nothing but increase Cain's anxiety. Questions slowly began to come to his mind, questions that should have been asked long before circumstances reached such a chilling point: What would he tell his father and mother? How could he explain Abel's absence? How could he face his brothers and sisters? What would God do to him? Why was he feeling guilt about a brother who brought about nothing but feelings of jealousy and envy?

He could tell the family that Abel was killed by one of the big cats that roamed the nearby trees, and that they had become increasingly aggressive over the span of time since the Fall and had finally resorted to the killing of a man. As he pondered the lie his heart hardened even more than before, reaching a darkness exceeded only by his late-night mentor. Now the thought that an all-knowing God would discover the truth seemed far removed from Cain's thinking. He reasoned that Abel was under the ground, so there was no living witness to the event. Neither God nor man would ever know what happened.

Just as these thoughts began to bring total peace to his core being, a voice from the heavens spoke, "Where is Abel your brother?"

God's voice in this instance had much the same effect as the rumbling growl of an approaching lion and startled Cain, leaving him momentarily speechless. When he found his voice he was too shaken to tell the planned tale, so he lashed out, "I do not know! Am I my brother's keeper?"

The Creator knew exactly what had happened, but gave the young man that one chance to confess. He failed the test and God, in a voice that brought Cain to his knees and caused his body to tremble, spoke ever so sternly: "What have you done! The voice of your brother's blood is crying out to me from the ground. That same ground that has opened its mouth to receive his blood will be cursed to you; from now on that soil in which you took such pride in working will no longer produce for you. You will become a vagrant and a wanderer on the earth."

Cain, still on his knees, was overwhelmed with the gravity of the situation he now faced, and with his hands covering a bowed head, gnashed his teeth and cried out, "My punishment is too great to bear! You have driven me this day from the face of the ground, and from Your face I will be hidden and be a wanderer and a vagrant on the earth, and whoever finds me will kill me! (Cain felt no sorrow over the murder of Abel; the sorrow that existed came only from the fact that he had been found out and would suffer greatly.)

God decided that he must live so that the punishment would be ongoing, and He told Cain that a mark would be assigned to him so that no person would dare to kill him. Immediately the skin that covered his forehead and his right hand changed color to a scarlet red, representing the blood of Abel. It would be immediately noticed and understood by all that the carrier of this mark was not to be killed and that a terrible vengeance would be taken on any who were disobedient in the matter. God departed, leaving Cain to wonder at the red mark on his hand and the words that were spoken to him regarding his safety and the future.

As soon as his weak legs again found their strength, Cain met with the family during the mid-day respite. The red skin on his forehead and hand was evident and several asked how it came to be. He told them little; only that he was leaving and taking Naomi to begin his family in the land of Nod (which was east of Eden). Rachel asked, "Where is Abel?"

He retorted, "Ask God!"

He quickly gathered together about a week's supply of food along with a few other items and put it all into a bag fashioned from animal skin; and of course he grabbed his favorite spear. Then a thought came into his mind and he made a request of Rachel: "Come with us and be my wife along with Naomi. I am strong and will be a good provider and protector."

The request took her by surprise as she had promised herself to Abel, so she promptly refused his offer wrinkling her nose as to a stench. He was irritated by her immediate rebuff and considered taking her by brute force, but Naomi's eagerness soothed his temper. Cain had seldom been known as a thinking man but even with all that had happened a bit of sound logic came into his mind, and he reasoned that this new existence would be very difficult, and it might be better to have only one woman in his care. Also, he decided, somewhat grudgingly, that for once in his life he did not want to force someone to bend to his will—not Rachel—not yet.

I was just returning home from working in the field when I was met by God and told of Abel's fate. I was sick with grief and anger. When God told me that the punishment for killing Cain was to be seven times greater than his punishment, I re-thought any plan of revenge. My mind was swirling as I tried to gain a hold on my emotions. I knew that the penalty would surely result in a life of terrible misery or painful death, and the family would be left without strong leadership, so a point was reached in which sound reason returned to me and at just the right time. I encountered Cain and Naomi on the trail. He saw me and had her stand still a short distance away. Though it nearly gagged me, I took the opportunity to speak to my first-born: "Why? How could you murder your own flesh and blood brother!?"

He snapped, "Because I hated him! I hated everything about him! And I especially hated the closeness that the two of you shared. His stature and strength were nothing compared to mine! Why was I not the favored one in the family?"

"You are so ignorant of what it takes to be a good son . . . or what it takes to be a good man! Your mother and I tried to teach you, from childhood, that things like obedience to God and an abiding respect for Him were of utmost importance; and near to that was a love for your family. You lost all interest in any of that while still a youth. I am uncertain of the circumstances that drove you, but it must be that Satan deceived you as he once deceived me. Your advantage was the fact that I was aware of his schemes and warned you many times to . . . well, no matter now."

"You speak of God and Satan, unseen phantoms who strike fear into men like yourself! A voice from the sky! Ha, that was the only evidence ever displayed to me—and now I am not even sure of that! Had either ever shown themselves, even once, I might have believed . . . but no more. I am a full-grown man, past the need of these childhood stories."

My daughter heard some of the dispute, and was puzzled. She asked, "What is he saying, Cain? Did you harm our brother? Do you not fear God? Is that the reason for the red mark?"

At this point I stepped toward my daughter, pleading, "Naomi, stay here with your mother and me, please! Do not leave with this . . . murderer who will treat you no better than a dog!"

Cain growled, "You would be wise to remain silent, Adam! She is coming with me and you cannot stop us!" He took Naomi by the arm and in hushed tones said, "Naomi, it was an accident. Abel and I were wrestling when he fell and hit his head on a rock. Your father would not believe me and will never forgive me. That is the reason for our sudden departure. And yes, the one who calls himself God does not believe me, so I suppose that may be the reason for this hideous mark."

The entire situation was beyond anything Naomi had ever envisioned. Was Abel dead? Death was an unfamiliar concept to her since she had yet to see someone die, but she instinctively knew that this would be a time of sadness like no other the family had ever faced. She also felt sorrow over the intense exchange between her husband and me; never had she or any of her siblings so spoken to their father. It was an experience she hoped never to relive. What should she do? More than anything she wanted to believe Cain and continue with their plan to be husband and wife. After a few moments of consideration, she let her desires have their way and respectfully replied, "You are wrong, Father. Cain loves me and will be a good husband; and we want to start a family of our own."

I knew that whatever Cain told her, it had been persuasive and a change of mind was not now likely. When she set her mind on something, only trial, error, and time could change it—and maybe not even then. I was also fairly certain that Cain could defeat and possibly kill me, should a fight ensue. There were too many other lives at stake to take the risk, but I made a last entreaty: "Why do you hasten to leave the family? Take thought before making such a decision. You have other brothers who will soon be young men. Any one of them would make a good husband. Surely you can wait a little longer!"

"Father, they are far from the time of fulfilling the role of a husband, and I have already waited a long while. I want to know the joy that Mother has known in bringing new life to this earth."

"My daughter, life will be so difficult for you . . ." There was a hesitation in my speech as I struggled to reach out to her but words failed me, and the look in her eyes told me where I stood. So, with a pain in my heart that matched the day's earlier news . . . we said goodbye. "I want you to remember that you will always be welcome here with us, no matter the circumstances." I gave her a hug to last the ages before turning to Cain. "As for you, I hope to never see your face again; and if, somehow, I find that you treat Naomi harshly, I will disregard God's warning!"

A smug expression came to his face and with Naomi walking on ahead and out of hearing, he back-tracked a few steps, came close, looked me straight in the face with eyes full of contempt and said, "Be careful, Adam. One member of the family has departed and I felt little in the way of sorrow." Then he smirked as though I would present no challenge whatsoever, and he mockingly added, "Of course, your death might cost me a few moments of sleep; then I would have to sleep a little later the next day to make up for it." This being said, he laughed in much the same manner as when he had defeated Abel in a wrestling match and rubbed his face in the dirt. He turned and followed Naomi, and they continued on the journey to Nod.

My heart so ached, making me weak and sick . . . sick to the point of vomiting. The events of this day would forever live inside of me, and I slowly made my way to our shelter. Upon my arrival I saw Eve and the remainder of our children waiting to eat with me. I had no appetite, but joined the precious group and told them everything as we sat around the fire. There was much in the way of grief at first, especially from Rachel and Eve; then, upon my urging, we reminisced: first of Abel, remembering his playful nature and also his skill at nearly everything important to life as we knew it, and then we spoke of Naomi's warmth and her reliability when existence seemed too tough to face. Eve also mentioned Cain, wondering how he strayed so far from the family and fretting that she might have somehow caused him to be the way he was. Later in the day, we went to the spot where Abel lay, and I dug a proper grave for him; then we all stacked rocks over it as a memorial. When the job was completed and after some words were spoken, several of Cain's younger brothers voiced the notion of hunting him down when they were older, but I gave them God's warning and added one of my own.

Work was more than strenuous once again as I had to make a concerted effort to compensate for the loss of the two oldest sons. Enosh was old enough to do a good day of work, and Eve more than held her own; Rachel, not normally one on whom you could depend, performed well though she was grief-stricken and not at her best for a time. The others basically took care of small chores and watched over each other.

Time passed, more children were born; many crops were planted and harvested. We finally reached a point in life where we were better able to deal with the loss of our son. The youngest members of our family now walked and talked; then, Eve was once again with child. At this same time two more of the children grew strong enough to work the fields and Enosh proved invaluable with his increased strength and stamina. So things came together in a timely fashion and Eve soon delivered another son.

There was something special about this child, an aura if you will; and Eve saw it from the moment she held him. She named him Seth and said that he would fill the emptiness in her heart and, to a degree, take the place of Abel. He was a good boy right from the start and my wife and I thanked God over and over for him.

Journey to the Land of Nod

I t was a long journey to the boundaries of Nod and along the way, early in the morning, Naomi and Cain came upon a low-lying valley surrounded by steep, rocky bluffs. The valley, viewed from those bluffs, looked to be a foreboding, mist-shrouded swamp with little to offer in the way of well-being. Cutting through the middle of it looked to be a quicker way to Nod, and Cain was always one to take what looked to be the easier route, even if the longer way on the ridge top would be safer. The climb down these rugged crags was exhausting and treacherous, more than he expected. And had Naomi been a lesser woman it would have taken much longer. They finally reached the bottom where the rocky terrain turned to a wet marsh and though the slog was demanding it was at least level.

There did not appear, at first look, to be much in the way of dangerous animal life in this land, mainly biting insects. But there was one creature, hidden behind some weeds and partially buried in the mud, that closely watched their every movement. Had they known the old serpent from Eden's garden had slithered to this land, they gladly would have taken the long way. The serpent was now old, but he had grown since the time of The Fall and was the largest of his kind by far, exceeding the length and girth of a mid-sized tree trunk. His brain was not as advanced as that of man, but among the animals he was superior and quite capable of a certain amount of reason. (Evidently, he was the only serpent given this gift because he had fathered many children and from my observation they were mindless, knowing only to kill, eat, sleep, and propagate.) The sight of a man and woman brought back vivid and painful memories of when he walked upright and was a handsome creature, later to be cursed by God. He still had no inkling as to why that happened; he only knew that, surely, humans were to blame. He was forced from Eden's garden, and now these two had invaded his territory and they would pay the price . . . and provide him an easy and needed meal.

Naomi, worn out from all the climbing queried, "Cain, are you sure that this is the best way to our new land? I know that all other trails would take longer, but the climbing and now this mud is draining the very life from me."

Cain, also tired and a bit testy, replied, "Just follow my lead. Once we get across this valley and you see firsthand the distance we saved you will respect my judgment."

"I do hope you are right, my husband . . . it is a wonderful feeling to the spirit inside of me to call you 'my husband.'"

"Soon, you will know the many good things that come with having a strong man to be at your side, to protect you; then you will count yourself fortunate to serve me."

That last remark was not made up of words that comforted her, but if that was her place in life, then so be it.

A little later, at Naomi's urging, they sat down to rest, though there seemed to be no spot particularly high and dry at this point, and nothing better in sight.

Of course, they had no way of knowing, but the spot where they sat was perilously near to the striking distance of the serpent. In fact, they were so conveniently close it was as if he willed them to their present location. He knew they were tired, and Cain laid down his spear, so this moment was perfect for the predator. Not that the spear struck any great fear into the serpent's heart, but even a small wound could cause some pain. The man seemed to be the logical choice for the first strike, as the woman would not handle a spear with any great degree of skill or power. He could quickly injure him and catch her before she could reach the rocks and a possible hiding place. "How good it would be to have fresh meat," thought the aging serpent. "This valley was never blessed with an abundance of suitable game for me. Most of the creatures here are too fast, too big and fierce, or too small."

As the pair began to drift in and out of sleep, it appeared a most opportune time to strike. The serpent slowly pulled himself out of the mud's grip, silently slipped through the swamp grass and opened his huge mouth to seize the man by the head; but then, he saw on that head the scarlet mark and a sense of terror pulsed through the many muscles of his body. It was a fear rivaled only by the experience with God's wrath in the Garden.

Why such a feeling he did not know, but instinct had always proven a trustworthy guide for him. He immediately pulled back and felt a calm return to the life inside him. Back into the mud he hastily retreated, with every intention of leaving that place with hunger still plaguing his body; then, another feeling, similar to instinct yet not as reassuring, returned to him. It was a feeling that he had known only one other time.

Satan, bearing a look of disgust, materialized in the muddy valley near to the sleeping couple whom he had been following in hopes of causing further torment. Once again, he had an idea to use the serpent in one of his evil schemes. He thought to himself, "If I could coax the creature into killing Naomi, Cain might feel the need to return to Eden, to forcibly take Rachel. That action would stir Adam and the others to disregard the curse of that mark and fight to rescue her. He mused, "Who knows how many would be killed or at least injured." But Satan did not want to indwell the serpent on this occasion. The thought of, once again, being inside what he considered a grotesque and inferior creature was too degrading to face, especially with his powers being limited by the body of whatever housed him. He had, in the past, taken possession of two creatures: once in the serpent, with excellent results; and once in a lion, which proved fruitless. When inside the mind and body of these putrid animals, he was unable to move as lightning, and unable to fly; his strength, though he could pass some of it to his host, was greatly compromised. His mind sensed the dumb-animal thoughts that came from such hosts, and that added to the humiliation. Lastly, he did not relish the thought of pushing God to the breaking point in this—what had become in his mind—high-stakes competition; and so far, that same line of reasoning had led him away from the attempt to indwell Cain. So he decided to give aim to controlling the serpent's behavior from the outside, by forcing his thoughts into the relatively simple-minded beast. As the snake slithered some distance away, still in retreat, Satan put forth the murderous notions of his heart. The serpent stopped and turned in obedience to its master, slithering back to its earlier position where it again readied those dreadful jaws, poised to grab, this time, the sleeping Naomi. He reared up so high it seemed that half his body was off the ground, and in earlier days from that position he had taken some fair-sized prey with his vicious strikes. But this time, in trying to be so certain of a killing blow he made a sound, just loud enough to startle Cain, who, seeing the monster, grabbed his nearby spear and drove it into the serpent's flesh. That brought forth an angry hiss which awoke Naomi and gave her an instant to dive away, barely avoiding death but suffering a blow hard enough to send the young woman flying. Because of Cain's strength, the spear penetrated the thick skin, but not nearly deep enough to bring about severe injury. It did, however, cause the instinct of self-preservation to override Satan's directives. The creature turned toward Cain and with incredible quickness threw a couple of coils around him to squeeze the very life from him. The thickness of its body was such that two coils covered the man's entire torso. Satan thought about intervening at this point to save the only human for whom he ever had any use, but on second thought, he found all this very entertaining. He watched intently as a game of cat and mouse ensued. He was somewhat impressed as he witnessed the myriad of muscles teasingly and steadily tightening their grip; life was ebbing away from the victim and the attacker wore an expression that could be described as almost sinister. But then, something unforeseen happened! Abject panic seized the serpent as, somehow, the scarlet mark was re-impressed upon its mind and at that moment an angel of God appeared and struck him with excruciating pain. It immediately released its coils and began to writhe in the mud. Satan, unaware of what had caused the suffering, mentally exhorted the creature to continue the battle, but within an instant he, also, fell to the ground tasting but a portion of the intense, burning pain. So, as he had done long ago, he fled and left his once-proud pet to face God's wrath, alone. That curse applied to animals as well as to men and the serpent was paying the ultimate price for his actions. Finally, as the sun was cut in half by the crest of the bluff, the creature, suffering and helpless in the mire could only watch as a revived Cain cautiously approached, raised his spear and with all his might drove it into the huge head. Never again did a serpent or any animal possess such a gift of cleverness—and the arrogance that came with it.

Cain, jubilant with the thought that his strength and stamina had defeated the foe, walked over to his wife who lay motionless, wondering if she had survived her injuries and what life would be like without her. Also, the thought that she might be nothing more than a burden from here on crossed his mind, but she began to stir as he rubbed her face and spoke to her. He coolly asked, "Can you walk or do you need more time?"

She shook her head, trying to focus her eyes and trying to recall the events of the day. She looked over at the still monster and in disbelief asked, "How on God's earth did you defeat it? After hitting the ground the last thing I saw was you in its coils and I drifted into sleep with the thought that this was our last day!"

"He almost squeezed the life from me, but he weakened during the struggle giving me a chance to pull loose from his grip . . . and I prevailed."

She had some doubts as to the likelihood of that story, but Cain's spear was sticking from that massive head and there were no other witnesses, so she had to believe it. All those childhood memories of him boasting about his exploits now gave way to an increasing amount of admiration for his fighting skill and a further belief that he would make a fine husband.

As the dwindling daylight gave its final warning before a change to the black of night, Naomi struggled to her feet and pressed Cain for a return to the top of the bluff. She implored, "While there is still enough light to find our way back to the safety of the rocks and the hilltop, let us make haste! The spirit inside me has no peace at the thought of remaining in this valley another moment!"

Cain snorted and replied, "Are you still a girl and afraid of noises in the night? Nevertheless, to please you, we will return to the hilltop and rest for the night." He spoke with his usual air of condescension, but hidden behind that was a feeling of relief that she expressed the very notion that had been in his mind. Unfamiliar territory together with darkness tends to alter one's thinking, especially in the heart of an inwardly fearful man such as Cain; but until she spoke, he felt as though there was no other choice. What if he had been the first to voice concern and she called him a coward? No, his pride could not have withstood such as that. So off they marched for the safety of that higher location that was theirs at the start of the day.

By the time they reached the rocks and a familiar looking path it was so dark you could barely see the ground ahead, but fear can provide incentive as was the case here, and they climbed for all they were worth until they reached a level spot just short of the top. They were both exhausted and gave in to the demands of the body rather than risk further climbing in that blackness. Sound sleep soon came to them, despite the unfamiliar high-pitched shrieks and loud guttural growls that would have kept them awake and ill-at-ease at any other time.

The sun was high off the horizon by the time they awoke, and even with all that rest they were still tired. Cuts and bruises were plentiful, but there appeared to be no serious injury; so the trek to Nod resumed, though it took a few moments for tired, aching muscles to get used to the idea of climbing and walking again. They soon reached the crest and stopped to gaze at the valley below. Odd looking creatures were making short work of their old nemesis. There were four-legged and two-legged animals, some with fur and some without it. It was quite a distance away at this point, but Cain recognized the hyenas with their peculiar stance, and there were also two large lizard-like animals unknown to him. When they made their appearance all fur-covered beasts slunk away.

Naomi, observing the feeding frenzy, said, "And we thought that this valley had little in the way of animals. If we had stayed the night where we were . . ."

Cain interrupted, "It does look like mine was a wise decision, to make for the rocks. Fortunately, this valley seems to be enclosed, otherwise I would have to spend all my time fighting to protect you."

A bit irritated at that remark she boldly stated: "I was never one to shrink from the many challenges this life presents. I can do my share of working and fighting—whichever is needed."

"Ha! You will certainly get your chance at one if not both, and then we will see if you learned anything from Eve. So far, you have shown yourself to be somewhat resilient, but we are just beginning. Your mother has lived through many such trials, over a long period of time."

As they continued along the top of the ridge, they found themselves more than a little nervous, hoping that none of the valley's predators could find its way up the steep, cliff-like area. On several occasions they cast their sight below and saw strange and beastly animal life. It was a world of violence unlike their home in Eden, with the smaller animals under constant threat of being injured or eaten, and large animals defending their territory with tooth, claw, and bone-crushing stampedes. Some of the violent activity appeared to take place for no other reason than sheer pleasure as slain carcasses were sometimes left to rot.

The sun had risen at least ten times on their journey and finally the couple reached the land of Nod. Why this land, Cain did not know, but it seemed that he was led here, and here he would probably stay (though the soil's lack of fruitfulness would cause him to move from one plot of ground to another within the country).

He had vague recollections of this land. It was eerily similar to the land Abel and he found while in their youth. They were in an explorative mood and had hiked into a wilderness so very like this, but by a different route. Being young, they had the stamina to move fast and for long periods of time. They traveled the distance in about seven days and never saw the cliff-ringed valley. There was little to see then, not much in the way of food and good water, of course they stayed only a short while before hiking right back to Eden with hardly a thing to report about their journey.

I took them to task at that time, telling them never to travel that far away again and risk not only their lives but all the lives depending on their various skills. And we made a trip to the whipping tree.

As Cain surveyed the surroundings, he was convinced that this was the same place. It was rocky in many spots, with a few plateaus, but there were parts of it that were low and swampy, dotted by springs. It was good that it had water, but the water did not have a pleasant taste—and that little detail came back to Cain upon his first swallow this time.

"Our provisions are nearly gone and there looks to be only a few fruit trees. The seeds that we have will be of no help for now. Perhaps we can find something edible from the marsh. The roots of cattails at certain times can be filling," Cain offered.

Naomi helpfully answered, "Here are some greens, much like what we had back home."

"This is our home! The sooner you get used to that, the better."

"Oh, of course. I suppose that the excitement of investigating our new setting caused me to speak that way. Here also is a plot of ground suitable for growing food."

Cain looked on disapprovingly and said, "It looks rocky . . . but I guess it sits up high enough to escape the water. It will be a lot of hard work with scant reward, but this is our lot and there is no changing it. Your god has done this! I wish I had the power to defeat him!"

Naomi gasped at the statement and with her hand to her mouth exclaimed, "How can you speak words against our Creator and expect to escape punishment? Do you not realize He has the power to bless and to curse?"

"He has already cursed me! What more can he do except to take my life? But that would be a blessing so it will not happen any time soon! If I had my way . . ."

Satan had reappeared in time to hear their exchange and he smiled.

Since Naomi was a good woman, God eased their suffering slightly and granted them a certain amount of favor concerning daily provisions. Had Cain been alone in this endeavor it would have been strictly hand to mouth and moment to moment, at best.

That first day they found a cave in which to live for the while. There were scattered groves of trees that would eventually add to their living quarters, but actually this cave was ideal in as far as protecting them from the cold at night and from any animals that might attack Naomi or fail to see Cain's mark.

The seeds that they planted in this rocky dirt produced a rather puny crop when compared to those in Eden—and that with much toil and sweat. Weeds and bugs took a toll on the plants and the soil was far from fertile, but later there was harvest enough to sustain them, most of the time.

The animals in Nod, especially the cats, had little fear of man and that lack of fear made for some perilous encounters. No one had yet lost his life to these creatures although Abel had killed one lion and injured several others that had attacked him in the field, which added some volatility to the territorial relationship between man and beast. Despite Cain's frequent outbursts of bravado, they often left him weak-kneed with their deep growls, angry roars, and the aggressive charges that stopped just short of a killing pounce. He quickly decided that it was best to keep a fire going at all times, especially near the entrance of the cave. Fire seemed to be the one defense of which all animals had at least some fear. After a time, the animals appeared to grow somewhat tolerant of the two humans. Cain assumed they were fearful of his spear and strength, but God, once again, communicated to the beasts that Cain was not to be killed. And so, the animals in Nod came to recognize and respect the red mark on Cain. Of course, certain pests still filled their bellies with food from his little plot of ground and from the fruit he gathered from the groves of trees. And insects made life miserable for the two, though it was not as dreadful for Naomi.

During the light of day, most of their time was spent preparing the ground for seed or gathering food from the wild, but occasionally they had time to explore this new land and get some close looks at the unusual wildlife. About a half-day's walk from their cave, near the low-lying, swampland they saw gigantic lizard-like creatures, much larger than the ones that ate the serpent, but not as vicious.

I had seen these creatures on my first day of existence, but only on rare occasions after that. The iguanas looked like babies in comparison, and although these creatures appeared relatively harmless they were so large it seemed wise to avoid them if at all possible. Even during times of apparent play they knocked trees to the ground. Other large animals were observed in this part of the land—enough to convince Cain that, despite the moisture, this was no place to grow food. And on the bordering plain traveling in herds were elephants, giraffes, zebras, buffalo, and many other animals that, given time, would have reduced the Garden of Eden to a barren wasteland. The ground here looked quite suitable for growing crops, but it would have been much too dangerous.

The birds were all shapes, colors, and sizes. Most of them flew, even some of the very large ones, but others could only walk; their weight proving to be too much for wings to bear. Even some of these birds looked to be dangerous with their large, sharp beaks and leg spurs that could slice a man into pieces.

There were also smaller animals that might, later, prove useful. Naomi befriended two young dogs and with such ease it appeared that God had made it happen. They were playful pups and she joyfully exclaimed, "They are so sweet! Surely we can keep them with us!"

"Do you think that the adults of their pack will not seek them? I have troubles enough without watching for wild dogs."

"But since they are young maybe I can tame them, as we did with the sheep and goats back ho . . . back in Eden."

"You foolish woman, dogs are not like sheep and goats. They seem harmless now, but after they become older and bigger, the wildness in their nature will drive them to attack and maybe kill you. And I will not be left alone for reasons of stupidity!"

"Just let me try it for a time. If they prove to be unmanageable or become mean, remember that I, also, know how to handle a spear and a stone axe."

Cain snorted, "Very well. But it will be your burden to bear. And they will not hinder our work or I will shorten their lives considerably."

Naomi playfully rubbed their heads and scratched their ears, quite confident that she could succeed in taming them.

Not long after that, Cain managed to capture some wild goats with the intention of taming them. In not too long of a time enough were captured to make for the start of a genuine herd. He proudly announced, "Now we have some animals worth our time and trouble.

We can keep them in the back part of our cave until they are no longer afraid of us. Then we will have milk to drink and hides for warmth. And those dogs of yours will not stir up trouble with my goats!"

Naomi, voicing her opinion with an infrequent display of irritation said, "I hope you realize the smell that they will bring with them until we can get them into outside pens . . . and know that it will be some time before the herd is large enough for your grandiose plans!"

"Yes, yes, of course," said Cain, bitterness filling his insides, "Why do you never appreciate my ideas? I am beginning an effort that will lead to nourishment and warmth for our bodies. You, with those stupid dogs, take food away from us!"

She knew that further argument was a waste of time and energy, so she respectfully ceased the practice.

They were able to keep the goats in the cave temporarily, but with the smell and the noise acting as incentives, even Cain hurried to complete the construction of outside pens. Of course, those goats had to eat, so the gathering of grass and weeds was added to the work load; later, Cain began the practice of leading them out of the pens to graze. It proved difficult to graze them without losing one here and there either to wild animals or to a goat's natural tendency to be on the roam, so Naomi mentioned the dogs that she had befriended. Taking note of their quickness, she wondered if they could be taught to keep the goats from running away. Cain, as usual, dismissed her idea as pure folly, but undaunted by his pessimism she began to work with the young dogs. It took a tremendous amount of perseverance on her part and she was near to admitting defeat, but with the revelation that bits of food, given as a reward, go a long way with dogs they soon began to learn the art of herding goats.

Cain was his old surly self throughout this experiment, constantly grumbling about having to do all the gathering of food: "I work from sunrise to sunset trying to provide enough food to fill our stomachs and you waste precious time with these useless animals; and to add to the wasted time, you have taken to feeding them our food!"

"My husband, they have to be given a reward so that they will better learn, and besides that, they will soon become quite skilled in catching rabbits and other small animals for their own food. They will not, then, eat so much of our bread and milk. But allow me just a little more time and I will continue to do the work of a wife and teach the dogs, also."

Fortunately, he grew tired of arguing, and though he would never admit it, he knew that things had a way of working out whenever his wife put her hand to something. He needed her, so he let her continue; then after what seemed like time never-ending, the plan succeeded, but instead of appreciation he offered nothing but fault-finding: "Those animals of yours are still eating too much of our food. Dogs found their own food before you came along, so let them eat only what they can catch. And their excrement is every where! I take as few as ten paces in any direction and it is there, always stinking—its odor worse than goats. Just waiting for me to step in it! We did just as well without them."

She snapped back, "Those goats of yours make a bigger mess than any pack of dogs!

"Those goats are providing things we need to survive!"

"Without those dogs our work would prove unbearable!"

Cain grabbed her by the throat and pushed her against the wall of their cave, then somehow managed to control his temper and released her. He then lay down on his mat to rest and brood for a while.

Naomi went into this life with Cain knowing of his ill temper but anxious to begin a family. She was certain that she could bring out the best in him, but after serving him during plantings and harvests, sweating beside him in the field, going on exhausting explorations of their new world, tolerating his foul attitude, and doing all the duties of a wife, defeat began to take up permanent residence in her spirit and she finally spoke her mind, "Why do you always look for the bad in every situation? Would it so hurt you to admit that my ideas and accomplishments have helped make a dreadful situation tolerable?" Her voice at first was weak and shaky, but it grew louder and stronger as she continued, "You have given me very little in the way of love and it scares me to think that I am gradually accepting it! If your attitude were only more like our father's . . ."

She started to say more but as the fiery anger was stoked inside him he found the energy to leave the comfort of his bed and leap to his feet.

He slapped her across the face, hard enough to knock her down, and then stood over her, pointing his finger and shouting, "You are never to compare me with him! He had no use for me, so I will not have him mentioned in my hearing! Do you understand?!"

Up to this point, their arguments had been relatively mild, mostly because she had seldom made her feelings known. The thought that Abel's death was not an accident once again crossed her mind, but she kept that thought to herself.

She was far from her former home, and the thought of giving up on her dreams of having a family caused her to take this pain.

Unknown to her, God had closed her womb for the present, giving her a chance to return to those who truly loved her, but she was determined and prayed nightly for children. God, against what He knew was best, but in order to grant Naomi's desire and reward her persistence, finally opened her womb and she conceived.

Cain, for one of the few times in his life, was pleased at the news and he displayed a certain degree of caring concern for his wife and future child. Naomi wanted to believe that things were changing for the better, but she was enough of a realist to withhold full confidence until more evidence was presented.

The day for giving birth came quickly and she so wished that her mother could be there to help her at such a time. Now, more than at any other moment in her life, she longed for her mother's presence, but she made the decision to leave and was not the type to cry out for support from anyone. And what good would it do since Eve was such a long, difficult journey away. She was not as prepared for this event as she would like to have believed with the pain intense and her husband out searching for food. Fortunately, she had been by Eve's side during several deliveries, so she gained comfort from the memory of those days. The situation was a rugged one to face alone, but Naomi was a rugged individual who had survived several of life's perilous episodes; then, the memory of her mother asking for God's grace and guidance came to her and Naomi prayed to Him. He, out of compassion, granted a successful delivery.

Cain returned as the baby was born and his presence, for once, actually brought some relief. Enoch was the name chosen for the little boy and Cain's face had a look of pride, and that expression, this time, was for something other than just his own accomplishments. And so it was a day to remember in more ways than one . . . but Satan, witnessing this display of tenderness thought to himself: "And to think of the approval I felt toward this one human. You turn your back for just a short while, believing that your work is far enough along to tend to other issues, then all these emotions of love, tenderness, kindness, and other such ignorance begin to creep into his mind. It looks as though a fresh dose of my influence is needed here, and from now on, I will not underestimate the power of these emotions and the circumstances which bring them to the surface. Maybe I will better use these feelings to my advantage at some point."

Satan remained true to himself and was unrelenting in his efforts to return Cain to the former days when murder was in his heart and tenderness was far from it. And it was not terribly difficult as the newness of a baby soon wore off after a few nights of lost sleep: "Can you not hush the incessant crying of that baby!? Is he a weakling or are you a poor mother?"

"He is just hungry. Be a little patient with our new-born son."

"If it is going to be like this every night, the two of you will have to move further back into the cave. And if that fails you will have to keep him outside."

"But what about wild animals!?"

"Then you will have to tend the fire, will you not? I have much work to do and cannot be slowed because of a lack of sleep."

Naomi, at that moment, so wanted to bring up the example of love and caring that had been set before her by their parents, but decided to conserve energy for the sake of the baby.

Satan and the New Scheme

A s God had warned, the land produced sparingly for Cain, and two
crops was about all they harvested from each new plot. No matter
how much care was taken to ensure healthy plant life, it was the same
old story. They would labor hard to clear the ground, work it up with
tools of stone and wood, then sow the seed. The plants sprouted, but
never could their growth be characterized as vigorous. At least the first
crops were not a waste of time, but the second crops were always less
fruitful and barely provided enough to meet their needs. They tried a
third crop on the initial plot but nearly starved. And God's words came
back to Cain: "You shall be a restless wanderer on the earth." Though he
was rebellious and stubborn, he was not a complete fool, so two crops
was the limit on each piece of ground; after that it was time to move
on to the next likely spot. Also, the grass did not long flourish under
continual grazing by their herd of goats. And along with the continual
search for arable ground came times of having to find other roofs to
cover their heads, as it made no sense to live far from the most recently
planted cropland and newly-discovered grazing area. One good thing,
though this territory of Nod was too rocky for successful farming, there
were a number of caves scattered throughout, and they always found a
new one within a day's exploration.

Now that a new soul, ripe for the tormenting had been brought
forth, the thought of other children began to look more promising,

and Satan, with the help of his demon subjects, worked on a plan. Said Satan, with statesman-like prowess: "Fellow fallen angels . . . I have the utmost confidence that we have captured Cain's heart and he will never be taken from us . . . and more than likely we will have his son's allegiance, also; but on occasion, Naomi seems to have a minor influence on the boy's thinking. Well, I have spent much in the way of time and energy to win total control of Cain. Now, true . . . we can continue this method of indoctrination with his children, but since it does require much in the way of time and effort—especially on my part—let us consider the possibility that there are other techniques which might prove more efficient in the capturing and holding of a soul. Now, as you are all well aware, with the conquest of Adam and Eve in The Garden, the human race was awarded to us . . . or more to the point, awarded to me. But God, in His misguided mercy, has given them an escape through the sacrifice of certain animals or first fruits of harvest . . . which is usually accompanied by sorrow for their wrongs. In short, He has made a way to win them back from me. So, for the time being, we have lost our strangle-hold on these humans . . . except for Cain. Oh, to be certain, the potential is there to capture them all, but we need a new course of action. Dagon, as one of my most trusted followers, surely you have a thought as to another means . . . with the same objective, of course."

Dagon, not accustomed to these situations, hesitated for a few moments . . . then blurted out, "Let us kill Naomi! She would then have no more influence with the boy or any others!"

"You fool! Do you think that, at the very beginning, that idea did not cross my mind?! First of all, she has God's favor and He will protect her, even to the point of imprisoning us before the appointed time. Also, our kingdom may never become great unless Cain has a woman to bear children."

Molech offered a thought: "Since all humans have weaknesses, could we not find some suitable candidates from Adam's camp. Some of them have reached adulthood and . . . I mean, would it not be better to work on two fronts?"

Satan thoughtfully replied, "That is reasonable, but I am not ready to overly confront that camp at this time. But I give you my solemn oath that their time will come."

Baal, who seldom offered an opinion without first exploring it from every possible angle, quietly said, "Is there something in blood . . . from which we might gain a mighty advantage over these humans?"

"Other than the shedding of it, I do not know, but I would be interested in hearing more. Can you take the thought a bit further?"

Baal took it a bit further: "I have observed during our stay on this earth that both, humans and animals, pass along certain traits—not just physical characteristics, but reactions, thoughts, and habits. Now, to be sure, it could be that God just makes them that way and that is the end of the matter, but what if those traits are passed along through something in the blood . . . or maybe intimacy? There appears to be a remarkable quality contained in blood, this red fluid that has never pulsed through our bodies. After all, Abel's blood cried out from the ground to God. Or maybe it is the intimacy . . . or a combination of the two. And if somehow this red fluid and that act possess some special significance in the passing along of these traits, could we find a way to disrupt the process and alter things more to our advantage?"

"I was not privy to the details concerning procreation, Baal." Satan, now deep in thought, continued, "And I am uncomfortable with the thought of this whole notion of yours . . . if you are thinking what I am thinking. We may be heading down a path that none would be willing to travel . . . Speak only a little more."

"Well, you are the only one, at this stage, who has the power and the skill to indwell another creature, to actually be inside its body, know its thoughts, and pass your thoughts and inclinations to it." (There was a pause as Baal studied the concerned expression on the face of his king and he felt his usual confidence slipping. The last thing he wanted right now was to say something that might risk his reputation for insight and force him far down the chain of command.)

Satan waited a few anxious moments mulling this over in his mind, and then ordered him to continue.

Baal, with misgivings, did as ordered: "What if you were to indwell the male humans during times of intimacy? Is it not possible that our traits . . . your traits, might be passed along to the offspring in a much more dynamic, invasive, and far-reaching manner?"

Satan drew a deep breath and lowered his head as though in intense, almost anguished thought. He remained silent for a time, to the point that Baal was certain of a harsh reprimand. Just as he was about to beg forgiveness for such a foolish idea, Satan spoke in a subdued manner and tone that none had ever before heard from him: "I am about to mention something that has been in the back of my mind for a long while; something that, as your king, I thought it best never to share. When I entered the serpent, on a whim of sorts, not only was there disgust in being inside such an inferior creature, but there was fear . . . a feeling of fear at the possibility of being trapped inside it; the thought that I might, for the entire life of the beast, be without much of my power. And a dreadful sense of the imprisonment that awaits me some day came over me. So then, after escaping its body, I thought never to try anything like that again. Later on, however, in the hope of inflicting harm on men, I entered a lion. Once again, fear came over me especially when I found that the brain of this animal was so deficient, and I could pass only a little of my strength to the beast; then, within a few moments, Abel's spear found its mark and feelings of intense pain pulsed through me until I managed to escape that animal's body. So I do not relish the thought of experimenting with man."

The subjects whispered back and forth to one another at this revelation and some quietly wondered if this small sign of weakness might open a door for them to someday gain power.

Satan, knowing the character of his mates and sensing their thoughts, fired out with a timely warning: "If any of you have notions of testing my strength and usurping my authority, let me remind you that in Heaven, Michael was the only one who could overpower me. All of you, acting as one, will not be able to defeat me in battle! You need a strong leader, otherwise you will be forever divided and of no consequence in the battle for the human soul. You will wander this earth in constant dread of God and in constant fear of attack from your fellow fallen beings. Flawed and lowly men will walk free of your persecution. Well! What is your decision?"

Fear, in this case being a great unifier, brought forth shouts from throughout the crowd: "Hail Satan! You are our only leader and king! Never would we war against you or attempt to overthrow you!"

Once again, knowing the character of his subjects, he placed no stock in their false, but noisy, words of praise and devotion; still he accepted it all with his usual smugness.

Baal offered, "Perhaps men will be less problematic to indwell since they are somewhat similar to us in physical appearance. Possibly the whole experience will be easier to face than that of being united with a common animal. Also, if found that you are able to tolerate being one with a man in spirit and body, perhaps then, you can teach us to do the same."

"I would not be so anxious to follow my footsteps in this endeavor were I you," said Satan. "It may be possible for some of you to perform the act, but to withstand the extreme anxiety that flows through every part of your being . . . that is the terrible drawback. If I do attempt what you propose and am successful, then at some point we may consider the who's, and how's, and when's of passing along such significant instruction. Baal, you truly have concocted a most brilliant plan. Though it is still in the experimental stage, and I am uneasy about rushing into the testing of it, the very thought of its potential gives me a hope welling up inside me, unlike anything I have known since Abel's death! You are, from now on, next in command and my closest advisor—even if the test fails. Just to possess the vision to put forth such innovative thought shows me that you can be counted on in the future—and I will, when necessary, seek your advice above all others."

Return to Adam's Camp

When last we spoke of my family, Eve had given birth to our son, Seth. He was a good boy and seemed to have more of God's blessings than any of our other children. He was obedient to us, not given to quarreling with his siblings and quickly he learned how to do many of the chores that were so essential to our lives. He had that positive attitude that made you enjoy his company. He also had a burning desire to learn about God and when we explained to him about the ways of our Creator, he listened intently in quiet submission, as though trying to retain every word, asking questions that were beyond one of his physical maturity. I knew that he would be successful in everything that his hand found to do.

Time marched on, oak trees went from acorns to full-grown trees, and many children grew from tiny babes to adults and had children of their own. I had the privilege of performing a number of weddings. The first ceremony involved Enosh and Rachel, and within a relatively short length of time, God granted them children; then, not that long afterwards, five more couples married and God provided them with little ones, also.

Something that we began to see—and how we dreaded those days—was the death of little ones. The first one nearly ripped our hearts to pieces. The third son of Enosh and Rachel was taken, despite our many prayers. They had, out of respect, named him Abel; after this, we all agreed to never give that name to another child.

I questioned God about such painful moments, trying to remain respectful: "Dear God, why is it necessary to hurt us in this manner . . . allowing these wonderful beings to come into our lives only to forever pull them away from our embrace?"

He answered me: "Adam, sin is creeping throughout the world and sorrow follows it like the smell of death. I have restrained its power to a certain extent but in order to maintain justice, death must have its way at times. And you were wrong to use the word 'forever.' You will see many loved ones again in a place where sin does not exist."

"Will death become a common occurrence from here on?" I asked.

"Not yet common, but when it does come to pass, it will almost always be painful; but until you are closer to fulfilling My command to be fruitful and multiply, I will bind the aggressiveness of death in your lifetime."

Unsure of my desire to know, I timidly asked, "Is the time of my death in the distant future?"

"I have not set a day thus far, but may it be a comfort when I tell you that there are a few more children and many grandchildren yet to come. Still, you will not live forever."

That last statement made me uneasy as the thought of dying was not something I wanted to face . . . ever.

God, knowing my every thought, said, "When it comes time to return you to the dust from which you were created, it will be painless in your case. And just to further calm your fears, Abel will be so very delighted to see his earthly father again."

That statement was like cool water on sunburned skin and seemed a likely place to end all questions . . . at least for this day.

Eve and I had more children, several sets of twins included, making for a total of 50. We were still strong and healthy but reasoned that we had more than done our part in fulfilling the command to "be fruitful and multiply." And really, the thought of more sleepless nights caring for infants caused us to wonder about the limit of our strength and health. Both of us had begun to see some gray hairs. I had seen animal hair turn gray, and many times the animal died not long after; so rather than have another child only to leave it orphaned, we agreed to cease intimate relations.

Of all the children God gave us to this point, only four had died: two sons and two daughters.

The rest of our days on the earth would be devoted to our ever-increasing family in as far as the planting and gathering of food, the care and nurture of children, and of utmost importance, the worship of God.

Seth was especially close to the Creator, even from childhood, and with Divine guidance, and Seth's enthusiasm, many of us in the land of Eden worshipped with a sincerity that had been lacking since the death of Abel.

To be certain, there were some in our company who cared little about God and His teachings, and despite harsh disciplinary measures, there seemed to be very little changing of their minds or hearts. I finally accepted the fact that sin was a part of the human nature and would remain a constant obstacle throughout the existence of mankind. But for those of us who loved the LORD, never would we surrender our loved ones without a bitter struggle.

There were now enough people in our land to become quite organized in our work. Yes, pests of every sort still made our lives far less than comfortable, but we had the numbers and the know-how to maintain good crops and healthy livestock. The men did most of the hoeing and digging, while the women watered, spread manure for fertilizer, and pulled bugs off the plants. Both, men and women, shared in the milking of livestock. The men usually had the duty of guarding against predators, especially through the night. We also had the duty of killing livestock in order to supply the women skins for making pouches, bags, blankets, and clothing. They became skilled in sewing the hides together in such a way as to make them look almost as good on us as they did on the animals. And of course, on certain days we gave the best of our animals to our Creator as burnt offerings. Whenever we did things that pleased Him, there was peace of mind and joy in our lives; then again, there were times when we sacrificed an animal that was blemished, or maybe we gave the best but did so grudgingly; at these times there were feelings of remorse as God spoke to our hearts—the conscience as He sometimes referred to it.

Life was not as harsh now as at the first; there were even occasional treats. We could always find fruit in the wild and sometimes honey. Eve could do wonders with those two items by mixing in some cream and putting it on bread. When the sun went down—except for those standing guard—we would often gather together in groups to tell stories, play games using small round stones, and tease the little children by hiding and letting them find us. Sometimes, on a rare day of recreation, the entire family would gather to watch the young men wrestle (and sometimes fist-fight when the losers were unconvinced) and run races. The women mostly cared for the little ones, or discussed the best methods of cooking, or made fun of the men. Sometimes we tried to play tunes by blowing through these hollow sticks that had termite holes in them; something we came across quite by accident one day when we heard a high-pitched whistle as the wind blew through one of them. Then someone decided to make up words that followed along with the tunes. That eventually added to our enjoyment . . . in most cases.

Quite often, after the winding down of recreation, the men became more serious and discussed things like weapons and the constant threat of the big cats, wolves, wild dogs, and other dangerous animals. Discussion often turned to action and we practiced self-defense with the spear and axe and learned the many advantages of working together to defeat these predators, and drive the fear of man into their instincts.

From time to time we experimented with different methods of defense, such as when to kill, when to drive an animal away, and when to run. As far as weaponry was concerned, I preferred the trusty spear and axe with their sharpened stone heads fastened to wood by leather strings or sinews. Some of the boys began to experiment with something they called a sling. It consisted of a piece of animal hide fixed with a pouch big enough to hold a small stone. They swung it in a circular motion above their heads and somehow released the stone at just the right moment to hit their target. At first it seemed only good for driving animals away, but at times that proves to be very beneficial. Enosh even took to fastening a long, leather strand to both ends of a slender, green tree limb from which he propelled sharpened sticks through the air. The sticks flopped every which way and I laughingly told him that it might be fine at just a few paces, but when you are that close, why not use a spear. He seemed bent on making it work.

There were other topics that interested us, such as the starting of a fire. That was one of the most important tasks in our camp. And once we got a fire going we did our best to keep it going for as long as possible because of the effort involved in starting it. We began with dry tinder—the drier the better. When we found a type that was particularly flammable, we stored some of it away for future use. The next step was the most difficult and that was creating enough heat to make a small flame. Sometimes we rubbed two sticks together, but that took a long, long time. Sometimes we placed the end of a stick into a notch on a piece of wood and spun that stick back and forth with our hands until friction caused enough heat to make the wood glow, at which point we placed it into the dry tinder and blew on it, the air making the glow even brighter and hotter. But the easiest way to start a fire was to make a spark fly into the tinder by striking two stones together; of course, not all stones created enough spark to do any good.

As for dissension, speaking for the men, I believe that most of us lived quite peaceably together. Some of the young men held rebellion within their hearts, and though they were often able to work through it with maturity, some could not—or would not—and there would be angry outbursts and occasional fist-fights. The one very important thought, somewhere in the back of their minds, that brought peace or held tempers in check, was the fact that there were too few of them to go out on their own at this point. There was safety, convenience, and a sense of comfort within the family. The dangers outside of it: vicious animals, shortages of food, loneliness . . . and also, though I was the most aware of it, attacks of a spiritual nature—the spirit within and spirits without.

As the father and most experienced in life, I was looked upon as the leader, which involved, among other things, the settling of some of these disputes. Fortunately, our lives were not complicated, and were it not for those rebels mentioned earlier there would have been very few major disagreements. Most outbursts of temper were settled in hand-to-hand fighting and involved wrestling and boxing. Whenever someone tried to go beyond that, to choking and gouging and such, one or more of us stepped in and put a stop to it. Usually, after exerting all that energy, the combatants calmed down and became family again.

There were three occasions in which no amount of debate, counseling, or fighting had the timely effect for which we had hoped. Two of those instances involved (as you might guess) marriages and which young man was to marry which young woman. As often as possible, Eve and I tried to match the oldest boy with the oldest available girl; and that almost always met with little or no argument. But on two occasions, those rebellious ones wanted the same girl and neither would listen to reason. Finally, it came to the point that we made the decision for them, and they could accept it or leave the family.

In the first case, the young man eventually, but grudgingly, accepted our decision; but in the second case, the boy totally rebelled and left us for a time. Lions and hunger finally brought him back, willing to accept our terms; but he held a long-lasting hatred for the newly-married brother. The third case involved a dispute concerning who was next in line to be in charge of overseeing a certain field. Even after much discussion there was no agreement and when it came to blows for the fourth time in two days I took control of the issue and made the decision based on the first-born status. That was a simple way of making a ruling, but it was the method of greatest acceptance. There was bitterness for a time, but that particular matter was taken out of their hands and soon was no longer a source of contention. These three examples turned out to be only the beginning of similar troubles later on in our life.

That gives you some idea of life as men knew it at this time. I will not pretend to know all that went on in the life of the women, as much of their work and conversation took place inside dwellings; but from the things I observed, Eve was held in high regard by all the younger women. She provided instruction on activity that was important to them such as cooking, sewing, caring for children, being prepared to fight off animals in those cases when the men were working the fields, or out gathering fruit or firewood. During her time on earth she had become skilled in dealing with wounds, rashes, ever-increasing illnesses. She had, by testing the leaves and roots of plants, discovered much in the way of healing remedies. And of supreme importance was her experience in the birthing of babies. The young wives were so comforted by her presence during these ordeals. And though she was a very busy woman, somehow, she still had time to talk with me at night, listen to my tales of hardship, and just generally let me know that I was loved. That meant a great deal to me and I shared some of those thoughts with the young men.

As the size of our family rapidly increased, the problems encountered in living together, peacefully, also increased. I found myself spending more time judging disputes than working the fields, flocks, and herds. Eve saw that I was becoming more and more tired with the passing days, and maybe, more importantly, she saw that life had ceased to hold any joy for me. She convinced me to call a meeting in an attempt to work out new arrangements as to delegating a few of our sons to positions of authority in order to allow me some time for rest. I took some days and nights to consider this and seek God in prayer.

Many of my sons already had positions of high responsibility, but my intent in having a meeting was to make their positions a little more official. Too often, my counsel was sought for matters that most of them could have resolved. They, mostly out of respect, seemed to fear that they might overstep their bounds by making decisions without my consent. This meeting—too long in coming—would clear up a few things.

Every man was at this meeting (we left the boys in charge of standing guard where needed) and all were curious. I began: "As all of you know, I have been the leader of this family for your entire existence up to now. I have given my utmost in trying to make right judgments . . . decisions made for the welfare of this family. Some decisions were such that it took days to decide; and some had to be made quickly. In looking back, I realize that my thinking was not always right . . . and despite my best efforts, there were times when you might have been better served had I chosen a different path. But it is easy to look back and ponder what might have been had we done things differently—much more difficult to choose rightly at the beginning. Well, enough of this talk: beginning today, it is with pride that I officially and publicly appoint several of you to positions of authority. Three of you will become family leaders to the extent that your decisions will carry much weight. You will take over many of the duties that have been mine. Of course, this does not take away the leadership and authority that each of you have within your own dwelling; but in order to maintain a developing, healthy society, there must be some guidelines and a few chosen men to oversee critical aspects of life. That was my foremost duty and desire until these last days. I will still be the final authority, should an issue of great difficulty arise, but you three, from now until further notice, will take my place in most instances. Enosh is the eldest son still with us and he will be second in command. I have observed his actions and heard his opinions long enough to know that he can be trusted in any area of life. Peleg is a good son and will be as fair in his judgments as is humanly possible. The third man is Seth, and though he is younger than some of you, he walks with God and has His blessings. You will find no better spiritual leader on this earth; skilled in everything worthwhile and able to teach that knowledge to all who will listen. Several more of you will be appointed to other positions as soon as we become accustomed to this change in our routine. I strongly encourage you to accept my decisions of this day without resentment."

Well . . . you might know that there was some dissension in the group. On the positive side was the fact that every man there was in favor of Enosh as the leader of highest rank. Most were in favor of Peleg, though there were two against him. Seth caused the majority of unrest because of his age. There were several older sons who thought it unfair that they were not chosen instead.

Abinidab argued, "I was nearly a grown man when he was but a child!"

Nadab added, "I was the one who taught him to start a fire and milk the goats!"

Seth stood there, feeling quite out of place, enduring their abuse— even agreeing with them and ready to refuse the promotion.

Feeling that this was not yet the time or the place for Enosh to make this decision, I stepped in once again and raised my hand for quiet to be restored. Quiet was quickly restored and it warmed my heart to see that, though there was disagreement, they still respected me. God had given me this blessing through numerous events and it offset many hardships. And now, at this moment, I silently sought His guidance, and these words came to me: "Young men . . . my sons . . . and grandsons from several generations. Let me say first, how pleased I am that this entire gathering has whole-heartedly accepted Enosh. Peleg has only two detractors . . . and that is very encouraging with the numbers here today. Now, let me explain to you that these three were not chosen by some wild, out-of-the-blue impulse. No . . . I asked our Creator for guidance in this matter and I pondered it through the work days and wrestled in prayer with it at night to the point that sleep all but deserted me for a time. The thought of Enosh as a leader seemed to bring total peace of mind and I was very confident in that choice. Then, I mentioned Peleg and several others to God with no clear answer at first. I went two days without food to prove my sincerity in seeking His counsel. My denial of food for the body was rewarded as God spoke to my conscience, telling me that Peleg was chosen. Seth, because of his youth, was not of my first-choosing; not that I thought he would be unable to handle the position, but because of what we have seen today with this conflict. Many of your names I brought before the LORD seeking the third leader, but with the mention of each name there was no peace inside. During this time, once again to prove my sincerity in the matter, I went three straight days with no food, the third day with no water; weakness nearly overtook me as I labored in the fields, and I wondered if it was all a wasted effort. But . . . a strange glow that started high in the sky, quickly descended, enveloping Seth and causing me to question my senses. I rubbed my eyes and temples, thinking that either my sight was failing or I was hallucinating because of my weakened condition, but there it remained, brighter than at first. I questioned God, 'Are You certain of this, LORD?' He spoke directly to me in such a still voice that, I only, could hear the words, 'Seth is chosen.' And the peace that was mine at that moment more than matched any I have had since those early, sin-free days. So . . . your disputes are more with God than with me."

Having said this, I searched their faces and saw no one who was ready to fight. The more rebellious ones were not terribly happy with the revelation, but seemed resigned to accept my account of the story and God's decision. How wonderful to see this through to a peaceable end.

Satan was not pleased with this turn of events, as he had labored patiently on stirring the rebellious ones to acts of violence, but through prayer his plans were thwarted, for now. Of course, he had sown many seeds of discord and some were bound to sprout at a more opportune time.

"I say to you all, it was so close to shattering into pieces—like a dry clod of dirt thrown against a boulder—this tribe of Adam's!" snapped Satan. "There were at least three young men in that group who had long grumbled that Seth was their least favorite brother and how they would not help him if he were in mortal danger. And now they accept Adam's words without a question or even a cross remark, inwardly cowering in fear at the presence of that . . . old man!"

Dagon remarked, "He does not look all that old."

"Oh, shut up you imbecile! If I say he is old then he is old!"

Dagon had, once again, opened his mouth without thinking and he wished that he could cast that last statement far away. Whatever credibility he once had in the demon world was slipping and he knew that his future comments had better be reasonable, in Satan's eyes at least. He truly gave thought to leaving the brotherhood for a while so as to never again be in a position where an unwelcome statement might slip from his lips.

Something New

I spoke earlier of Enosh's new toy which consisted of a slender, but strong tree limb with a long, thin strip of rawhide connected to both ends. One day, preparing to practice, he hung an animal hide in a tree, then sharpened ten sticks, and an idea came to him. He cut notches in one end of the sticks so that the leather strip would better hold them in place. Then, as usual, with his left hand holding the middle of the tree limb, he used his right hand to grab the end of the stick held by the thong, and pulled back. The limb bowed and he released the stick. As usual, it flew out awkwardly and at less than twelve paces hit a tree and broke into pieces.

Nashor, stepping quietly to a spot just behind the marksman, watched with amusement and asked, "Were you aiming at that tree?"

Enosh whirled around in surprise and blurted out, "I certainly was!"

Trying to muffle his laughter Nashor retorted, "My mistake. It looked like you were aiming at that hide hanging on the thorn tree about five paces to the right."

"Fine, fine! Have your laugh now! When I perfect this weapon you will not be laughing anymore!" He was embarrassed but as Nashor's laughter continued, he soon found himself laughing. After the light moment he became serious again and stated, "I am so certain that this will eventually be useful to us and not just a toy. If I could only figure a way to make the, arrows, as I call them, fly straight. You are usually quite clever in solving problems, Nashor . . . how about an idea for this?"

"I have to agree with our father and tell you that the spear, axe, and maybe the sling are the only weapons that will ever be of use for defense."

"You would mention the sling, since you had a part in its making and are skilled in its use."

Nashor stared into the distance for a time giving the matter fair consideration, then replied, "Well . . . two thoughts come to mind: Could the weight of those projectiles make a difference and . . . can we learn something from the birds?"

"Hmmm . . . we have stumbled onto dead birds in the forest and examined their bodies, finding that their bones are hollow, yet strong. That would make them less heavy. But I doubt that a hollow stick from any type of tree would be very strong. In fact, a heavier stick might make for truer flight"

Nashor thoughtfully answered, "Probably true, but I was thinking more about the feathers, a feature possessed by no other animal. They surely play a major part in flight."

"That seems reasonable, but how could we fix feathers to the arrows?" asked Enosh.

"I have no suggestions at this point, but maybe a thought will come to me at a later time."

Enosh then offered an idea: "Speaking of finding birds in the woods . . . I remember finding broken eggs on the ground from time to time and on some occasions, the egg yolk that ran onto sticks and such, dried and seemed to hold them together. Do you see my meaning?"

"I believe so," answered Nashor. "You think that it may be possible, using the insides of an egg, to stick feathers to these arrows in such a way as to aid them in straight flight."

Enosh shrugged his shoulders and continued, "At this moment, many of our ideas are unproven and it will take much in the way of trial and error before reaching any definite conclusions. Different sizes of arrows and different types of wood to find which is the most suitable; and whether to use an arrow with only a sharpened end or to try and fix a stone point; and should the feathers cover the arrows from point to butt, or just in a few sites along the shaft. And what if in the end it all proves fruitless and my time wasted?"

"Defense of the family is a worthwhile endeavor, so do not let the doubts of others stifle your . . . creativity. I am being serious, now. May it turn out to be what you hope it to be and God's blessing upon it."

The two parted company realizing that their leisure time had gone on too long and their labor was needed in the nearby fields.

Cain's World

Not long after the weaning of Enoch, another child was born to Naomi and Cain, a very pretty girl who was named Tamarah. Her hair was reddish and her little features were straight. Upon viewing the tiny child and seeing a resemblance to Rachel, Cain's mind began to, once again, entertain thoughts of returning to the land of Eden and capturing his first love. It seemed impossible for him to put her completely out of his mind for any extended length of time. As far as any true fatherly love toward the little one, there was not an abundance, only a little less irritability on this day.

One day, after a time of healing, intimacy appeared to be nearing the foreseeable future judging by certain words and actions which were not missed by Baal. He soon began to encourage Satan to indwell Cain so as to test his theory concerning human blood and intimacy.

"I am telling you that they are not far from resuming physical closeness and we do not want to miss this opportunity as we did with the last child."

Satan, becoming weary of this whole notion answered, "You talk as though this is nothing more than deceiving a child or outwitting Dagon! I tell you there is more to this than you know. When the time seems right, then I will involve myself in their sickening rituals. I have not forgotten your theory, but let me take care of matters in my own time."

Baal came close to overstepping his limits and he respectfully replied, "Of course, of course . . . curse my anxiousness in this matter.

Seldom do I ever have a shortage of patience, so I beg your forgiveness my king."

Coldly, Satan replied, "Forgiveness is not a quality near to my heart . . . if I had one. Tomorrow night has been on my mind all through this day. We will see, my second in command . . . possibly tomorrow night."

With that comment, Baal's hopes were high and during the evening he secretly led the young couple into an argument, ensuring there would be none of the "two shall become one," on this night.

Tomorrow came. Early in the day, Baal, in a moment of weakness boasted that Satan was ready to try the experiment that had been discussed earlier. The word spread all through the camp, eventually getting back to and irritating the master demon again, putting him in an uncomfortable situation in which there was no graceful way to do anything different. Satan put a firm hand on Baal's shoulder and with those cruel, fiery eyes that could make the insides of the bravest being turn to water, sternly took him to task: "Baal, my trusted assistant . . . just what is your idea in spreading these unconfirmed statements! 'Possibly' was the word used if memory serves me. Now, if in any way I fail this test, my leadership will again be questioned and I may have to display my superior strengths to the entire band once more. Since the day you were appointed as second in command, your abilities in assistance have diminished."

Baal, unable to meet his leader's gaze replied, "I have displayed weakness as of late, but I only told two others and . . ."

Satan motioned with his hand and in uncharacteristic fashion said, "Let not your mind be troubled. Call the others—all of them—for a meeting and let us face this situation immediately before rumors and unrest rule the day."

Baal, somewhat surprised, but certainly thankful to have escaped his captain's anger, did as ordered and assembled his fellow demons for the meeting.

All were curious about the reason for this gathering as meetings had become a rarity of late, called only when an issue of great importance was imminent. Satan, with Baal at his right side, prepared to speak: "I called this meeting for two reasons, the first to tell you that I will be attempting an indwelling of Cain tonight, provided that he and Naomi are feeling amorous . . . of course, that mood can be facilitated by the skilled use of my powers of persuasion." (There was a pause, and polite laughter initiated by Baal spread through the fraudulent group.) "I am quite confident of success in this matter because of the power, ambition, and craftiness that are mine . . . essential qualities in the make-up of a triumphant leader. I know you will all be supportive of me in this endeavor; and the support of underlings is of utmost importance . . . which brings me to the second reason for this meeting." The word "meeting" had barely left his lips when he backhanded Baal with terrible force. The blow lifted his feet off the ground and he landed on his back. Stunned and startled, the lieutenant remained motionless for a bit and Satan continued: I have sensed the beginnings of rebellion in our midst . . . minute as they, presently, may seem, I offer this *demon*stration for your benefit. A word to the wise, if you will . . . just in case there are others of you who desire to usurp my authority."

Baal, finally able to arise to a sitting position, blinked his eyes over and over, trying to regain his focus, and as his vision cleared, his temper flared and he lunged at the back of the still-speaking master. Satan, with uncanny intuition, grabbed him before he could strike any kind of blow and began to slap him across the face in humiliating fashion using his palm in one direction and his backhand in the other. Baal was so outmatched it was embarrassing to watch; like a youth against a full-grown warrior. And Satan, at once smiling and then laughing the entire time, administered one of the more cruel beatings any of them had ever witnessed. As Baal would try to block the blows Satan either powered right through the uplifted arms or used the arms against his weaker opponent to continue the slapping, saying, "Why are you hitting yourself?" Most of that crowd cheered wildly at the violence and humiliation, deriving an odd pleasure from witnessing it, but a few who were closer to Baal and who blamed Satan for their circumstances, thought to turn away or leave. Immediately, the beating ceased, but only for a moment, while a long and imposing finger was pointed and shaken as a warning to stay put less they receive the same. Then the activity resumed and went on for some time with no let up in the severity of it or the frenzied delight of the aggressor and the onlookers. Finally, more out of boredom than anything, the lesson came to an end. Baal was weakened to the point he was unable to get to his feet for an extended period, and his pride was more than crushed.

After the passing of a few days, around the time of Baal's partial-recovery, Satan appeared at his side to discuss their future.

Baal, still sulking, his ego all but destroyed, was unable to lift his gaze from the ground. His voice trembled at first, from fear, intense dislike, and maybe frustration. When his regained some control, he spoke in a guarded tone, as one on the verge of lashing out, but who knows (similar to a vicious dog that once fought against a tiger) the consequences of such an action. "I will step down as second-in-command, immediately . . . if that meets with your approval."

"It does not. You made a series of thoughtless blunders, but now that it is over, the lesson displayed for all to see. I want you to remain in your position. You see . . . I unwisely allowed a certain amount of closeness to creep into our relationship, forgetting that no one is to be trusted and that to be a strong ruler I must reign with total ruthlessness. Yes, I could drive you away from this kingdom, but your insight and counsel are still the best of the lot . . . and I was impressed with that moment that your temper controlled your actions. I like that. Now that you have been properly punished, I assume you will not fail me again. And know this: God still speaks with me from time to time, as He does with all members of the angel hierarchy, and though I am misguidedly considered the lowest of the low, He still, on occasion, asks of our comings and goings. And He continues to consider me to be above all of you. Now, if I earnestly requested an early imprisonment for any of my subjects . . . well, can you take such a risk?"

Doubt and dread were driven deep into Baal's psyche at this revelation, and without hesitation he replied, "You have my allegiance, for as long as we exist on this earth."

There was a slight pause as Satan weighed the meaning of those words; after the pause he elected to accept Baal's promise at face-value.

As he started to leave, he offered to Baal some words of encouragement: "You might like to hear that the indwelling was something of a success, though I am not yet certain where it will lead."

Baal had totally forgotten about the testing of his theory through the course of recent days and he somehow found the strength to jump to his feet, and the enthusiasm that seemed long-departed, never to return, came rushing back causing him to temporarily forget the humiliation. There were so many questions that came to his mind and he nearly blurted them out, but remembering that many of his troubles began when he failed to keep a tight hold on his tongue, he restrained his eagerness and forced a more reserved demeanor. "So . . . to what would you compare the experience?" Then, with excitement nearly causing him to, again, let his tongue stir up trouble for himself, "Wha . . . what was it like?!"

"Once I fought through the anxiety . . . in several ways it . . . was unlike anything I have ever known. At first, all I sensed was from Cain's feelings of sheer pleasure, and I began to think that, maybe, these humans have one advantage over me, but then, I sensed Naomi's spirit, and it utterly ruined the experience. Evidently, she still feels love for him, despite his total lack of concern for her. But, at least I now know that any tender word or deed from our dear Cain comes about only to use others. Right now, he needs her, but that will one day end. And I will continue with these experiments from time to time, in order to test your theory. But to lose so much of myself for even a few moments is hardly worth the risk." (Satan momentarily goes on a tangent.) "I tell you they are mindless during these interludes—oblivious to all reason! But . . . there is a certain amount of deception taking place, especially from the man, and that element makes it somewhat tolerable. Still, because I am duty-bound to destroy them . . . but am forced to use this act of indwelling to further my cause, I hate them even more than at the first!"

Satan, momentarily returning to a more composed self, tries to stay on the earlier subject, "Well . . . whether or not your ideas are proven true, my fondest hope is that this obsession . . . this intimacy, will turn out to be the ultimate weapon in my arsenal of wiles. I will use it to stir up jealousy and suspicion; cause guilt, tear down friendships," (voice rising with each new category) "disrupt family unity; and then, with the family torn asunder . . . their societies will fall!" Calmness again returns, and a slight smile as he mulls it over in his imagination. "If I just remain patient, they will disobey God because of these desires."

Satan continues, "Now, once again . . . to our earlier subject: I realize that it will take time to come to any conclusions—several children will have to be born . . . and grow. It will take time, a great deal of it. Patience . . . that is the one characteristic in which God and I are in agreement in as far as the part it plays in success."

Over the course of time, more children were born to the couple from Nod, two boys and two girls joined Enoch and Tamarah. Cain and Enoch were fairly large as toddlers, but the two newest boys were large at birth—and one of their sisters was not tiny. Others were born as God allowed, until there was a total of fourteen—seven of each sex. Four of them were physically large at birth and the other ten of a more normal size.

God, speaking to Those closest to Him, said, "Have You taken notice of the children born to Naomi? Satan has managed to disrupt and taint the reproductive process and important qualities carried within that process. If I was not so well acquainted with him, he could surprise even Me. It was my hope that this course of action would prove too distasteful for him, but hatred for men and selfish ambitions have evidently had their way, yet again. I believe, though, that Naomi's days of child-bearing are finished. Her prayers for children have been answered . . . but she will receive little in the way of joy from most of them . . . bless her spirit."

Rearing of Children in the Land of Nod

L ife passed, and Enoch grew up fast and of a fair size though not as large as Cain; and unlike his father, he was not totally lacking in true wisdom. Cain taught him things about fighting, planting crops, milking the goats, gathering fruits and greens, and starting a fire. All these were important to their life in Nod, but Naomi wanted to teach him things like sharing, thoughtfulness, and the art of conversation, which most of Eden looked upon as significant in such a simple life-style. She tried to instill the importance of respect toward elders in the event that he might someday come into contact with his grandparents, and even more importantly, respect toward the Creator; but like most boys he observed and followed the example of his father. And Cain made it a point to cast Eve (and her father) in a negative light. Also, God—if He existed at all—was painted as unfair and never to be held in high regard. So the boy, at the beginning, came to be big and strong and full of contempt, pleasing his father and those with like beliefs. Cain had some feeling for Enoch, and the two of them built a city which Cain named after his son. It was nothing to boast about as far as beauty and excellence of carpentry, but Enoch was proud of it.

Enoch and Tamarah were half-grown by the time the others arrived, but the newcomers—the ones born big, soon caught up and grew even larger than Enoch. Then, after only a little more time, they grew nearly as large as Cain; and only his experience and ruthless tenacity enabled him to defeat them in wrestling bouts. Enoch was a bit quicker and that allowed him to keep his edge over them, but he had to wonder how long that would last?

Two of the girls, Tamarah and Adah, had respect for their mother, but nearly all of the other girls had little if any. Other than Enoch, (and he kept it hidden) none of the boys had respect for her, and her once-hardy spirit, along with the light in her eyes, diminished more and more with the passing of life's episodes. She eventually had grandchildren, many of them, but received even less in the way of love from them as they followed the ways of evil with a continual desire for more. Try as she might to make a difference for good, her life had turned out to be nothing but a continual disappointment, with Tamarah and Adah her closest friends. Witnessing, day after day, a society that did as it pleased with no boundaries, she found herself becoming hardened to it and somewhat accepting of it. She wanted to escape before losing anymore of herself.

She had not seen her mother and father in such a long while, and she truly struggled to remember our faces. Finally, the day came that drove her to make a decision she should have made long ago.

One morning, Cain came to the dwelling finding nothing but fault with the food that she served before him, and Naomi had her say: "I want you to know that I am so very weary of being unloved and totally disrespected by nearly all in this poor example of a family! I want to return to my mother and father—to people who fear God and obey His teachings—and by so doing, have love for one another."

Cain, in his usual hateful tone responded, "You have no mother or father. They died long ago when they ventured into our territory and we killed them." Her eyes intently searched his face to see if there was any truth in the statement. He glared at her for a time, torturing her before that wicked laugh of his.

"That is a lie and one of the most evil you have ever told!"

"So what if it is? Besides, you could never survive the trek back to Eden and you know it. You also know that there is much in the way of work here and you cannot be spared for even a day."

"My only purpose here, it seems, is to be your slave—preparing food, making sandals and clothing, training dogs, caring for goats, and taking care of little ones that will grow to be worse than their parents—with your full support. I am making plans to leave, soon; if I die along the way than so be it."

Cain stared off into space and gave another of his sarcastic comments, "Of those tasks that you mentioned—privileges actually—one is missing and has been for a very long while."

"And it will continue to be that way for my part; and add to that, the fact that you have taken some of our daughters and made wives of them, setting a pattern that all our males now follow. We no longer know who fathers which child."

"All this talk of 'wives' and 'husbands' as though there was something special about it. They are just words that hold some *wonderful* meaning for you. There are very few pleasures in this existence and I intend to fully enjoy the ones that are available—with no rules except those that I deem necessary."

"I say again that the point has been reached where I am no longer needed, so I will soon depart for Eden and I truly do not care what happens to me along the way!"

Cain slapped Naomi to the ground, and in a fit of rage pointed his finger and through slobbering teeth seethed, "You may soon perish, but it will not be on a journey to Eden! If you try to run away from me, I will have you tracked down and brought back to Nod! And you will regret the day of your birth."

Cain was convinced that he no longer needed or wanted her, but if she were to leave him it might lead to a loss of respect within the male ranks . . . and he would not stand for that.

Naomi remained silent in order to avoid further abuse, but her plan to leave was now fixed in her heart, and her mind was set. She soon went to the only ones she could trust, Tamarah and Adah, and told them of her plan to leave. They also hated life in Nod and had often hoped for some sort of deliverance. This looked to be their only chance.

The Escape

It had been generations since Naomi made the journey from Eden. She had doubts mixed with some fear, but anything would be better than what she now had. They made their plans and part of it was to leave as soon as possible. She knew that Cain would never suspect an early departure since he had so forcefully warned her, and in his mind, scared the rebellion out of her. They would leave in the morning, after the men left to tend the flocks and fields. Sacks containing some fruit, vegetables, and a few other essentials would hopefully get them through a good portion of the trip, with the hope of finding more along the way. If anyone saw them carrying these sacks they would pretend to be out gathering food for the family.

Sleep was in short supply this night as she went over and over the plans in her mind; and there was anxiety, not so much for herself but for the safety of her two daughters. There was anxiety, but there was also excitement and hope at the prospect of escaping this life of near-torturous captivity. Excitement . . . yes, that was it—a feeling she had not known since she began the journey to Nod with the man that, at the time, she loved and who seemed to hold promise for a wonderful life together as husband and wife. She searched her memory for something positive in that youthful relationship, something she could point to with joy, but other than a moment here and a moment there her dreams never materialized. And she had more than lived up to her end of the arrangement.

She came to her senses at this point and cast these painful memories from her mind, never to think upon them again. Now it was time to make use of the one thing she had gained from this relationship with Cain, and that was the cold, hard fact that there are times when you have to utterly forget your pride and admit to abject failure—not an easy thing for a strong-willed woman.

Finally, the early rays of sunlight announced their daily victory over the darkness, and most everyone in the camp arose, grudgingly accepting their lot within the miserable borders of Nod. Even Cain was willing to put forth labor digging in the soil, the one area of life in which he derived a measure of satisfaction.

As was her custom, and to be certain of avoiding suspicion, Naomi made the men a tasty morning-meal, one that should have received praise, with eggs gathered from the nests of water-fowl, bread, fruit, wafers with honey, cheese and milk from the goats; not surprisingly, all of it taken for granted. The only words spoken were coarse and concerned the fields and goat herds. As the men set forth to take part in their daily labor, they griped and cursed as they walked. And the women began their day with the customary whining, arguing, and cursing. This particular morning saw a hair-pulling brawl—activity in which Naomi, in times past, intervened . . . but not this day. She thought to herself: "Maybe the fighting will provide an excellent diversion."

Tamarah and Adah, carrying their sacks of goods, were more than ready to begin, and with the fight now quite heated, their mother calmly led the way down a little-used trail that ran back to old dwellings and exhausted fields, long abandoned. Confident that their escape was seeing, at least, initial success, they stepped up the pace and maintained it for a good while. They were just short of mid-morning when they heard the barking of dogs on the trail not far behind them. Fear seized the hearts of all as they wondered whether to run, hide in the bushes, or climb a tree. Tamarah blurted out, "Mother! Do you think that someone knows of our plans?!"

Adah, nearly in tears asked, "How could anyone have known? What will happen to us?"

Naomi, not prepared with an answer at this point, was nearly in a panic herself at the thought of being discovered so soon. All at once, two dogs burst through some bushes. She had grabbed a tree limb to use as a club and had drawn back, ready to swing with all her might when the look of fear and concern on her face quickly faded, and was replaced with one of relief and affection. It was Mal and Keber, Naomi's best friends in the animal world. Dropping to her knees she hugged them and lavished words of praise, "Oh, how good to see the two of you! I did not think to bring you with us, but how wonderful now that you are here!" Those dogs wiggled from nose to tail-tip, a display of love solely reserved for Naomi's eyes, and as she petted them they licked her face and jumped on her. "We will be so grateful to have your keen eyes and sense of smell!" She looked at the daughters and with tears of thankfulness streaming down all their faces she said, "We have a much better chance of success with them! With all the training devoted to these companions since their puppy days, how could I not have given thought to their usefulness at a time like this?" Being still on her knees, and with the two daughters following the example, she gave the first of many "thanks" on their journey.

Then, Tamarah timidly offered, "We did decide this quickly. We probably needed a little more time to be thorough." Her voice rising, "But I do not blame you for wanting to leave as soon as possible!"

Naomi sensed a weakening of her resolve and spoke sternly, "Girls, this is no time to for second thoughts. If we were to change our minds . . . by the time we got back, there would be nothing but punishment of the severest kind awaiting us. Choose now! You know what lies behind—beatings to be sure, and very little chance to ever escape again. Only God knows what lies ahead, but I am willing to take that chance with or without you."

There was no further discussion as all three were, again, of one mind; hoping for something better but ready to lose their lives if need be.

It was soon mid-day and some of the women began to be curious as to the whereabouts of the three. Judith said, "I saw them walking toward the trees carrying sacks. They are probably gathering fruit and let the time get away from them."

That seemed to satisfy most, though a few wondered if wild animals might have attacked. But all were in agreement that Naomi could send a lion scurrying for his life and after several crude, derogatory comments along those lines, all talk ceased for awhile.

When it was nearing sunset and the men came in from their labors ready for food and rest, the women asked of the missing ones. None of the men had seen them. Cain, at this point, began to get suspicious, but he did not want to discuss female rebellion in front of the whole camp so he snorted and said, "They probably got lost searching for food. You know that none of the three have any sense of direction. We will send out a search party in the morning. They will pay dearly for not having food ready for us tonight!"

Several of the men were not quite convinced as to the reason for their absence, but their leader seemed mostly under control, just his usual ill-tempered self, so they ate and, soon, fell asleep. Despite his outward act of relative calm, Cain laid awake planning revenge of the worst kind upon these three, possibly even death.

———————◆◆◆———————

Daylight had nearly given over to darkness by the time the women got a fire going. They allowed plenty of time, but there was little in the way of flint rock (the best for creating sparks) around their camp, and by the time they found a few pieces it was sunset. The night animals were just beginning to growl and shriek when the flames gained strength enough to provide protection. The younger women breathed a sigh of relief, but were still worried. Naomi told them she was about ready to climb a tree, only half joking.

Adah asked, "Do you think they will come after us tonight?"

Tamarah chimed in, "Will they send their dogs after us? Some of those dogs are truly ferocious! How many men do you think will take part in the chase?"

Naomi, after a few moments, thoughtfully answered, "Cain will rest tonight, being confident that we will be quickly overtaken. And though he is not overly wise, he is wise enough to know that wild animals could make a meal of them from the darkness of the forest, even with the use of torches. Also, he will want some daylight to be better prepared for the hunt. And yes . . . they will use dogs. Mal and Keber can hold their own against most of them, but Cain has two that he and Enoch trained to be quite vicious.

"We will have to be mentally alert and on our guard at every turn on this venture, because he will use any and all means to gain his revenge. As far as the number of men is concerned . . . he will not send more than four or five, figuring that there is too much work to be done to spare any others; and, he will be certain that three women will be easily subdued by the men of his choosing." Naomi paused, and then smiled, causing the two to question it. She answered, "I was just thinking about the punishment that awaits those men if they do not succeed."

Tamarah started to ask another question, but Naomi changed the subject and asked, "Who wants to take the first watch?" Two sets of eyes filled with dread stared at her. They were quite familiar with night watches, but usually the men took care of that. On those occasions that the women were involved there were several of them armed with spears and plenty of dogs to assist . . . and, in such cases, men were not far away.

Naomi explained, "One of us has to be awake at all times, tending the fire and watching for the expected and unexpected. The dogs will help us, but they need protection, too. Lions would love to snatch any or all of us. Keep in mind that it is of utmost importance to stoke the fire and maintain its present strength. During your watch, if either of you feels that she is on the verge of falling asleep, awaken me. I will watch the entire night if need be."

Adah volunteered to go first and she did well; then Naomi took her turn and nearly lasted until dawn. But she eventually reached the point of extreme fatigue and woke Tamarah. She was difficult to rouse, but when she finally gained her senses she did well, and that allowed her mother a short, much-needed rest. At the rising of the sun, and the insistence of the dogs, the three were quickly on their way. Naomi knew they could not waste a moment and hope to stay ahead of the strong, young men who would soon follow. The thought went through her mind that she definitely could travel faster alone as the gravity of the situation seemed not to strike at the heart of the younger ladies, judging by their occasional lapses into laziness. Naomi implored, "Adah! Tamarah! Walk faster! Do you not realize that this is surely life or death!"

Adah answered, "But we have not yet heard the bark of a dog. Maybe they think we are lost and not all that far away from camp. And we have come to at least three places where we had a clear view of the valley trail far behind us, and there was no sign of anyone."

Naomi almost screamed at her, but managed to control her temper, "If they get that close, we are in grave danger, especially if they see us in the distance. They would, then, redouble their efforts and catch up with us long before we reach Eden. We must travel for at least seven more days at this pace to reach our goal. It will be a test unlike anything you have ever known."

The two appeared to better understand their plight after this admonishment and the pace quickened until near-sunset, at which time they collapsed at a likely looking area to spend their second night. It was at this time that Naomi took three straight tree limbs and sharpened the ends, making spears. They would have to do, as there was not enough time to sharpen rocks and fix them to the ends of the limbs. At least they now had some means of self-protection and would no longer rely just on the dogs and the fire.

They were in an elevated, rugged setting this night and flint rock was plentiful here. A fire was soon ablaze and Naomi took the first watch while her daughters fell sound asleep. Too tense to really relax, she remained vigilant well into the wee hours of the morning, continually watching, straining to see through the darkness with only the fire, a partial moon, and the stars for illumination. Finally, she was near to surrendering her position as night sentry when off in the distant valley a tiny speck of light caught her eye. Was it a star? No. She fixed her eyes on that one spot, unwilling to shift her focus elsewhere. Her own fire had died down, allowing her to see more clearly. Just a little while longer . . . she stared into the night, hoping to gain a clearer knowledge of the distant, flickering, orange light; a light that soon quieted to a dim glow. She rubbed her eyes, hoping that, somehow, her imagination was the source of the glow, but after a few more moments of examination her fear was confirmed. She reasoned that since she saw their fire, they saw hers, and would be off to an early start in the morning. There was now no sleeping for her, so she let the others get a good rest while her eyes remained fixed on the now-faint, far-off light. She prayed that they would not take up the chase while it was dark, and never did she see torch light, granting her a degree of much-needed comfort.

At the first sign of dawn she woke her daughters and told them of the situation. The womens' campsite was at the edge of some trees and on a ridge overlooking the valley. It was still dark enough to see a speck of the distant fire, but light enough to get a fix on its location. The men would surely catch them in two more days—well short of Eden—unless by some miracle they could gain a man's stamina or Naomi could figure out a different plan of action. There was a shortcut . . . by way of that awful valley. Not many things truly frightened her, especially after living with Cain, but her insides became weak and her legs shaky as her mind pictured walking through that terrible place. It was not so much the thought of facing death, but the way they would die: being torn limb from limb and ending up in the intestines of some loathsome creature; being utterly defeated by a mindless beast driven only by instinct. All remnants of inner peace would abandon them the moment their feet left the safety of the cliff tops and touched the marshy ground of that basin.

There was a good reason for that lack of peace: Of all the places on Earth, Satan had a fondness for this valley with its, seemingly, never-ending suspense and violence. He took such pleasure in the anguished cries of the weak as they were crushed by the strong; and along with the suffering was the notion that this valley was his creation, in a sense. This was Satan's retreat, and his tyrannical presence was felt by Naomi—a most significant gift and one she did not really recognize or appreciate at this point.

The three were soon on their way and by the light of early morning the women anxiously looked down from the cliffs into that fog-shrouded gorge, each wondering whether they would have the strength of body and nerve to descend into the source of Naomi's greatest fear. She was far from certain as to whether she could force herself to go that way, even as a last resort.

Two more days passed, and they maintained a pace that none thought possible, reaching a mark that looked to be about the halfway point of clearing that abyss. They had not seen a sign of their followers since that early-morning campfire. Could it be that the men were tiring; after all, they were human, too? And Naomi had prayed for deliverance, a fact which she was not shy in sharing with her daughters. Surely this was a situation that God fully understood and to which He would readily grant success. Tiring men and tireless women could well be part of that answer.

Naomi now felt a boost of confidence as they further persisted into this new day which saw them climbing and hiking over rugged terrain. Maybe their quickened pace had made the difference and their stamina and resolve would outlast that of their pursuers. Now, with her mind more at ease, her imagination began to run wild and she could almost picture the joyful celebration in Eden at her return. Well, that tender thought lasted all of twenty paces, and then a dampening chill ran down her spine at what sounded like a dog's bark. It was not Mal or Keber as they were right there in plain sight. Of course, there were many strange noises that came from that area, maybe it was a wild animal. She stopped, then raised a hand as if to say, "Quiet! Listen!" The dogs' ears perked up and their back fur bristled. They growled, but Naomi gave the order for silence, and they obeyed. There it was again—a distant bark. And the confidence that was theirs only a moment ago vanished much quicker than it came. They now had to do some strenuous climbing to get to the top of the ridge that presently challenged them, and with abject panic acting as a motivator they soon were quite close to reaching the highest vantage point of the entire land; from there they would have their best view of the trail behind them. Their blood ran cold as they glanced over tense shoulders and saw two dogs sniffing the ground only a hilltop away. The dogs were right on their trail and seemed to gain in strength and speed as they sensed the nearness of their quarry.

The men were yet further behind, unable to keep up with the dogs, but close enough to recognize the now-frenzied pitch in the yelps and howls. That would enliven their tired bodies and prove the difference between young men and even the heartiest of women. They were not going back to Cain empty-handed to face torturous punishment and, worst of all, the taunting from their brethren.

The women, after pulling themselves and the dogs over the last ledge of the steep, rocky bluff, had reached the high point of their surroundings and the low point of their outlook. Taking a few moments for rest and to cast one last wistful look at the neighboring hilltop (so as to be more certain of their situation) they promptly saw four men moving at a trot. Naomi's voice, with barely a trace of the dejection in her heart, was still strong and she charged, "We will not give up, now or ever! They still have to climb this cliff and they will find it difficult, just as we did! All three of us are hardened from our journey—much stronger than at the beginning. Let us run wherever possible and climb hills as though lions were at our heels!" (Inwardly, she wished that it was a lion they faced.) They were somewhat dispirited, but hope was still present within their now-calloused souls, and they would fight until the end, whatever that might prove to be.

The Pursuers

The men, for the first time on this mission, were able to rejoice as they caught a glimpse of the runaways at the crest of the challenging mount just ahead of them. "Climb! Climb for all you are worth!" commanded Nergal. But Hamath, gasping for his next breath, cried out, "Wait!" They gladly followed that order, stopped and stooped over with their hands upon their knees.

Nergal, near the end of his strength and taking a breath between every couple of words, anxiously asked Hamath, "Why do we . . . stop now when . . . we are so close . . . to our goal?"

"If we continue like this, bodies already weakened, and even more so by the added burden of helping dogs crawl over these crags, we will gain very little by day's end. However, if we take a time of rest, eat some food, drink a little water, we will, in the long term, gain considerably on them. Maybe . . . before night falls . . . they will be in our hands."

"What if they continue to out-distance us?"

"They may for awhile, but with our vigor restored we will move twice as fast as before and more than offset the lost ground."

Hamath was the eldest, wisest, and by far the largest of the four, standing nearly a head taller than his mortal father, Cain—and they listened to his voice. While they rested, talk was lively and flowed freely for the first time since the start. "I never would have believed that those three could avoid our capture for this many days."

"Naomi, maybe . . . but not Adah and Tamarah!"

"She must have willed them to travel at her pace."

"You know . . . I do not relish the thought of fighting inferior women, but we had better be prepared because Naomi will be prepared." All nodded in agreement.

Lamech added, "Cain wants them returned alive, so we must not lose sight of that order."

Edom fired back, "If they want to step into a man's sandals, they will have to accept a man's punishment!"

Nergal said, "The dogs will reach them well before us; so it may amount to nothing more than pulling them down from the trees." There was much laughter as Cain's trait of overconfidence began to show itself.

Nergal was a tough, aggressive man, stocky in build with a heavy, dark beard and a mis-shapen nose that had been broken more than a few times.

Edom was the youngest of the lot, red-haired and average in size and looks. He always talked a good fight, but at every stage of his life he usually backed down when pushed. He wanted to be like Nergal, but it just was not in him.

Lamech was the only one of the group that might be spoken of as handsome, though not by a vast majority. He was tall, but nowhere near Hamath's height; and he was somewhat rangy in build. He was one of the very few in Cain's camp who, given a different set of circumstances, could have lived in Eden and done well. He was quiet, usually trying to avoid controversy, but when pressed, could hold his own in tests of a physical nature and in debate.

The break in action was not terribly long, but each man seemed to display a surge of vitality. Their dogs proved unable to scale the rugged rocks ahead and they waited impatiently at the base. The men soon arrived, and with their new attitude, men and dogs proceeded at a faster clip. Up the rocky ledges they scrambled like goats, and with a determination that had been lacking since the second day. If they could maintain that mood, Hamath would look like a prophet. As soon as the dogs were helped over the last hump, they were off again as though Cain was behind them with a thorn-switch. The four ran at a fast trot in an attempt to stay within earshot of their trackers.

The Decision

The ladies, under the circumstances, had been quite successful in putting that last mount well behind them. The terrain since then had been relatively level and the only drawback in that was the fact that the followers now enjoyed the benefit, also. While on the run, they ate the last of their fruit—plums that they found in a thicket just before the rise in elevation and the soil's transformation to near-total stone. How glad they were that they had taken the time to gather a few extras, just in case; without those, their strength would now be completely spent.

It was well past mid-day and their pace slowed considerably. Naomi knew that they had given their all and that they had to rest for awhile. There was no food and they had not had water since that spring at the base of some cliff, prior to being sighted. It felt so wonderful to get a much-needed rest. There was no conversation, as all seemed to understand the need to conserve energy; then again, there was not much desire to converse. Of the three spears that were sharpened early on, they managed to save one, and there were no trees anywhere in sight to make more.

While the three rested, all face-down on the hard ground, trying to remember the last time they lay on something soft, the dogs' ears suddenly perked up and their heads raised looking off into the distance. Even Adah and Tamarah now recognized the warning signs of impending danger and they jumped to their feet. Naomi listened intently and after a few moments the distant sounds came closer, leaving no doubt as to the source. The realist in her overruled her hopeful heart and she faced the truth: "Daughters, barring the unforeseen, they will overtake us by nightfall. Their dogs seem to be moving at a greatly quickened pace, as though Cain implanted his very thoughts into their minds. Our dogs, even on their finest day, cannot best them in battle. If by chance we could make skillful use of the remaining spear and hurl rocks with all our might . . ." Realism quickly returned to the good woman and a decision had to be made. It was a decision that she dreaded with all her heart. "We have only one choice . . . to climb into the valley below and, hopefully, avoid capture by means of stealth. There is no easy way down; it will take agility as well as courage."

"Will the dogs be able to go with us?" asked Tamarah.

"I am not certain. This will be even more challenging than our previous climbs."

Adah looked at her mother with sorrow in her eyes and Naomi answered sharply, "Do you think I want to leave them to face a violent death to those four-legged miscreants of Cain?" Then her mood softened and she touched Adah on the shoulder and offered, "If there is any way to get them off this ridge . . . but I will not trade our lives for them."

That seemed to be of some comfort and attitudes at this point were still solid.

They searched along the cliff's edge about a stone's throw and found what looked to be their most likely chance for a successful descent. It was a narrow pathway in the rock face that was somewhat camouflaged by coloring and shadow, and not straight up and down. Also, there were several small trees, somehow growing out of fissures in the rock; and there were scattered hand and footholds. The dogs actually made out as well as the humans most of the way with only two spots that required assistance. All had nearly reached the bottom when those distant barks became quite distinct. Naomi hurried the others along with strong words of admonishment: "They will be at the edge, shortly! Do not now become sluggish with us so near our goal! Hurry! We may have a chance to hide before they see us!"

Very near the base, they dropped a short distance to the ground with nothing more than a few scrapes, but as they began the run for cover, Naomi stopped them with a word and a raised hand. She did not want to rush from one crisis only to stumble into another. She cautiously ran her eyes over the landscape searching for possible trouble. The search proved fruitful as they found the spear that they had dropped while at the crest. She grabbed it and led them into a brushy area.

At the top of the cliff, two highly-anxious animals saw their quarry and it seemed that nothing would stop them from making a fast, downhill-charge. But the lead dog proved overly zealous for such a steep grade and he plunged end over end down the rocky slope, managing to hit one of the small, protruding trees which made for a slight buffer. He survived the fall, but was badly injured, barely able to crawl into a marshy area where some tall grass offered only a little in comfort or protection.

Naomi, with relief and a certain amount of satisfaction said, "If only the other one had done the same." In her mind she thought, "I should take the time to finish him, but we must avoid all unnecessary noises to survive in this valley."

Mal and Keber also wanted to move in for the kill, but under orders Adah and Tamarah held onto them. "Mother, there does not appear to be another living creature in this God-forsaken valley. Let our dogs have their revenge."

"By all means, Mother! That creature deserves to die!"

"Hush! The still, small voice inside me sends forth a warning to remain very quiet. My last visit to this place was one of great stress with nary a moment of calm. And do not think this valley is devoid of creatures or God-forsaken—you would be very mistaken on both counts."

Naomi's words of warning and the look of command in her eyes left the others with a much-needed reassurance.

Tamarah, always curious, quietly asked about the last visit, "Please, tell us what you saw here. You mentioned it once when I was a child, but that was long ago. Can you remember it?"

"Yes, I remember." She stared into the distance, her mind searching for the details, sorting truth from hazy memories. She told of the noises, the strange animals and their vicious ways, the clash with the serpent, their hasty retreat, and the peaceful sleep after reaching the upper ledges of the cliffs. She had not spoken of these things in a long while. The daughters, after listening intently to every detail, were now more than ready to trust their mother's leading through this ordeal.

Meanwhile, when Timna, the more cautious dog, saw its obsessed brother's plummet down the steep slope, he trembled and whimpered for a while, and then slowly worked his way back to the top. Upon reaching solid footing, he swiftly backtracked to his approaching masters.

Said Hamath, "I see Timna, but Tema is not with him. Something happened to him, for they would not otherwise separate."

Timna ran up to them whining and barking, running a few steps ahead then coming back. The men understood its behavior and wasted no time in following.

Naomi, crouching . . . progressing cautiously, motioned for the rest to follow. They managed to slog their way through shallow water, mud, and rotting vegetation until they reached a grove of small trees, which provided one of the few relatively dry areas in this marshy lowland. It was still moist, but at least one could lay down to rest and not wake up in a puddle of water. Also, it gave them a chance to check each other for ticks, leeches, and other bloodsuckers. And as unpleasant as it had been, walking through that green, crawling, sour-smelling cesspool, there was a plus in that their scent would be hidden from Timna.

It was nearing sunset at this point and down in that basin light would quickly vanish behind the cliffs. In the battle waged daily since the Creation, darkness was soon to be the victor, and strange howls and shrieks sounded a victory cry that would continue as long as darkness had its way. The daughters wanted to attempt the building of a fire, but Naomi, after some consideration spoke against it. "Let us not build a fire . . . not tonight, not ever in this valley. The men are too near and the animals here are of a different breed and may not fear fire; in fact, fire may attract them. I do not know that . . . but I sense it. We must huddle together and quiet the dogs so as not to tip our presence to anyone or anything."

Through clenched teeth Adah exclaimed, "Ow! The bugs are terrible here! My face and arms are covered with welts."

In a whispered, exasperated tone, Naomi rebuked and advised: "Hush! Rub some mud over your skin. That will offer some help. Ladies, this will be the longest night of our lives! There is a possibility of peril at every turn. If we are to survive it, we must remain completely still, and the dogs, too. They are brave, but they will lose their lives in any confrontation here. Notice their unease; they sense the danger all around them. They are to remain still. They must . . . for all our sakes."

Decisions of a Different Camp

The men soon reached the cliff's edge and as their eyes searched the valley below for some sign of the three women their hearts dreaded the downward climb and the amount of time that had to be spent in such an inhospitable place. Over the last two days they had heard the strange noises and caught some brief glimpses of animal life that was beyond the familiar.

"Cain swore to us that of all the places on earth, Naomi would never go there again! Once more she has done the unexpected."

"Maybe we could tell him that they fell to their death."

"Yes! Or maybe we could tell him that we watched as wild animals tore them apart!"

Hamath gave a disapproving shake of his head and answered, "What are you thinking? Are we to be defeated by the likes of these three? If they are brave enough—or more likely—desperate enough, to enter there, shall we be outdone? I tell you they are within our grasp; success is ours if we do not weaken! I will not return to our people without their live bodies—or pieces of their dead bodies."

Lamech was of the same mind and added, "We must hurry! Light will be in short supply by the time we accomplish the descent. They have surely made camp by now and, hopefully, we will see their fire. We may even risk a night-time capture."

Nergal spoke, "To get a fix on their fire is well and good, but to risk travel in this unknown swamp is foolishness. After we reach the bottom, let us get a fire going—if we are able to find anything dry—and then search the surrounding darkness for signs of their fire."

At the top of the ridge, there was still moderate light, but by the time they reached the bottom they were in heavy shadow. Dry anything was scarce, but the top sections of swamp grass proved a good bet to get a fire started. They soon found what looked to be a large pile of manure, and nearby were some small limbs, so they had enough to keep a fire going for a time.

Edom observed, "I have never seen animals use the very same spot over and over like that. That manure pile, I mean. What animals behave that way?"

Lamech laughed and said, "Of course, I am not sure, but that may be from one animal . . . and one time."

Three of them had never been far from the fields of Nod, but Hamath said, "Once, Cain led several of us toward the swamp land, some distance north of our present home site. Upon our return trip, we ran across a creature that he called an elephant, and another that was called a hippopotamus. Their manure piles were about half the size of that one. Grass and green plants appeared to be their main food . . . but this has some bone fragments in it."

"Who cares what comprises the manure! It all stinks and it all makes for a fire!" snapped Nergal.

Hamath slapped him hard across the face just to remind him who was in charge. He jumped up as though ready for a fight, but he was smart enough to back down, for now. Hamath was the stronger fighter and this was no time to wage a battle between tribesmen.

They had a few pieces of flint rock with them, brought down from the top, and that looked to be a wise move as there was none to be found in the swamp. The fuel—grass, manure, and sticks—proved adequate for combustion and within moments of applying their expertise in the matter, a flame blazed away. Timna was darting here and there with his nose to the ground and he quickly found the women's scent. There was hardly enough light to see tracks of any sort, but while Lamech tended the fire the others searched for any clues as to the womens' whereabouts. They walked a good distance and despite animal sounds that caused these stout-hearted men some angst, the hunt continued with Timna in the lead. They soon reached the swamp water where Timna's nose lost the scent. At this point they could only guess as to their next step, so they thought it best to get back to the fire. Black of night now made its presence known and if not for the glow of the fire near the cliff's base, they would be lost.

"What was that?!" Nergal nervously whispered as a rustling in the brush caught his full attention. Hamath heard it, too, but acted as though it was nothing.

Edom, possibly the most uneasy of the group, then heard another noise in the brush—a low, guttural growling. The three readied their spears, and Timna, usually ready for a fight, was timid in this case, remaining close to the men. "You heard something that time, Hamath. Either that or you picked a fine time to practice your spear wielding."

Hamath, to change the subject and in his bravest voice said, "We are near the fire. Let us make haste and check on our brother, Lamech."

Edom gave a shout: "Lamech, are you safe and . . ." His question was cut short as Hamath shushed him to silence.

"Stupid simpleton!" Hamath hissed through his teeth, "Any chance there was to avoid danger by stealth is now gone! We will have to fuel up the fire in order to make it large enough to ward off this valley's creatures."

They soon made it to the safety of the fire. Lamech had well tended it and with the anxious addition of fuel by six other hands it now burned bright.

The presence of these intruders was sensed by more than just flesh and blood. Satan, on a late-night inspection of his most-beloved site on earth, felt the unfamiliar vibrations emanating from their bodies. As only he could do, with precision, he stared out into the darkness and picked up their heartbeats, distinguished their feelings of fear, and gauged the exact location of the source. He materialized to a spot just outside their camp . . . and observed. There was little in the way of conversation because of Hamath's orders to be still, so he gained no information in that way. He reasoned within himself: "What are Cain's people doing here? Cain surely warned them of this place . . .

unless they ran away from the land of Nod to escape him, in which case they may have stumbled into this valley by chance. No . . . there must be a reason for their presence here. Is it possible that they are on a mission to scout Adam's camp in Eden . . . to prepare for a battle? Oh, if only that would prove true! That might account for taking such a risk; to sneak into Eden by a way no one would suspect." He stared intently and listened into the air, slightly sensing something else, but nothing of which he could be certain. Animals from the outside, on rare occasions, found their way into here, but being unfamiliar with the ways of the land, they did not last long. Soon, a slight smile parted his lips as he recognized the danger lurking in the darkness. It had been a long time since his creatures had provided their self-imposed master with violent entertainment of this scale. Once again he reasoned within himself: "If only these men belonged to Adam . . . but they are Cain's offspring . . . at least, partly. I *could* interfere at this moment and send my pets elsewhere; after all, I want these men to live in order to see them do battle against my hated enemy; then again, entertainment is woefully lacking on this earth. I desire to witness some violence. And, if these were never to return, Cain would surely send a large force to bring war to Adam's territory—especially with some timely instruction from me."

The Sleepless Night

Not a single word had been exchanged between the three since pitch-black set in on their campsite. The dogs, so far, were obeying their mistresses, being unusually still—which was much against their nature. The night air was unbearably heavy with tension and the incessant drone of biting insects. All three coated their exposed skin with mud and though that made a difference, some bites still came through causing intense misery; a misery that brought even strong-willed Naomi close to surrender. She could see the faint glow of the distant fire. Perhaps it would be best for her daughters if all surrendered, and took their chances in Nod. She, of course, would probably not be allowed to live, but at this point she was willing to do anything to get back to the cliffs and escape this place of unending torment. Just at that moment, Tamarah took hold of her right hand, and Adah took hold of her left, neither knowing of the other's actions. Not realizing the extra strength that adrenaline produces they all squeezed so tightly it caused pain, but it was a different type of pain . . . and it was welcomed . . . and she was comforted by it. So, not a sound came from any of them as though they intuitively understood that there was one who would hear the slightest whisper. They dared not sigh or sob—just prayed, silently.

The Camp Fire

Panic causes people to make mistakes. The men, in their anxiety, had used about every available particle of anything combustible in order to keep that fire blazing big and bold. They dared not leave the security of the flames to venture even a few steps into the brush in search of more fuel, but it could not last until the morning light. What could they do? Finally, Hamath lifted the ban on speaking deciding that communication was now of the utmost importance: "How much longer before the fire dies?"

Lamech, the expert on fire, answered, "It will not last the night at this rate, but if we could find one more armload of sticks, tend it wisely, and huddle close, we might have protection until the morning."

There was an awkward silence as each man looked at the other and then looked at the ground. Nergal nervously offered a solution: "Here are a few small sticks that have not yet burned. Let Edom hold four of them in his fist with each of us drawing one. The man who draws the longest stick will win the right to step into the brush and search for more fuel." There were some puzzled looks with more silence, and he added, "Does that not seem just?"

Hamath, after some anxious moments, broke the stillness and spoke quietly, but straightforwardly: "It is just . . . but the longest stick would hardly be a reward."

The four agreed and Edom closed his eyes, rubbed the sticks between his hands, put them in his fist and arranged them in such a way so that no one could tell their measure. He even wrapped his free hand around the fist to better hide the high-stakes game pieces. In his own mind was the thought that never before had four tiny pieces of wood held so much significance.

Hamath bravely drew first. It was the shortest one of the four.

Lamech took a deep breath and drew second. Not knowing how long the sticks were, his heart sank as he pulled out one that was half-again as long as the first, but when Nergal's draw proved to be longer yet, Lamech gave a quiet sigh of relief—quiet enough that he would not be accused of cowardice.

Needless to say, Nergal was not overjoyed, but he seemed ready to accept his fate.

Edom could barely contain his delight and had to put one hand over his mouth to hide a smile. He had held the sticks in his hand and knew that Nergal's was the longest. Imagine how that feeling of elation came crashing down when Edom opened his hand and saw that his stick was the longer . . . by a fingernail. "Now wait . . . we must measure to be certain!"

There was some doubt at first, but Hamath and Lamech both agreed that Edom's stick was the longest.

While sitting closest to the fire, Edom broke under the strain and cried, "No! I will not go into the brush! If we tend the fire carefully . . . it will last. Please, do not force me from the safety of the flames!"

The raising of his voice caused some growls in the darkness, further weakening Edom's resolve. Nergal grabbed his spear and said harshly, "You will search the brush for wood! We all agreed to the terms! You will abide by them. Yes, you may die out there, but you will most surely die here if you continue to sit by that fire."

Edom was panic-stricken, and ready to fight his brother to the death rather than face the unknown. He grabbed the spear nearest him and assumed a fighting stance. The other two tried to reason with him, but he was out of his mind at this point.

Satan was overjoyed with the chaotic scene being played out right in front of his gleaming eyes, and seemed to gain strength from the intense anger and fear, but he had something else in mind: "If I let the fight continue it may be possible that both men will be killed, and though I relish the notion of human death, my pets will be deprived of a live kill." He pondered the situation for only a few moments. "They have been restrained long enough: Attack and feast!"

With the fire still blazing and providing abundant light, three of the valley's most feared beasts burst out of the darkness, finally showing themselves and giving the four terrified men a fearful and open look at the source of the deep, rumbling growls that made hungry lions sound playful. The men, for a moment, stood frozen with fear! They were now so close to the fire the flames literally licked at their flesh, but they felt only a chill which penetrated their bones.

Standing erect, the creatures were nearly twice as tall as Hamath, and bigger around the middle than the largest tree trunk. Their two, huge legs looked like sections cut from the Serpent's body, and their heads were like that of a crocodile, but much larger, with mouths full of teeth. Their arms were not terribly long, in comparison to their height, but quite muscular with thick, heavy claws at the end that could rip flesh with ease. They had large, powerful tails anchored by strong, wide muscles, designed to knock their prey off its feet in a given moment. And lastly, their hide was extremely tough, making it difficult to drive a spear, or any pointed object, deep enough to cause injury. They had never seen fire and with whatever guidance Satan could force upon them, they would overcome any instinctive fear of it.

They were like cats playing with mice at this point, sensing the deep-seated fear of their prey and seeming to derive such pleasure from it. The men finally came to their senses enough to know that they must put up a fight even though they were all dead men.

Shaken, and weak from fear, they readied their spears, but had no confidence in them. Two of the creatures lunged forward, snapping those sharp teeth. Hamath yelled, "Drive your spears into their lower belly!" Nergal followed the order and found that the flesh in that area was a little softer—still tough, but their weapons got through the thick hide and went in far enough to at least cause some damage. The creatures became enraged with pain and reacted with a deafening roar and a surge of energy that said there would be no more games. The largest one bit into Hamath's mid-section and lifted him off the ground as though he was a child. Hamath screamed in agony as the eating process began, but with his last dying act he drove what was left of his spear into one of the monster's eyes.

That caused it to temporarily release its hold on Hamath's lifeless body while it dealt with the loss of sight in that eye. By now the third creature, which was not as large as the others, had taken up the battle with Lamech and Edom. Edom, to his credit, fought well, mindlessly and repeatedly thrusting his spear into the belly of his enemy. But though this beast was smaller their spears had not the desired effect; apparently not sharp enough or sturdy enough to reach vital areas. But the two men continued to plunge away, keeping the animal at bay, until it turned and gave a swish of that powerful tail, striking Lamech full-force and sending him flying into the dark underbrush.

Nergal fought valiantly, at first using only his spear; then, blinding himself to suffering, he grabbed burning limbs from the fire and threw them into his tormentor's face. Glowing embers found their way into its mouth and eyes causing great pain, pain that had never before been experienced by this seemingly invincible brute. But it also infuriated it, adding to its unmatched, killing power. It grabbed Nergal by the torso and tossed him into the air where he was ingested, head-first.

Seeing that his brother was, now, silently disappearing from sight into the gullet of some hideous, unknown creature, Edom lost all courage and fled into the same darkness that terrified him so just awhile ago. As he ran blindly through the mud and the stinging branches of the underbrush, with the smaller of the beasts not far behind, he was able to take *some* hope in that it appeared he had gained a chance at survival. Ten or twelve more strides . . . now he would rest. He could hear the creature splashing through the swamp water and, thankfully, it had lost his trail. He collapsed face-first behind a bush, tightly covering his mouth to stifle the gasps for air, his heart pounding so hard he was certain that every living creature dwelling within that valley could hear it. He was wrong about that. There was only one who could, and that one decided to give another of his subjects a bit of assistance. Satan directed one of the big cats—a male lion—into the vicinity. It could see quite clearly in the blackness. Edom's nerves had only begun to calm, when he heard a more familiar, rumbling growl. Not as loud as the earlier ones, but just as frightening and plenty enough to, once again, set his heart pounding violently. He shifted to his side covering his head with his hands, hoping that he could, somehow, make it to dawn . . . but he just had too many things against him on this night. The lion leaped onto his prey, sank his teeth into Edom's neck and dragged him off into the night.

Lamech, beginning to regain consciousness, repeatedly shook his head trying to clear the cobwebs from his mind. In the darkness he momentarily questioned his whereabouts, but as he felt the misery inside an injured body, his memory returned. It was so difficult to take a shallow breath, let alone the deep ones for which his body craved. Struggling to his knees he slipped quivering hands into the tall grass and parted it enough for a better look at the campsite. By now, the fire's glow appeared much dimmer as the brush and manure had about given their all. As he peered through the opening and with the moon's light coming over the cliff top, he could make out the two larger creatures. They, to Lamech's disgust, were finishing with what was left of Hamath and searching the ground for any morsel that might have been missed. He was quite certain, from what he now witnessed and what had taken place earlier, that his brothers no longer walked the earth. He was also quite aware of the need to vacate this area immediately or he would be the next meal. But as he sought to pull back, he fell forward, and out of reflex threw down a hand to catch himself. It did not seem like much, but the quick movement and the extra rustle of the grass caught the attention of his brothers' killers. The biggest one jerked its head around at the sight and sound. Lamech remained in the kneeling position with his hands at his side and his upper body in a forward lean. These creatures were incredibly wary and he knew that he must not so much as blink his eyes. The big one, Hamath's spear tip protruding from one eye, stared directly at him. "Does he see me? He is not charging my direction. Maybe he is back to cat-and-mouse games! I cannot out run them, so I will take my chances on remaining still."

The other one saw its partner focused on something, and it also stared in Lamech's direction. They watched with great patience, instinctively knowing that on more than a few occasions a nervous quarry flushed after a time of waiting.

Lamech remained motionless—not a blink, or a twitch. Insects bit and stung his skin, causing grave doubts to rise up in his mind and soul. His inner thoughts spoke: "How can I stay a moment longer in this position! My muscles are beginning to cramp . . . and I must not clench my teeth! If only I could scratch at these bites. Bloodsuckers! Many more bites and the blood will be drained from my body by the littlest of creatures. Ohhh . . . the misery is unbearable!"

Finally, after what seemed about as tolerable as a lashing while staked face-down in the hot sun, the creatures' interest was diverted elsewhere. Their backs turned to him, he pulled back into the tall grass and lay quietly. How wonderful to let the neck, back, and legs, relax. It felt wonderful to rest, even if only for a few moments, to stretch cramped muscles; but the chest pain, once again, made its presence felt and he knew that the longer he lay there the harder it would be to get to his feet.

The cliff was not that far away, and though his body was suffering, and other unknown dangers perhaps lurked in the darkness, he must make for it as quietly and quickly as humanly possible. Of course, even with a body free of injury his chances of escape would be less than good, but what choice did he have? So summoning every bit of fight that his flesh and spirit could provide, he slowly, silently, crawled away from the grass and, struggling, made it to his feet. Once upright, he at first tip-toed, slowly but surely putting some distance between those things and himself. Patience was needed now, more than ever, but at this point was not a strength possessed in abundance so he broke into the darkness at a run. The two predators heard something crashing through the underbrush and though it could have been one of any number of animals, their senses led them to investigate. Fortunately, their hunger was reasonably satisfied, so the desire to kill was somewhat subdued, for now. Their pace reflected complacency as they walked in the general direction of Lamech's path.

The first glow of dawn was beginning to color the horizon, but did not provide much light to aid the escaping fugitive. Somehow, after falling twice and stumbling over half of the vines in that setting, Lamech found the correct trail and emerged through the worst of the underbrush, his eyes beginning to make out the cliff base. The adrenaline flow now accelerated, and hope welled up inside him masking the agony of his injuries. Then, he heard a rustling in the weeds just behind him and a snarling growl. This growl was not quite as fearsome when compared to the other sounds heard in this land—to be certain a smaller animal—but from what he had already seen he braced himself for an all-out attack. Suddenly, Timna bounded from behind a shrub onto the trail. His hair stood on end as he snarled and snapped at the man. Lamech knew that the events of this night had driven the dog to act in this manner and he tried to soothe the animal's madness with tender words and actions. It was difficult to get down on a knee in order to call Timna to him, but he managed it and saw success in the endeavor. The dog returned to a calmer temper, and it was time for both to find the place where they first disembarked.

Satan, after basking in the glory of his lion's lop-sided victory over Edom and the subsequent feasting, revisited the campsite to be sure of four dead men. A smug expression on his face, he thought to himself: "Where are my champions? Surely they have not overlooked the body of Lamech . . . maybe they have already finished him, depriving me of one last pleasure for the evening." He walked over to the place where Lamech had been launched and there was nothing there. He thought, "There is no blood, no sign of a struggle?" He stared into the darkness, listening so intently, with a sense of hearing and intuition possessed by no creature in the animal world . . . bent on finding proof of Lamech's destruction. He could hear the satisfying sounds of many animals as they made their final kills of the night just before a return to the light and heat of the day. Satan wanted to believe that Lamech was finished, probably swallowed whole; but his suspicious nature would allow him no peace on this early morning. He continued to search the air . . . then, there it was! He sensed the location of Lamech . . . "He is near the cliff! He must not be allowed to escape and thus cast a pall on all that I worked for this night!"

Satan flew to the vicinity of the rock face, where he saw Lamech and Timna approaching it at a run. His beasts were moving that direction, but at much too slow a pace. He thought, "How should I organize this? I could cause the rocks to fall on them, but I want to see my pets finish this!" He sent his thoughts into their animal minds as best he could and it appeared to make a difference as they now ran—determination evident in their every stride.

The two fugitives made it to the rocks where they quickly found the steep, mountain path. Lamech heard his pursuers smashing through and over everything in their way and he was terrified. He grabbed the dog and tried to lift him to the first shrub which was more than head-high. The dog struggling in his grasp and the man's body so hampered by pain, made for a next-to-impossible situation. They would not escape this way, but Lamech tried to grab Timna for one final attempt. Timna pulled away and ran back down the trail, directly into the path of the predators. And Lamech, in his present state, was also not thinking clearly. In somewhat of a state of shock, he wildly scrambled and clawed, loosening rocks and finding no solid footing whatsoever. It was climb up a body length, then slide back down nearly the same distance. Satan was quite confident that the escape would not take place and he watched, eyes glowing, mouth grinning, fists clenched in anticipation. Timna, by this time, was crazed with fear again, and had no comprehension of the fate he was about to face head-on; but somehow, he was by-passed as neither of the pursuers paid him any mind. Their killing natures so focused on the man, they ran past the growling dog, their giant feet stepping just beside and slightly over the confused canine.

Lamech recognized his failing and the need to think clearly, so with a renewed mind he took a few precious moments to truly focus on the logical move. He jumped high enough to grab the shrub, then pulled himself to the first solid handhold; and with one foot soon on the shrub and the other in a crevice, he then planned the next step. The monsters approached with roaring loud enough to cause a man's shaking legs to give way. And it looked as though they were about to seize him, making a perfect night for their master, but Lamech leaped over to his left and grabbed tightly onto a small but sturdy limb, and it also held. He was then able to use his strong right hand and grip the all-important hold at the limit of his reach. His pain went unnoticed through all this exertion as the largest of the creatures, seemingly right at his dangling feet, reached to swipe him to the ground. Lamech, adrenaline flowing and his hand securely wedged pulled himself up to a foothold that was just high enough to avoid the first lunge. The animal was frustrated in its initial attempt and redoubled its efforts, trying again to capture his prey. A little higher he climbed this time, maybe enough to make the difference; but the rocks began to crumble away under the tremendous weight. Still, he was able to make an upward spring reaching one arm as high as possible and swiping those heavy claws. This time, it made contact with Lamech's foot, enough to rip away the sandal and slice the flesh near his heel. Pain now racked every fiber of the man's body, inside and out, but somehow he lost no ground to the blow. Upon the creature's backward slide, Lamech looked for his next move. He was just below the point where the slope of the rock face became a little gentler. The monster, seething with rage and totally bent on killing this hairless ape, once again, began its climb. And through it all, Satan delivered strength in abundance, as much as the creature could accept.

The sun's rays were now bright enough to lend aid in finding hand and footholds. With his very life depending on it Lamech trusted in the present foothold enough to bounce upward and grab the only ledge on the face—narrow as it was. His relentless adversary, despite the unstable footing, climbed again and made a last, desperate lunge stretching that neck upward and snapping those massive jaws in an effort to sink its teeth into that enticing, bloody foot. But once again, even at Satan's continuous urging, with his full counsel, the animal came up short. And despite its great weight causing the ground to tremble, and stones to give way, the man was not dislodged from his perch. Not built for this type of hunting, the creature lost its balance and fell backward upon unforgiving boulders, with many loosened lesser stones adding further injury. Again, the hillside trembled, but Lamech maintained his lofty position.

The added pain from the injured heel was now so intense the man struggled to keep his grip—mentally as well as physically. Still, he managed to overcome all that this experience threw at him. He took a few deep breaths, put his healthy foot on a newly-created crevice, and pulled up to the gentler slope. There he rested a moment on the ledge and watched with utter delight as the injured beast limped back toward the swamp with its mate. Despite the pain, Lamech managed a smile; but the smile was short-lived and probably his last one for some time.

Satan, definitely not expecting this outcome, shook his fist as he pondered some of the options at his disposal: "I could cause the rocks to fall from under this trespasser! Maybe I could call one of the big cats to climb the rocks or I could . . . Hmmm."

On occasion, Satan's pride caused him to miss an opportunity, but he restrained his acts of revenge this time and gave the matter more thought: "Maybe it would be better to have a witness to report to Cain. And . . . knowing him as I do, he will probably beat or kill Lamech for failing to spy out the land of Eden. But even if he does not, the man's account concerning this expedition should bring the possibility of war that much sooner. After all, if I killed him, Cain would waste much time waiting on and wondering about his men, and he might waste more time sending another small group to spy out Eden. Yes . . . this will make for a better use of my wisdom and power: allow one to live for now, for the chance to watch many die later." Satan, his mood improved, departed the valley to reunite with his demon followers.

The Long Night

As the never-ending night wore on, the women kept a tight hold on Mal and Keber. The every crackle of twigs and rustle in the undergrowth caused their hair to stand on end prompting Naomi to gently scratch their ears and very softly shush them. Though ready for a fight as they sensed danger and the unease in their mistress, they also took great pleasure in the attention paid to them. Being working dogs and not accustomed to this, they wholeheartedly accepted it and had a continual desire for more; and if obeying her wishes brought about this attention, they would comply until their dying day.

Loud noises in the direction of the men's camp immediately grabbed the interest of all. There were the unmistakable sounds of anguished human cries, a barking dog, and roars so loud they first thought an entire pride of lions rumbled at the same instant. They were tightly holding on to dogs and hands and all the while staring wide-eyed in the direction of the distant fire. They saw what looked to be sparks rising upward and wondered what brought that about. There were more terrible roars and one last, faint cry—then silence. The creatures all around became quiet, at least for a little while—and that was welcomed. The women wanted, so much, to discuss the situation, but remained silent.

Animals soon resumed their nighttime communications, but thankfully that lasted only a while as the early stages of morning began to quiet them. The ladies noticed the change and at first were uncertain of the reason for it; then Adah saw a flicker of light through an opening in the limbs. She excitedly grabbed the arms of the other two and pointed it out; within a short time, sunlight spread across the distant horizon and spirits soared; howls, shrieks, and roars all but ceased. Smiles and whispers were once again permitted and spontaneous, despite intense thirst, insect bites, and fatigue. They had survived the longest night of their lives, though they each understood that there was still much to be done to get back to the safety of the cliffs, but they now had a fighting chance.

Tamarah smiled, but sometime during the course of the night she had become ill with fever, nausea, and cold sweats. Naomi was hopeful that nervous strain was at the root of it and that the sun's light would bring better health. It was not something she ate as they had next to nothing. Since no one else was ill they tried to come up with a reasonable answer for her affliction. Naomi and Adah passed at the chance to drink the marsh water—despite terrible thirst—but Tamarah gave in to her body's need (and promptly vomited much of it back into the slough).

There was little that could be done for the woman in their present setting so they struggled to their feet and prepared for the task of seeking a better place.

Showing concern, Adah said, "The dogs drank with no ill effects . . . but I suppose animals are more adapted to such things. You will recover, soon!"

Naomi asked, "Are you able to walk out of here?"

She answered weakly, but without hesitation, "I will escape this valley if I have to be cut up and hauled out a piece at a time!" The remark brought a smile to all.

It was, of course, slow going as they slogged back through the filthy, green water, but there was mostly hope in place of fear and uncertainty. Adah and her mother, at the beginning, helped the failing Tamarah along by standing on each side and supporting her under the arms. She was very weak but her spirit was steadfast, and her eyes were fixed on the outlying cliffs; her heart on the freedom she would possess upon scaling them.

They were optimistic, but each knew that daylight did not guarantee safety and that every step was a gamble, every bush a hiding place for peril, the slightest of sounds something of which to be wary.

A Day of Testing

Lamech's every body part was throbbing with pain, adding to extreme fatigue, but he still managed to pull himself to the top of the ridge. He crawled a few feet inward, away from the ledge just to be safe, and then cast one last look at the valley of death that claimed his three brethren and the two most valuable dogs in all of Nod. Many of the males in Cain's line are not terribly close as they are often uncertain of their father's identity, so brotherly love is not desired or encouraged, but he felt a tight kinship with these, made more so because of their common struggles. So it was with an ache in his heart that he finished the viewing and reminisced about the successes and failings of the expedition.

A paralyzing stiffness attempting to set in, he thought it best to struggle on his way while there was still ample light. And though quite weak with hunger, he was more concerned about finding water; not only to drink but to rinse the dirt out of his wounds. The condition of his foot as it was would make for a long trip home—if he could make it at all—so to have a better chance he desperately needed clean water. Surprisingly, that was a teaching he recalled from Naomi.

If memory served him, there was one small spring about a half-morning's journey away—probably double that with the injured heel. He reached down inside for all of the strength left in him to get to his feet, then began the longest walk of his life. He had lost one sandal, and had no spear or stick of any kind for support. It was excruciatingly painful to put any kind of pressure on his wounded foot, so along with slow, tortured steps, there was hopping and limping and crawling. He could see some small trees off in the distance and planned to make use of a limb or two. The one good thing about making such slow progress was the fact that he had time to look the ground over for sharp rocks that could be used for cutting, and he found several.

Working As One

"So far, we are making progress," was the thought that came to Naomi as they neared the weeds at the water's edge. The women managed to painstakingly slog their way through the shallow swamp water, narrowly avoiding some sort of lizard, probably a small crocodile. They saw several snakes but fortunately, none near the size of the original serpent. Those that they saw were more interested in sunning themselves, so paid no attention to the three. Of course, the sight of such wretched creatures brought feelings of revulsion and Naomi's memory was refreshed nearly to the point of carrying Tamarah the rest of the way at a brisk walk. Finally, they emerged from the stagnant, stinking, liquid waste, only to be rewarded with a walk in ankle-deep mud for a time. When they reached solid ground, even Tamarah was able to pick up the pace a little and their spirits were bolstered. Under Naomi's watchful eye and cautious supervision, they worked their way around potential land dangers such as several sleeping lions, and some of those peculiar looking birds that were similar to emus but much larger. They had lethal spurs on the backs of their legs and wicked-looking beaks that would surely tear flesh to pieces. The women restrained the dogs by holding tightly onto the fur at the back of their necks. Eventually, they reached the men's former campsite where they observed huge imprints, and areas of ground that was worked up as though whatever made the tracks was involved in serious action. They also found a sandal, pieces of broken spears (one with a stone point intact and long enough to provide

Adah a weapon), and—much to their distaste—part of a hand. In a way they were relieved to know that they were free of their pursuers, but after all, they were of the same tribe.

Unknown to the three, there were some other creatures that stirred in the daylight: four hyena-like animals had picked up their scent and were silently stalking them. It came about as the women and dogs waded out of the water, where two of the hyenas were getting a drink and watching for easy prey.

Hyenas, on many occasions, are a cowardly lot, but can be vicious and at certain times able to defeat even the big cats. But their skittish nature restrained them this time as in their animal minds they were uncertain of the three never-before-seen creatures walking upright. Other creatures that walked on two legs had proven dangerous in the past, so they had to gauge size and strength. The fact that one of the three was crippled did not go unnoticed. As to the pair of four-legged creatures, they were not terribly large and should make for easy marks. But they would wait a bit before an attack—for a more opportune time.

The women left the men's camp and as they began making their way to the cliff they recognized the lay of the land and saw a familiar path with a few of their tracks from yesterday. Naomi stopped to investigate some other prints and said, "I hope that what I am seeing means nothing, but these first tracks are made by man, and a dog's tracks are here also."

Adah bemoaned, "It can not be true! Surely they were made yesterday!"

Naomi was uncertain at first but after further examination answered, "They are headed toward the cliff . . . and look at the huge tracks following . . . one step to every ten of ours! If these are two-legged creatures there may be more than one. And their path through the underbrush is cut as though it was nothing more than tall grass. Be on your guard . . . our troubles continue."

Naomi readied her spear and Adah did the same with her remnant. Their actions cooled the killing-instinct that was about to be displayed by their watchers. Tamarah, staying between the other two, was doing all she could just to stand. They carefully continued on the trail before them, following the sandal prints toward freedom. Not a dangerous sight or sound did they experience all the way through the brushy growth; then finally . . . full sunlight! They reached the cliff at the same spot from which they entered this nightmare.

After some inspection, Naomi remarked, "There has been a rockslide since yesterday. I pray that there are enough hand and footholds to assist our escape. Now the next question: How do we get these dogs to the top?"

They did some looking, some figuring, then reasoned aloud and came up with possible solutions using vines for the dogs and spears extended downward for human assistance. But the foremost act Naomi desired to accomplish was granting Tamarah's wish to depart this valley. Adah, in good health and the stronger climber, exchanged spears with Naomi assuming that she would be more adept at extending the longer spear within reach of her weak sister. With the agility of a cat she began the climb and was soon able to grab the sturdy, lower shrub, where she pulled herself atop while keeping the spear tucked inside her leather garment. From the vantage point of the perch, she located several cracks in the rock face for her right hand. Once secure, she used her free hand to extend the spear to Tamarah. Naomi was crucial to the process, lifting and supporting the younger woman to the point where she could take hold of the butt end of the spear. With the diminishing strength left to Tamarah, she maintained her grip and Adah pulled her up to the main crevice. That was a big step and a time of rest followed. She then managed to crawl to the shrub, and with some assistance, was able to straddle the main part of it and hold her position. Naomi, with rocks sliding past, barely missing her head, offered words of instruction. It was a good plan, and it looked like the worst was over. The long process was made somewhat easier when Adah reached the gentler incline; from there, with Adah above and Naomi below, the struggling woman pulled up to the relative safety beyond the narrow ledge.

Adah was proving to be quite skillful in scrambling over rocks, while continuing to use the spear to pull Tamarah, both women using all the energy their bodies could provide. And just before that moment when all strength cruelly abandons ambitious endeavors, they reached the top. Adah hugged her sister and understood when the gesture was not returned; but Tamarah's smile, weak though it was, spoke words of utmost gratitude.

After catching her breath, Adah retraced her steps back down to help her mother with Mal and Keber. As she reached that wonderful lower shrub, Naomi threw to her one end of a vine. She had twisted some vines together and tied one around Keber's middle. As Adah began the strenuous climb back to the top, Keber did his part to aid in the ascent, making for an easier trip this time.

Naomi grabbed Mal and began to prepare him for the same. He became uneasy and backed away, his fur bristling. She started to scold him for his rebellion when there came a snarling from the brush, and before she could grab the spear remnant, Timnah charged from a nearby hiding place with Tema close behind. Tema, though greatly slowed by injury, was still dangerous and had two desires: to kill and eat. Naomi reached the broken spear in time to ward off the injured dog for the time being, but she also wanted to help Mal. She screamed at Adah, "Pull Keber up that slope and do not come down for any reason!"

Adah was so startled she lost all ability to think for herself; uncertain as to what was best at this moment, she obeyed. Adrenaline surging through her, she was able to man-handle the load capably all the way to the top with strength left over. By now her judgment had returned and, disobeying orders, she started back down to help her mother.

Naomi yelled at Mal to come to her, thinking they could stand side by side with their backs to the cliff and have a better chance of survival, but Mal had been restrained from his natural tendencies for entirely too long. He continued to fight in the open with an intensity that would persist until he or his enemy was dead. At that moment, Naomi made a rare mistake, so sure that Tema was no longer a threat she dropped her guard for an instant. Tema saw the opportunity and rushed in, grabbing the woman at the thigh and knocking her backward. The animal was still powerful, wounded as it was, and it shook its head back and forth to better deliver the bite and maintain control. Naomi's grip was loosened, but she held on to the spear and began to thrust it into the dog's chest, not a deep wound, but enough to cause him to yelp and release his hold. She jumped to her feet and was, once again, able to keep him at bay.

Just as Adah reached the lower shrub, ready to jump down and enter the fray, the four hyenas charged from the underbrush. They had been waiting for an opportune time and this was it. The dogs were taken completely unaware, but with the fight that remained in them they gave all they had—even Tema. But it was, for the most part, a slaughter as the hyenas were too large, too strong, and too vicious. Naomi was momentarily stunned by the scene, but Adah's shout soon caught her attention. The daughter lowered her spear and Naomi, leaving her own weapon on the ground, took hold of it and at the same time began to climb. One of the hyenas saw that fresh meat was escaping and ran toward the figures on the rocks. Naomi was successful in reaching that beloved shrub, but in an awkward position with her feet and legs dangling. The hyena leaped high and snapped, just missing the woman's feet. He tried again, and again he came up just short as she curled her knees enough to foil the attempt, but so close she felt its nose touch her skin. Straining with all her might, her heart pounding, she pulled herself up to and crouched on the main branch, hoping to regain her wind, but she became light-headed and her foot slipped. She found herself, again, on her stomach, legs dangling. The hyena saw another chance and climbed higher than at first. Seeing that the woman's legs were within reach he readied his leap. She knew that the animal now had a definite advantage and many thoughts raced through her mind: "I must pull myself back to where I was . . . but my strength is nearly gone, and all that is left of leg and arm muscle is cramping. Look at him—if he was human his expression would clearly be seen as gloating. No more . . . for the first time in my life there is little desire left in my heart to continue fighting. He has me. The only option left is to release my grip, fall to the ground, and try to grab the spear—if I am still able to move. Hmph—a lot of 'ifs.' God help me!"

The animal, jaws slobbering and snapping, crouched for the killing leap. The legs surged from bent to straight, quick as the strike of a coiled snake, and his body became airborne. Suddenly, with precision timing and unusually good fortune, a series of head-sized stones that Adah managed to dislodge from the heights, hit the disgusting predator. His trajectory was greatly altered and he slammed into the ground, sparing Naomi's life. The moment of the ground's impact saw him roll to his feet and run with his tail tucked. He was finished with the *easy prey* and hurried back to his companions, hoping to share in some of the food that could no longer fight back.

Adah lost her spear in all the backbreaking activity, so they were without weaponry at this point, but there was no way that either would climb down to search for any.

The exhausted woman slowly worked her way back on top of the shrub and just stood there for a while, almost gasping for every breath. When she felt some strength restored, the climb continued without a spear for assistance. The going proved tedious until the enterprising Adah returned to the summit, grabbed the vine-rope and lowered it to her mother, greatly aiding her. As soon as all were safely atop the rugged climb, there was time for thankfulness and reflection.

Tamarah, terribly weak but still somewhat alert asked, "Where is Mal?"

Naomi looked off into the distance and after some hesitation quietly answered, "He was killed by hyenas that attacked at the bottom. He saved my life by fighting off one of Cain's mongrels, the healthy one, while I fought the one that was injured from the fall. The hyenas, during the incident, charged and finished them in short order . . . but it was long enough to allow me to escape death . . . with the help of your sister."

Tamarah was too exhausted from sickness and exertion to show sorrow. Fever still plagued her body and had she any moisture left in her flesh it would have found its way to the surface.

Naomi massaged her daughter's forehead and soothingly promised, "I will walk to the nearest spring and somehow get you some water. The last time I was in this area there was a pool not too far from here."

Tamarah touched the woman's wrist and in a voice so quiet, spoke words that only Naomi could hear: "It took a very long time . . . but I believe your gift of intuition has finally begun to blossom in me."

"What a strange thought to have at such a time," a puzzled Naomi answered with a slight smile.

"What makes you believe such a thing?"

Speaking haltingly and in tones barely audible, "I am quite sure . . . you will have to . . . go on without me."

"No, dear." she answered confidently, "You just need some water and a night of rest; tomorrow you will be strengthened.

Still in a whisper, but loud enough that Adah could hear, "Thank you . . . thank you both, for getting me out of that . . . that awful place." All at once, eyes widened, she grabbed Adah by the arm and with a final, surprising burst of energy, blurted out, "Bury me away from this ledge! So . . . I will never . . . have to look at . . ." With that she fell back and breathed her last.

They were so taken by surprise that they looked at each other in disbelief. Naomi shook Tamarah's lifeless body and rubbed her face and hands while a concerned Adah looked on with her fist against her teeth in shock and anguish. This went on for some time, but finally, after a respectful silence, Adah tugged on her mother's arm and softly said, "It is of no use; she is gone."

Naomi did not immediately give up, but reality soon re-entered her consciousness and she sat up, staring hopelessly, first into the sky, then at the ground. Keber sat beside her and offered a whine of sympathy. She lightly stroked his coat and then held him close. Not a word was spoken for a while. The surviving women were so weary—mentally, physically, and spiritually from their ordeal, that no tears were shed. Although Tamarah's burial was of utmost importance, they had to have some water, and then something to eat or they would be too weak to accomplish the task.

Adah said, "We could walk to that spring you spoke of, drink our fill and return to take care of Tamarah."

Naomi snapped, "No! We will not leave her at such a time!" Then softer, "If you will watch her, I will look for water."

"How will you carry it back?"

"If nothing else, I will return and tell you the location of it, so that you can go and drink your fill. Somehow, God will provide. And . . . I will also find us some food."

Adah, though beyond weary, shook her head approvingly at all those words and added, "If only we could catch our food, like Keber. Oh, but the thought of eating flesh nearly causes me illness."

Naomi smiled faintly and remarked, "Cain and a few of the others have already sampled flesh, but thus far the practice is not widespread." Her words brought a look of disgust to the daughter. That being said the good woman headed toward Eden and the general vicinity of that remembered waterhole. She walked and walked in the heat of the day, the sun bearing down on her head, seeing nothing but rocks until her thoughts became disoriented and her legs wobbly. She began to hallucinate. Never had she experienced this, but she seemed to recognize that things were not as they should be and sat down to rest. She began to wonder aloud, "Where are the girls? What was it I came to find? Oh yes, water . . . and maybe food. I cannot . . . cannot remember . . . the way."

She now crawled on all fours, searching the ground—but for what? Seeing some small trees in the distance, she pulled herself along in their direction, not for any rational reason, but because she was drawn to them. Closer and closer she came, her final goal in life to reach those trees; and when she drew to within a stone's throw she managed to stand and walk, and then, somehow to run. She ran with everything that remained in her, oblivious to the fact that when she succeeded in reaching her goal, there would be nothing left. It would all end at that point. "Look at those trees! The prettiest in all the earth; and Tamarah, Adah, and I will sit in their shade and laugh and talk and enjoy life!" Just as she stepped forward to take hold of a leaf, she plunged headlong down an embankment. Sliding on her belly, arms extended, she came to a stop. Everything went black as exhaustion and malnourishment had their way.

Slowly, consciousness returned to her. Touch seemed to be the first of the senses to catch her attention. Her hands were in . . . water? She shook her head, trying to clear the delusions from her mind. But it *was* water! She wriggled to the water's edge and plunged her face into the life-giving elixir. If there was anything better than this . . . no, there was nothing better than this! She drank to the point of excess, stopping just before her body rejected it all. As she lay there, on her side and still weak, she lifted up her eyes and saw what looked to be melons. Once again, she shook her head in an attempt to sort out reality from imagery. Another glimpse and they were still there; light green and so full and healthy in appearance; not like the scrawny, bug-infested ones that grew in Nod. She struggled to her feet and made her way to the vine where she grabbed one of the melons and broke it open. Oh, the red flesh was sweet and satisfying. Clearer thinking was returning with the intake of fluids and nourishment; and with it came the desire to get back to her girls. An idea came to her to hollow out one melon for carrying water, along with a whole one for Adah's nourishment. But just before beginning the return, Naomi thought it best to do something with the dog bite on her thigh. Through all of the day's events, it seemed the least of her concerns. Thankfully, the bite marks were not terribly deep, but something she had learned with the passing of time was the use of clear-water mud in the treatment of wounds. Figuring that there may not be a better chance than this she sat down at the water's edge, took mud and applied it to the damaged area. That done, and the sun approaching the horizon, it was time to go.

The sight of her mother in the distance was such a delight and a relief to Adah. She was nearly beside herself with worry. "What took you so long?! I truly did not know what to do; whether to bury Tamarah myself and then search for you, or to reason that you were dead and begin the walk back to Nod! What are you carrying? Melons!"

Naomi first handed her the one that held water and Adah nearly drained it before Naomi stopped her. "Not so fast, daughter. Save a little for later." She then broke open the other melon and the poor girl devoured its contents with much the same enthusiasm.

The two rested for only a short while when Naomi glanced toward the sun and said, "I strongly suggest that we begin the burial now. Fortunately, we are on top of the cliff and will have later light to work, but we can wait no longer."

They lifted Tamarah's body and, as requested, carried it far back from the ledge where she would, figuratively speaking, never have to look down on that valley of misery again. They found a level spot that sat up higher than the surrounding area to lay the body. Earlier, Adah had folded the lifeless hands across her sister's chest in anticipation of this action, and with the knowledge that should she wait too long it would be difficult to bend anything. It was a burdensome task for either of the women to place those first rocks on top of Tamarah. They wanted to use heavy stones so that no animal would ever reach her, but the thought of crushing her under all that weight was, at first, too much to face. Finally, Adah gritted her teeth and placed the first of the ten largest ones around the body. She then took smaller ones to place directly on the body. When there was no longer any flesh to be seen, Naomi took part. In fact, the action begun, Naomi worked at a furious pace to beat the darkness and to finish before her emotions rendered her useless in the matter. Darkness settled in, but if there was anything around this land in strong supply it was rocks, so they worked diligently until total blackness and increasing fatigue stopped them. They placed their hands against the tomb, now higher than their shoulders, and leaned against it to rest and to bid farewell. A full moon rose high into the night sky and provided enough light for them to see the haggard appearance on each other's faces. They had been through a nightmarish ordeal, beginning with the day they left Nod. Soon, they would find out if it was all worth it . . . but how could it be? Exhausted to the point of death themselves, losing their beloved sister and daughter, watching helplessly as the brave Mal was cut to pieces and eaten before their very eyes, and to this point no certainty about their future. Would they ever make it to Eden? Would they be accepted or killed by those who did not remember or ever know Naomi? The moon's light continued to expose the feelings (especially of doubt) that were carved into their faces. They clasped hands and looked at each other with a love and appreciation that only those who have shared such times can understand.

Finally, Naomi broke the silence and prayed, "Dear God, why did I not pray for her in her time of illness? I was so sure that she would be healed. Surely, You who watched over us to this very day could have prevented her death had I only asked. But why should I need to ask concerning such matters?! You already know of our problems and the solutions to them! But I will take the blame . . . and ask Your forgiveness for my thoughtlessness . . . and also, my bitterness. Help us to find peace. Into Your safe keeping we officially hand our loved one, Tamarah."

The prayer completed, they collapsed to the ground in sorrow and exhaustion, with nothing but rock on which to lay their heads. But whether on sand or boulders, they were out in an instant and did not stir until the sun was high in the sky the next day. Upon awakening, they stretched and rubbed their sore bones and muscles; then sat up to gather their thoughts. They were still tired, but much better off than the previous day. It would probably take several days of rest to recover completely, but they had not the time for that. There were a few sips of water left in the melon, and after finishing it they threw away the empty rind.

Keber had his nose to the ground on a path leading back to Nod. He stopped every few steps, his tail wagging with purpose, and whined as though he was on to something important. Naomi, at first aggravated and wanting to get started, decided to check on the reason for the dog's anxious behavior. She saw spots of blood. It had been there long enough to turn dark brown, but she had dealt with blood enough times in her life to recognize it at a glance. There was also a small island of soil amidst all the rock where a man's footprint was visible. She raised her voice to Adah, saying, "It appears that one of the men did escape. We saw the tracks yesterday, but it was my hope that something caught him before he reached the cliff."

"I saw no sign of blood while we were climbing."

"Naomi, with a quiet laugh responded, "We were a little too engaged to look for such things, yesterday. Well, he will most likely survive the trip back to Nod . . . the bleeding looks to be negligible. He may not survive once he arrives, of course. Assuming that he does complete his return, Cain will either send another group to look for our remains in that valley or reason that we were successful in our return to Eden, in which case he might organize a war party. Probably the latter as he will not believe any story concerning my death without bodily evidence. He knows me too well . . . and I know him. Yes, that is it! So let us be on our way to warn our relatives in Eden . . . if only they will heed our warning."

Second and Third Thoughts

L amech found two stones that were unusually sharp and he was wholly convinced that chance was on his side this day. It took a while, but after he reached some trees he was able to cut a fair-sized limb and make it into a walking stick. The effort, no more than it was, took all that was left in him and he slept through that day and evening, well into the next morning. Upon awakening, he saw that there was a mass of flies covering his injured foot. The sight of it nearly turned his stomach and had he anything in it he would have vomited it up. They had laid their eggs and maggots were already eating their fill. With all the energy of a man fighting off a swarm of hornets he flailed away and picked at the grisly sight before him, nearly offsetting all the good of his long rest. It was frenzied for a bit and so difficult to mentally deal with the image of those parasites using him. But on the bright side he had to admit that, somehow, the gash on his foot looked a little better. This too was, at first, looked upon as just another in a line of good fortune.

He felt rested, but weak with thirst and hunger. Now with his wits somewhat returned, he saw a familiar bend in the trail ahead and was certain that water was near. As he struggled forward his wits did not betray him and he soon saw the clear, cool spring that refreshed them all before they arrived at that terrible valley. Using his walking stick at first, it proved too awkward and he soon cast it aside and hopped at a runner's pace, whereupon reaching the pool he jumped in with all the enthusiasm of a young boy, drinking as much as his common sense would allow. Again and again he dove under the surface of the cool, wet, invisible gift from . . . Who knows what! And his spirit was lifted higher than at any other time in his life! You see, in Nod, one lives life in the constant search of physical comforts . . . and there are few; not much that is considered pleasure other than food, rest, and women. But Lamech was beginning to sense that there were other, possibly more noble goals in life: overcoming adversity, finding real freedom, and beginning a search for something larger than Cain or himself and, ultimately, in charge of everything. He was ignorant of Godly intervention, but thoughts from the long forgotten came back to him from those few occasions when he was a child and heard some of Naomi's words concerning Godly matters. Of course, it seemed that Cain usually intervened to ridicule such notions, but the knowledge that Cain had been proven wrong in many areas of life left Lamech to search his soul for the first time. He was being courted, in a way, without any understanding as to the Source.

He soon left those deep thoughts to concentrate on more immediate matters, such as the pain in his foot, finding something to eat, facing his fellow countrymen as a failure, and arriving home in one piece. "Hmph. Home . . . as though that was anything desirable. I know there will be punishment, and I have faced it at other times, but . . . what if Cain kills me this time? Would I fare any worse in the land of Eden? Still . . . miserable as it often is, Nod is my home and I am more comfortable at the thought of going there than anywhere else. I *would* like to see Adam someday . . . just to see for myself if all the good things Naomi spoke about him are true. I have many questions to ask about life; things that I would never ask Cain or any of the other men in my land. Maybe I will see him someday." He made his decision and continued the walk east, toward Nod.

It was a long and arduous trek, especially with an injured foot; but at least it was healing, and after ten days he was able to put all of his weight on it. His attitude was much improved with the healing that had taken place and even more so when he saw the patch of evergreen trees that were on the outer borders of Nod. He had seen them on only a few occasions, and there were no other stands of evergreens anywhere in the land. When he saw a giant pine tree standing somewhat isolated on a rise at the east edge of that stand, he was totally assured of his whereabouts. He soon found an old goatskin left over from an earlier time when goats were grazed in that area. He took it and fashioned a makeshift moccasin using a sharp stone to cut it and a vine to tie it around his foot; now with both feet protected his pace quickened and he threw the walking stick away. Maybe he was facing dire punishment, but he was so happy to be in familiar territory that all dread was put behind him for now, and he began to truly appreciate his escape from certain death.

An Unpleasant Reunion

I t was two more days before he had contact with his fellow countrymen and each asked the same questions: "Where are the others? How did you survive? Have you talked to Cain, yet? Did you kill the women?"

He soon grew irritated of hearing the same words over and over and he was frustrated that not one person was glad to see him. Cain eventually heard of his return and actually rushed toward the approaching Lamech to hear details of the trip. "Well! How did you kill them?" Lamech looked at the ground in shame and fear and gave no reply.

"They must be dead or you would not be here! Where are the others . . . ?" "Hamath . . . Nergal . . . Edom?" Anger was building after each query and Lamech continued to remain speechless. Cain, now in a softer tone but total disgust seething just behind the clenched teeth asked, "Could you not even overtake and defeat three women?" There was a pause before the eruption . . . "Answer me!!"

By now a crowd of men had gathered around the scene, shaking their heads and voicing their contempt (mostly in an attempt to curry favor with Cain) when Lamech finally found his tongue: "We saw them from a distance and chased them into the valley, where you killed the serpent. We followed them and were close behind when they went into the swamp water . . . and the dog lost their scent. It was dark by then and we made camp. Even with the fire blazing, three giant lizard-like creatures attacked. We fought valiantly. I watched as Hamath was eaten and am quite certain the same end came to Nergal and Edom. I was knocked senseless into the brush and came to in time to see the creatures as they scavenged the ground for pieces of my brothers. Somehow, I managed to escape . . . but am certain that the women could not have survived the night!"

Cain retorted, "Those three women escaped from four strong men and two fierce dogs. What makes you think they could not survive that valley? Or do you ever think? Tell me . . . what are you thinking now?"

Lamech lashed out, "Do you not believe my story? You of all people! You have been there!"

Cain called for his whip and in a calm but heartless voice responded, "I believe you, but you failed and must be punished. Also, there is something about you that irritates me; nothing to which I can point and say, 'That is it!' It is just something deep within you that clashes with what is deep within me; so the act of showing mercy will not begin this day . . . and certainly not with you. However, since I do believe your story, you will be allowed to live . . . most likely. So much depends on whether I tire of the activity.

Lamech's foot was not in condition to run, so he tried to mentally prepare himself. Several men grabbed him and dragged him to the usual tree where whippings took place. They stretched out his arms and tied him face-first to the huge oak tree. Cain's whip was brought to him and he looked admiringly over the only invention to which he could claim as his own. Others had innovative ideas from time to time and often he puffed up with pride when he took credit for them, but this particular whip was solely his, fashioned from the hide of a cow, a rare animal in Nod. He truly enjoyed making use of it and there were many scars and blood stains on the trunk of that tree, each with a story to tell of pain administered and endured. None had yet died there, though it was close on three occasions. Lamech hoped that piece of history remained unchanged after this day. Cain, standing just out of the shade in the hot sun, reared back and unleashed a blow that made even the more hardened of the onlookers wince. Lamech cried out in agony and wondered if he could withstand ten lashes of that same magnitude. Ten was the number that Cain usually struck, the exceptions being the three that nearly died; but it seemed to most of the witnesses that this first blow was especially severe and they secretly thought that no one could take nine more like that. He reared back and struck again with the same intensity and the outcry was heard by those watching over the goats on the far outskirts of the camp. With his scarlet-red forehead glistening brightly, even more than usual because of the exertion and sweat, he struck the fifth blow and brought such pain that Lamech fainted. When the victim received the sixth with silence Cain gave thought to reviving him with cool water, to be certain that he would feel the last four strokes. But he was, indeed, tiring from the activity, and so finished the job stopping at ten. The men of the camp walked away, some marveling at Cain's power and proficiency with a whip, others joking about the bone showing through Lamech's flesh. A few watched only because they had to and remained silent, afraid to say anything that might be taken as weakness. Just before dark some of the women untied him and administered a concoction made from leaves and roots as a salve. He was conscious and very much in pain, but water was his main need at this point and he took in all they offered.

Though his mind was clouded to some extent by suffering, many thoughts crossed it: "How long until the pain eases? Was this punishment final or is there more to come? How long before my body heals? What would it take to kill Cain? Was there any truth to that story of a curse upon the one who kills him? If I flee the land of Nod, would those in Eden grant safety to me?

He would further consider these issues at a later time; surviving this night was more critical at the moment. Thankfully, some of those same women who were not totally without caring and concern (and who also were attracted to him) continued to see to his needs. After they washed away most of the blood, sweat, and grime and tended his wounds he was able to struggle to the nearest lean-to where, despite the pain, he quickly fell asleep. The next day was a trying one, seemingly without end, but at least he was able to joke with one of the young men as he remarked, "The pain in my back causes me to forget about the pain in my foot." The young man laughed and admired him for his strength of heart.

Another day began and the pain was now tolerable. As the morning neared its end, Cain approached the lean-to as though all was forgotten and said, "I have been giving the matter some thought . . . and I have decided to organize our men into a fighting force for the purpose of seizing the land of Eden and killing any who get in our way. It has come to me in a vision that there is much in the way of unfinished business that must be set straight . . . and you will guide me since you have recent knowledge of the path that leads there."

Lamech was puzzled and asked, "Why go to all that trouble? Do we not have more than we can handle here? Who will watch the herds and tend the fields?"

"You would not understand!" He paused, then continued, "But . . . since there is nothing you can do to stop me . . . the unfinished business of which I spoke concerns capturing and punishing Naomi, killing Adam, taking back land where I labored long, and . . . the memory that has obsessed me from the time I left Eden—taking Rachel to be my woman—with or without her consent."

"Who is Rachel?"

"She is the younger sister of Naomi and the most beautiful woman you will ever see."

Lamech had never seen Cain react in such a manner, as though a juvenile smitten by one of the young females. He stared off into the air with a light in his eyes and a slight smile on his face. It was so out of character for this tyrant that Lamech felt very uncomfortable being made a part of the moment.

It lasted only a moment and Cain returned to his senses and to his usual self, at which point he put his finger in Lamech's chest and said solemnly, "We will work hard the next two days, getting herds and fields up in shape, then on the third day, leaving behind a few men to be in charge aided by the women and children, the majority of the men of our tribe will begin the trek to Eden. I expect you to help beginning immediately, and do not tell me of your injuries." That being said, he gave Lamech that cold glare that made men's hearts turn to water within their chests. Standing over him, impatiently waiting, he fully expected the recuperating young man to jump to action.

Lamech knew that he had to arise or risk more punishment, and somehow he made it to his feet and headed toward the fields. Fortunately, he managed to get with a couple of the more sympathetic men in the camp and they shielded him from Cain's sight which allowed Lamech a chance to go easy and let that back heal. By the end of the day, even with light duty, he was in nagging pain, but it was better than the preceding day.

Several of the men, by Cain's order, gathered together that evening to go over the next day's plans. Cain was not overly intelligent, but he did have a knack for knowing which man would serve best in a certain role. As much as it irritated him, he put his hand on Lamech's raw shoulder and announced to the others, "This man was the last to travel the route we are about to take, so he will walk beside me in the lead. Now . . . what supplies should we carry on this journey?" He paused a few moments to look over those gathered and they seemed to be unsure of themselves in this matter. Reluctantly, he turned again to Lamech and asked, "How much did the four of you take and did it seem to be enough?"

"I lost track of the days, but it seemed that it took nearly a week to reach that valley, and we traveled at a solid pace. Each man took a leather sack with enough bread, cheese, fruit and vegetables to last a good week, with the belief that we would find ample food along the way, thus stretching our supplies several more days. We also carried spears and Edom packed a hatchet which proved useful for chopping wood . . . until the handle broke . . . and we took some flint rock for starting fires."

Cain mulled it over in his mind and was uncertain as to what was best. Cainan, one of the largest men in the tribe, nearly a head taller than Cain, and about half as clever, boldly spoke out, "Let us take even less than did Lamech and the others! We will find food along the way and when we get to Eden we will take their food! I say enough of this 'planning!' Well . . . are you hearing me?!" Almost every man present rolled his eyes.

Onan said, "There were only four of them. There are 120 of us, and food from the wild will be in short supply. I believe we should pack as much as we can carry." Several voiced their support for his statement.

Cain agreed in part, "That sounds reasonable. Of course, it has been a very long time since I walked that trail, but that valley should be nearly half-way to Eden. So, by my figuring, if each man packed a little more than what those four started with and carefully conserved the food, making use of all that the wild provides, we should arrive in Eden with some to spare. What say the rest of you?"

Everyone there knew that was not a question, but an order, and pity any man who dared be a naysayer. So there was a lot of commotion in favor of Cain's words, with back slapping and loud shouts meant to energize all who were in attendance, and each trying to get louder than the next! The women and the men who were watching the herds thought for a moment that Eden had attacked first. After swelling with pride at all the noise in favor of his opinion, Cain stood up by the fire, the flames illuminating him, and with the men cheering he shouted, "Start packing tonight! Tomorrow at sunrise we begin!" The shouting continued for a while longer, then gradually died down as the men attended to the business of readying themselves for the march.

The Long March

T hrough the course of the evening, the men checked two and three times to be certain they had all they needed for the march to Eden. They packed so many supplies it left the women and children short, but theirs was a noble effort and sacrifices had to be made.

After a short night with much tossing and turning, they left at the first hint of sunrise and quickly found that the walking was difficult as they stumbled on rocks and tripped over each other in the early light. By mid-day, they learned to walk side-by-side, single-file, whatever the trail allowed, and they made some progress; of course a smaller group could have traveled more efficiently, but it was adequate for such a large body of men untrained in military maneuvering. And when you take into consideration the fighting that broke out at every stumble which inadvertently jostled another, I suppose one could say the progress was above average. Cain, after the fifth altercation, threatened bodily injury to those involved in further delays . . . and he would personally see to the punishment. That was enough to control tempers for the rest of the first day.

As darkness approached, they were still within the borders of Nod and in territory that was quite familiar to many of the older men. There was much in the way of, "I remember when so and so did this and that right over by . . ."

The decision was made to set up camp and many smaller fires were kindled, their glows dotting the earth like small stars and contrasting sharply with the moonless sky. The vast majority elected to go with numerous small fires instead of a few bonfires, using the experience they gained from keeping watch over herds by night. A bonfire was good for keeping predators away, but a small fire was better for staying warm; and there were enough men that creatures of the night were not likely to attack. They were all quite tired from the lack of rest over the preceding days and most of them slept well . . . except for an ill-favored few whom, by Cain's orders, tended the fires.

They were up at sunrise, and after eating a bite ready to face this new day. Their marching skills were much improved and there was but one outburst that was quickly put to rest when Cain cast that cold glare their way. In hushed tones there was still some dissension, such as: "Well, you just wait until this is over, then we will see who is the better man."

Days three, four, five, and so on passed by with hardly a snag at any point. The men marched willingly over rugged terrain, the same springs that served Lamech and his three brothers were still flowing and supplied the 120 with drinking water, though they were too small to accommodate swimming. They found scattered fruit trees, enough to provide minimal nourishment and a welcome treat to break the monotony of the same old rations that now had to be forced down because of age and bruising. Day seven arrived and patience was now in short supply. Fights erupted on a regular basis and Cain now watched with amusement instead of rage. They were nearing the dreaded valley, probably a day out, but were not aware of it as yet. Lamech recognized the surroundings, but elected to remain silent hoping that fatigue and frustration would cause them to give up on this notion. Maybe there would be a total mutiny against Cain and he would be killed. If events pointed that way, Lamech planned to do his part in support of the rebellion.

"Lamech! It has been seven days since we left. Are we nearing the valley?" inquired Cain.

"There may have been darkness when we passed through here. Nothing looks familiar," answered Lamech.

Others asked him the same question, irritating, yet bringing a measure of amusement to Lamech who played with their minds. "Surely this is the right trail. You know, I was injured and close to dying of hunger and thirst; so perhaps I was delirious and we are not even going in the right direction."

Cain grabbed the young man by the throat and lifted him off the ground, holding him there and staring into his bulging eyes. His teeth clenched, he quietly, but coldly warned, "If by tomorrow your memory has not improved, I will cast you over the nearest cliff and continue the march relying on my recollection of this area."

Lamech, choking and sputtering, was beginning to black out when Cain dropped him to the ground. Some of the onlookers pointed and laughed, others made haste to get out of their leader's line of sight, lest he take out his wrath on them. Whatever was going through their heads at this moment, the foremost thought common to all was that mutiny was out of the question.

That night, as they all slept, right on the border of that valley of which only Lamech was aware, a visitor silently dropped in on the camp. Satan had been out for a walk in his refuge and sensed intruders. He quickly picked up on the vibes emanating from their camp and traced them down. Seeing their fires from a distance he instantly emerged from the darkness and stood on the outskirts of the camp admiring what could loosely be described as "his workmanship." He dropped to one knee and stroked his chin, smiling much the same as when he witnessed the murder of Abel. The smile turned into a quiet chuckle and he mused: "It took them a little longer than I thought, but at least they are here. There are many of them . . . maybe enough to do irreparable damage to the family in Eden. Ohhh I could be of great service to these, if God would only let down the protective hedge around Adam. Ha, it is wonderful to never have the need of sleep!"

He moved unseen through the motionless collection of humanity, stopping here and there to whisper words of anger, hate, and deceit . . . even rebellion, though that might prove an obstacle to Cain's tyrannical hold on this tribe. But rebellion was Satan's specialty and he relished the thought of seeing it in action, knowing that, whether it be Cain or someone else in the leadership role, he would have control over them. He soon stopped beside Cain's sleeping body, whispering advice and instruction: "It has been too long since last I visited you, but it looks as though my teachings have been retained. Remember to trust no one and show no mercy. Lead by violence and be ready to display ruthless ways to underlings . . . do that and you will lead for a very long time . . . and I will be with you . . . at least until another idea proves more entertaining." Again he laughed, and then left to continue his night walk through the dark and foreboding valley, but he would return before they reached Eden.

It was sunrise and Cain's troop prepared for the day's march beginning with a rather meager breakfast. Their supplies were nearly depleted, even with rationing and finding what nature supplied. Cain walked straight to a still drowsy Lamech, stooping over he grasped him once again around the throat and lifted him into the air leaving his feet dangling and dancing. He pressed him for answers, "Well, have you had a good rest? Do things look more familiar in the morning light?!"

Lamech could not speak at that moment and frantically motioned to be released. Grinning all the while, Cain watched him suffer a good bit, and then released him. He fell to the ground coughing, gagging, and struggling to get his breath. His answer was too long in coming to suit the taste of his tormentor and Cain reached down and snatched him by the hair with the intention of further injury. Lamech was jerked to his feet, but just before those huge hands had their way he managed to force out a few words while holding up his much smaller hands in a compliant gesture. Cain backed off and with a still-mocking smile said, "Are you sure that you are ready to talk, or do you still need more time to think?"

Lamech hoarsely spoke, "Ready . . . to talk. We are . . . at the border of the valley . . . where the women were lost."

"You mean where *you* lost the women!"

Looking down at the ground in shame and frustration, he took a couple of deep breaths, shook his head and said, "Sometime tomorrow or the next day, will find us . . . very close to the spot where we followed them down the cliff face."

"It is indeed good to see that your memory is sharper today!" Cain cast a pompous, expectant glance at those surrounding the little scene and it was followed by boisterous laughter that was too quick in coming and too long in lasting.

Lamech, under orders, took the lead with Cain close behind, and after marching another two days, they reached the memorable cliff that overlooked the infamous valley. Lamech saw the monument built for Tamarah and began to investigate it. Cain and several others walked with him their curiosities stirred by the huge pile of rocks. They were asking each other: "What is this? Did the women build this? It is surely for one who has died, but why would they take the time and energy to build such a thing?"

Cain, trying to display intelligence, stated, "The first question is . . . did they build it before they went down into the valley or after they came up out of it?"

Lamech was irritated by that and let his temper control his tongue, "If you had listened to a word I said about my journey you would know that we were right behind them and they would not have had time to build such a structure on the way into the valley!"

Like the strike of a snake Cain backhanded Lamech and with such force one of his sandals was left in place while the rest of him went flying through the air. Cain seemed quite pleased with himself and a little surprised at his display of speed and power. He said in his heart, "You will still be leading this tribe when all these here today are long dead." He then stood over Lamech, and calmly offered, "You are slow to learn, but I am a willing teacher."

Lamech was woozy, barely aware of something huge standing over him, so whether death was imminent he cared not at this point. Cain thought that he might still need the young man and he let him rest for a time while he plotted his next move with some of the others. Onan had a skin of water and squirted some of it into Lamech's face, enough to stimulate the senses and restore awareness. He squatted down and quietly said, "You are as thick-skulled a man as I have ever seen. You know . . . if he begins to think he has no further need of your assistance, he will kill you for standing in his shadow . . . and in his mind that covers a meadow."

Lamech was alert, but groaning as he now pulled himself up on hands and knees. He weakly replied, "Controlling the tongue is a skill that has eluded me thus far."

Surprised at this sense of humor during such a time, Onan replied, "Yes. Will you live long enough to ever master that one?"

Lamech laughed a little, though his entire body ached. He countered, "Well, at least I am becoming accustomed to pain. Maybe it will be like a callous and I will gradually toughen to the point that Cain can no longer hurt me." Sensing that Onan was one of the few who looked at life in a similar light, he asked him, "Tonight, if I sneak out of camp and run to Eden, will he even bother to chase after me?"

Onan hesitated, then whispered, "Be very careful. While you were on the ground I overheard Cain telling several of the men, Cainan among them, to keep watch over you in the event that you tried to escape. It was as though he knew what was in your mind . . . and hoped you would try it. So if you run . . . use every tactic that your mind can imagine to avoid capture—especially by Cainan. He lives to be like Cain, so if you are captured, your life is finished"

"Maybe I can pretend to have a spirit of cooperation until we arrive at Eden and . . ."

A doubtful look on his face, Onan quickly interrupted, "My suggestion would be to run as soon as you see an open opportunity. Several times in my life I have seen the expression that comes on Cain's face shortly before killing dogs or men that he deems no longer fit to breathe air . . . like the one he is wearing today."

Lamech thought for a few moments and quietly said, "You may be right. That expression has been on his face all day." There was a pause as a series of next-moves went through his head. "When the opportunity presents itself, I hope my legs will be able to do what I want them to do. Your thoughts are appreciated, Onan." The two men spoke nothing further at this time, not wanting to raise suspicion.

Cain wanted to know who was buried under the rocks and he gave the order to tear down the monument. The men, being somewhat superstitious concerning dead bodies, were at first careful in the dismantling, but just one impatient glare from their master and they began to grab and throw. They soon reached the bottom layer of stones and removed enough to see most of the body and Tamarah's face. Cain was slightly disappointed, hoping that it was Naomi. He now gave the command to resume the westward march.

Other than Naomi, Tamarah was the only female for whom Lamech had any feeling. And though he was part of the group that worked so hard to capture her, it now troubled him to see her lifeless body. And the thought that they would walk away and leave her like this was equally disturbing. "Wait! Will we not replace the stones?!"

Cain snapped, "No! There is no time for that. Besides, she does not deserve any special treatment after running away; let the birds of the air enjoy themselves."

Lamech exercised self-control at this point and managed to keep his mouth shut, but he truly began to see what Onan had seen—that look in the big man's eyes along with the tell-tale glances being cast back and forth between Cain and a few of his closest followers.

They resumed the march at a brisk pace and as they tramped along on the rugged rocks Lamech made further plans. Since the desecration of Tamarah's remains, he had been considering how he might return to the site to rectify the wrong that had been done, but the how and when of it was challenging with so many watching his every move. Finally, darkness nearing, the men began the job of starting some fires; but there was very little of anything for fuel close-by, so they had to spread out and walk some distance. Cainan, and a few of the other ringleaders seemed to bunch together to avoid carrying wood, and that allowed Lamech some wiggle room in the ever-darkening evening. He grabbed some sticks while with Onan and a few of the others, to make it look good, and that group soon blended in with another group of wood gatherers. Meanwhile, Cainan walked in their direction, anxiously doing his best to keep his victim in sight.

Lamech edged ever closer to a small grove of trees about twenty paces to the west when Onan cleared his throat and gave a jerk of his head, indicating that there would be no better time to run. Lamech gave a tight-lipped smile and a nod, touched his chest and gave an open-handed gesture to show appreciation; then quickly and silently blended into the night heading toward Eden. After traveling westward for some distance and purposely leaving a few tracks on scattered areas of soil, he then back-tracked until he was, once again, on solid rock. This area was strewn with large boulders which would provide him with cover.

Nearly all trace of twilight now gone, Cainan could no longer make out images in the darkness, so he dropped the few sticks that he had gathered and ran toward the grove of trees where Lamech was last seen. All the men who had gathered wood near that grove were on their way to the campsite when he anxiously stopped them and asked of Lamech's whereabouts. They all looked at each other, then looked back toward the grove and with shrugged shoulders said they were not his keeper. Cainan ran wildly into the trees looking here and there calling out Lamech's name. Enoch, Cain's first-born, and some of the others arrived and also searched, to no avail.

As much as they dreaded the thought of it, they went to Cain and told of the escape. There was no time for beatings at this point so he gave the order to take some small logs from the fire and using them as torches, try to find his tracks. The moon was now coming over the horizon and it was nearly full, which provided some light to assist in the search. Ten men, lead by Cain, headed off into the night where they soon came upon tracks pointed toward Eden. The men continued that direction at a trot, hoping to catch sight of Lamech or maybe even find him at the bottom of a gulley with a broken bone. That would be ideal! Cainan was now at the back of the line, having lost his place among the elite.

The Chase

As he sulked and fell further behind the others, he decided to catch his breath, and as he stopped and leaned over, putting his hands on his knees, a sound caught his attention. He did not have a torch, but by the moonlight he caught a glimpse of someone appearing from behind a boulder and running back toward the east. It looked like Lamech's stride and after moving a few steps and seeing him again, he was certain. Cainan thought to himself, "I need to call for the others." He placed cupped hands to his lips, took a deep breath and reared back, but stopped. "If I was to capture him by myself, maybe my favorable standing would be returned. Yes . . . there is no doubt that once my hands have taken hold of him he will be like a young boy in the grip of this man. Ah, I can see it all in my mind." A self-assured grin on his face, he ran toward the figure, trying for now to just stay close. He would bide his time and catch him unaware because just as sure as he was of his advantage in strength, he was also aware of Lamech's advantage in foot speed. As Lamech crept from one boulder to the next, Cainan followed, keeping his distance but not so far as to lose sight of him. Chance, he reasoned, was on his side with the moon beaming down imitating the twilight at early evening.

——◆——

Lamech rejoiced in his heart when the searchers walked right by the cleft where he was hiding. After they disappeared over the ridge he stepped out into the moonlight, certain that he was unseen. So many feelings and notions were pulsating through him: "I did it! Two of them were so close I could have spit on them. Oh, my heart is pounding much the same as when the beast in that valley nearly finished me. Hmm . . . as I think about it, Cain and Cainan would fit rather well in the company of the valley's creatures. How I would love to see them have that chance. Well . . . enough of this dreaming. I have to be careful that no man in the camp sees me. If I stay about a shout away from the fires . . . that should do it. Far enough to avoid being seen, but close enough to, hopefully, avoid predators."

Cainan closed the gap between them, preparing to make his move. It was difficult for a man of his size to remain unseen, but there were enough large rocks to make it so.

Lamech, confident of his situation, stopped to rest, and as he did he gave thought to his success in staying alive and pondered the "what if's" of these last days. There was a sense of relief and peace inside, but also of wonder. He had felt this way before—on the long trek back to Nod and the hardships that were overcome. He stared off into the darkness not looking for anything material, but searching for answers. Just then . . . he heard a noise behind him. He was quickly brought back to his wits and thought, "What was that?! Do not look over your shoulder. Just listen for a bit, act as though nothing has changed, and do not show fear. Is it an animal . . . or man? Which would be better? Or was it anything at all? Maybe my mind is playing tricks on me."

He remained very still with his head slightly cocked so as to gain an edge in hearing. He heard nothing more at this point, but sensed a presence out there. He decided to pick up the pace, though he would have to be somewhat cautious—to fall and injure an already tender foot and ankle, or to break a leg would be his end if there was anything behind him. He wished for his spear or hatchet, but Cain had taken them away, leaving him with only his intellect for comfort. He broke into a trot, stopping occasionally to listen. The first two times he heard nothing, but it was hard to hear with his heartbeat hammering away in his ears. He stopped again . . . this time he heard the sound of footsteps! There were many rocks on the trail behind him, but the moon's light was too dim to see anything clearly. He looked at the trail ahead and saw that it was reasonably smooth; also, the top of the next ridge was situated so as to be entirely in the moon's light. Once he was over that ridge, his view would be free of obstructions and enough in the light to get some idea as to the identity of his follower . . . or followers.

He jogged up to the crest of the ridge, acting as though that was to be his normal stride from there on, but just as soon as he cleared it he broke into a lope hoping to put some extra distance between himself and his pursuer. The moonlight was quite bright now and his path was well lit. When he had gained enough space to ease his mind, he stopped and turned to observe. He was standing beside the only rock on the slope big enough to offer some cover and he crouched behind it, waiting for what seemed like a very long time; so long that he began to question his senses. Then . . . there it was! The silhouette of a giant slowly appeared up on the horizon and momentarily froze in place on the ridge, standing so that the moon was directly behind him, eerily illuminating his form and causing the resolve of an already weary young man to further weaken. The distant figure began turning his head, first left, then right, as he searched ahead for his quarry. There was now no doubt that it was Cainan; the very one of whom Onan had warned. Seldom had Lamech, in earlier times, thought of him as an enemy, though maybe a competitor; after all, they were of the same tribe. But just now, the memory of Cainan defeating three men at a time during some rather serious clashes within the tribe came back to his mind. So there was no longer any feeling of kinship. What to do?

The big man had run a long distance, but was not terribly winded. As he surveyed the smoother surface ahead he thought, "Lamech must have heard my steps and is now hiding. The moon's light on this hill is such that I would surely see him had he continued at his earlier pace. There is that one rock in the distance, but to have reached it already . . . Hmm, with that foot barely healed and all the abuse that he has taken, how is he *able* to continue? Well, if I must chase him all the way back to Nod, I will."

Lamech watched the giant as he resumed the chase, and at a near-run. And though he desperately needed rest, it was run or die; so he vacated his hiding spot and, now knowing what was behind, took up again the race for life. He tried to think as he ran: "Tamarah's grave is about a ridge away; if I can continue this run that far, maybe his endurance will give out . . . but what if it does not? All those times when we worked the fields . . . he was the one who complained of fatigue and acted as though he could hardly pull another weed or walk another step. But during wrestling matches and contests of strength, stamina was never lacking . . . just like tonight. Well, I can make it to the gravesite, but not much further. I must be prepared to make a stand of sorts right there, while I have enough energy to at least throw rocks. I might consider descending into the valley, as a last resort. Madness must be near to taking me to even consider that."

"Ah! He was behind the rock! It looks as though his pace has slowed. I will overtake him by the next hilltop and end his life there. Cain will indeed be pleased." Cainan's adrenaline level increased as he saw the distance between the two fast closing.

Lamech made it to the ridge with time enough to hide, mount a defense, or begin the downward climb, but whichever he chose it had better be quick. Then a thought came to him, though it nearly turned his stomach. He ran over to the grave, briefly hesitated, gritted his teeth and then laid down in it, feeling Tamarah's cold, stiff, rotting flesh touching his hot, sweaty flesh. He did not remain that way for long as the whole situation caused his blood to run cold and sent shivers throughout his body, even more so as Cainan lumbered into the area, barely ten steps away.

Gasping for breath, but a smile of victory beginning to break across his face, Cainan growled, "I know you are up here! Your pace was like that of a turtle at the last!" He began to talk to himself, "The moon's light is still bright and the trail beyond the grave has only a few rocks big enough to hide a man. There is no visual sign of Lamech up ahead and no distant sound of footsteps on loose rock." His eyes searched the area and his finely-tuned ears listened to hear breathing—maybe even a heartbeat if Lamech's heart was pounding as hard as what Cainan deemed likely. He resumed the thought process: "I was close behind him. He could not have continued to run on that bad foot . . . and stumbling and lurching as he was, I would be able to hear him on the rocks ahead. He is on this ridge, somewhere. Come out, Lamech! I know you can hear me! Come out and death will be swift . . . but continue to anger me and I will break you bone by bone!"

Lamech was shaking with fear, knowing that he could not run, and could not fight against such a brute with any hope of success. Cainan's growling, bellowing voice by itself was like that of a hungry male lion and added to the torture of the situation.

Then, Cainan's confidence began to fade ever so slightly as he considered the possibility of climbing into that valley. The thought took root in his head that Lamech's only hope was to make the descent. He was not familiar with the climb as was Lamech; and after hearing all the stories, and hearing the animal noises coming from below over several nights, the bravado that made up the majority of his personality slipped away allowing a more down-to-earth attitude to surface. He slowly walked toward the edge, to possibly see some sign of his quarry, and to decide if Cain's praise was worth the risk of following any further.

Lamech was up on one elbow as he peeked over the edge of the grave and saw his best chance for survival. With the moon now sinking below the horizon, he quietly crawled out to an area of level footing. Legs still shaking, he picked up a large rock, heavy enough to do damage but light enough to be thrown; and he silently made his way toward his tormentor. As Cainan intently studied the steep slope, Lamech reached a point several paces behind and carefully, with all the focus and strength he could muster, threw that rock at the upper part of the giant. He reasoned that even if he hit him in the neck or shoulders, the force of the blow might knock him over the edge. The rock felt good as it left his hand and appeared to be on the right path. It struck the top of the giant's head, glancing off into the canyon. It was not nearly enough for a kill, but it did have an effect. The big man dropped to his knees, holding his head and cursing Lamech's name. His vision was blurred and he jerked his head from side to side, all the while rubbing his forehead in an attempt to regain his bearings.

Lamech was terrified as he watched Cainan struggle to his feet. Assuming that recovery was only moments away, he instinctively ran headlong into the huge mid-section, delivering a blow that, only a short time ago, would have seemed impossible. Cainan staggered backward only a step, but the rocks at the edge gave just enough to cause him a loss of balance. He threw those long arms forward, grasping at anything, and he caught Lamech by his hair, dragging him downward. The hair pulled out, but not before the two continued the slide on the upper slope with Lamech clawing at every crevice and outcropping that his hands and feet could find. Finally, his downward momentum slowed and his hands locked around a lone rock which protruded from the slope like a large human hand. He hugged it as though it was a cherished possession and then chanced a look at the screaming, sliding figure below him. He knew that Cainan was right at the last foothold of the upper slope; once past it, the remainder of the cliff was quite steep. And how his heart longed to see him slip past that ledge. There was little in the way of light now, but in the near-darkness . . . was it possible? The huge figure came to a stop as he evidently was able to grab and hold on to that ledge.

Cainan, in an instant, went from terrified to arrogant, certain that his great arm strength saved him from death, and he began spewing out threats as he slowly pulled himself up from certain death.

Lamech could scarcely believe what had happened and the joy that was his for too short a time seemed to plummet into that valley. But anger welled up, took the place of despair and he thought to himself, "I did not survive up to now by giving in to the likes of this dog! He is unfamiliar with this slope and is not built for climbing, so he will be a while in reaching the top. Perhaps a few more well-placed stones will take the conceit from him . . . forever!"

Lamech scampered upward, not having to pull anywhere near the weight of his large relative. He quickly rounded up the only plentiful resource in the region and began rolling them toward the slobbering, cursing Cainan. Fortunes had reversed and Lamech now with the advantage did not waste the opportunity. The first few missed, but still struck panic into the struggling bully. The fourth and fifth stones, which were larger, hit their mark and took the legs from under the big man causing a downward slide right back to that ledge.

Lamech had him where he wanted him and was very confident of success at this point, and even though the moon had disappeared for the night he could tell the man's location by the screams and curses that continually spewed from his loud mouth. He rolled stone after stone, even throwing when they were small enough; and he continued until he heard a noise like a soft thud, and then a particularly loud scream that grew fainter as the distance between the two men rapidly increased. He could hear the sound of falling rocks and of Cainan's body hitting obstacles on the way down. It was a sweet sound to Lamech's ears and a peace rose up inside him at the thought of this victory . . . or was it yet a victory? He was just in the process of returning to Tamarah's grave, but his ears picked up a distant moaning, which turned into an anguished cry, "Ahhh! Lamech! Lamech, I know you are up there!" Amazingly, he survived the plunge. He was injured and dazed and . . . out of some sort of instinct still able to speak abusively. "You have not yet defeated me! When daylight comes, I will climb out of here and there will be no place you can hide that I will not find you! Do you hear me? Answer me!!"

Lamech, in a sense, marveled at the big man's resiliency and questioned, "How could he possibly have survived a fall from that height? Did the small trees growing out from a few crevices cushion his plunge? He surely broke bones . . . but maybe not. If he is able to climb he will eventually find me . . . and he will not give up until he does. I have to look at this as though he will succeed, and again hunt me to the death."

Animal noises were plentiful from below on this night and that gave Lamech an idea. He began the art of taunting, something at which he was quite skilled, "Cainan! Are you hurt? Speak to me, old friend!"

"Old friend?! When were we ever friends?! You thought, and hoped, I was dead. I not only am alive, but still well enough to snap your neck—when I get my hands on it—and I will get my hands on it!" Cainan, at this point, was in and out of awareness. He was badly bruised with many cuts and scrapes on every crook of his huge frame. His mind was still in a state of confusion as he lay motionless on the rocks trying to sort out the details of how he ended up where he currently was. As near as he could recall, he fell blindly through the darkness using his hands and feet at every opportunity to slow his descent. The blows he took were of a glancing nature and he could only guess at what saved him from certain death. It felt like tree branches and he heard occasional sounds like the snapping of limbs, but he hit so fast and hard and was so disoriented that many of these thoughts were only a blur. After a sufficient time of rest he was coherent enough to remember his foe and his goal, and so continued the tirade. He lashed out at Lamech and after listening to each returning insult his anger increased. His adrenaline flow was at its peak and forced all pain out of his senses. He truly could have climbed at that moment had he any light to see.

Lamech persisted, knowing that Cainan's pride and temper would never allow his tongue to remain silent. Though he was beginning to tire of wasting his wit on a man so short on wisdom and understanding, he tossed down one final barb: "Why, those are some terrible things to say to your kinsman! I may have to report to Cain how easily you were tricked and how I defeated you in battle!"

"Defeated me?!" he retorted in a voice nearly loud enough to be heard throughout the known world. "You will do well to still your lying tongue!"

Finally, what Lamech had hoped for happened, and that deep, bellowing, voice attracted much in the way of undesirable attention.

"You will see, I . . . what . . . what is it?" By some hidden reserve of strength deep inside the big man, he jumped to his feet. As tall as he was, what he was now facing dwarfed him. It hissed violently and lunged forward. His legs were weak and quivering uncontrollably; his heart pounding so hard it nearly came through the rib cage. Never had he seen any creature like this. He did not know it, but it was the same one that devoured Hamath. As it grabbed him with those incredibly strong arms he had only an instant to react. He managed to get his hand around what was left of a broken limb and with all of his might, as the monster's jaws bit down on his middle, rammed it into the creature's eye. Again and again he thrust it into the lone, unprotected bit of flesh, but with each succeeding stroke his strength gave way and the blows, from first to last, appeared to have little effect. In the end, the same lizard-like creature that devoured other visitors from Nod found its way to Cainan's final resting place, and dined to the sound of tortured screams and the crackle of bones. It walked away, nearly blind from previous and present injuries, but for now, feeling little in the way of pain and hunger.

Lamech, at first grimaced hearing the shrieks and cries, and even the faint but distinct sound of splintering bones but soon, a wry smile came to him as he considered the past: "I knew his loud mouth would be the end of him . . . down in that valley, anyway. I always hoped to live long enough to see him humbled . . . well, I was unable to see it, but I can well imagine it. This valley has redeemed itself in my mind. If I ever pass this way again there will be one, worthwhile, fond memory to go with all the nightmarish ones."

In fairly short order, quiet returned to the night and he walked back to the grave; though far beyond weary he rebuilt the monument over Tamarah. As he stood there, leaning against his handiwork and remembering how she used to watch over him when he was but a boy, an abundance of strength somehow returned and his muscles and joints felt as they did before any of this. He looked at his hands and repeatedly stretched out the fingers and closed them into fists, feeling no pain. His legs were ready at that moment to march in whichever direction the mind dictated. Life was reasonably good again, but he had been on the go for a long while and did not want to put his body to the test without at least a little sleep. So he found a small area of soil and slept until dawn. He arose and trotted toward Eden, uncertain of his role in that which was ahead, but sensing a purpose.

The Return

Naomi and Adah, accompanied by Kebar, walked at a slowed, more relaxed pace now, not only because of fatigue but also from knowing that they were free, temporarily at least, from those who troubled them. They continued toward Eden for four days before Naomi began to recognize the lay of the land and certain familiar sights which brought a widening to her eyes as she pointed toward them and made remarks like: "That looks to be the tree . . . it is! I used to climb it as a girl and it is now huge! There were other trees beside it . . . large ones . . . but it appears many have died and nearly rotted away. And there is the meadow where Abel first kept flocks! And off to the east . . . the clear, cool brook that we waded when the sun was particularly hot . . . oh what precious times. We should be seeing our kinsmen soon."

Adah was nervous and asked, "Will any of them remember you after such a long separation? What if they do not? If your father and mother are no longer living, who is left to recognize you? And if they do not know you, will we be killed . . . or abused and enslaved?"

"Calm yourself, Adah! You ask too many questions and have too little faith in life."

"What good things have ever happened to me that I should have such faith?"

"You were one of the fortunate ones that I was able to teach concerning the good things that God has in store for those who trust in Him . . . you and a few others . . . until Cain damaged and destroyed so much of my teaching."

Adah was silent for a while, then asked, "Did you fashion those stories about your father and mother . . . and that garden? Did your father speak truth when he told you of the early days of Creation . . . or was it as Cain said—things just appeared from out of nowhere and no one really knows of the beginning?"

Naomi, instead of being angry at her daughter's questions, thought carefully regarding her next words. Silently she asked for assistance, and then proceeded: "Everything I have told you is based on the things I heard from my mother and father . . . and witnessed myself. Maybe the way I recall it has some minor flaws—there being no person with a perfect mind—but after spending so much time with me and seeing the examples I have laid before you . . . and after seeing the life that Cain has displayed . . . which of us will you believe? Do you not see a difference? Do you not understand about right and wrong?"

"I . . . believe so," began Adah, "but there were so few in our tribe who followed your example in even the slightest form, I was left to wonder which ways were best . . . to wonder about the meaning of right and wrong. Day after day, for the vast majority of my life, I watched as the cruelest and strongest of our tribe prevailed in nearly every endeavor . . . and for the most part those methods seemed to me the way to live. But now, after being so near to you through all these trials, and closely observing your actions . . . I am being persuaded that your ways are best."

Naomi, her face glowing with a seldom-seen expression of joy and pride, gave her daughter a long hug and said, "I pray that my mother and father are still alive; then, instead of hearing a lot of words you will see real-life demonstrations of 'right' and 'love' and 'joy.' And you will be free from the constant cynicism that came from the people of Nod over anything spoken of as 'good.'"

They walked all that morning and began to see signs of human activity: crops, fruit trees, freshly-planted fields. They were not aware of it, but they were being watched. Two men were hiding behind some trees, carefully observing their every move.

"Are you sure you have never seen either of them?" whispered Dedan.

Javan, the younger of the two answered, "I know that our tribe has grown considerably in these later days, but I do not recognize them."

"I am long past my youth, but the older woman is not familiar to me in the least. The look of her covering is different . . . the hide is not cut the same; and it is tattered as though it has seen better times."

"She appears to be older than most of the other women. What if they are spies from some other people? We could attack them!"

The older man put his arm in front of the younger to restrain his youthful aggressiveness and calmly stated, "They do not have the look of danger about them. Let us confront these two, peaceably, and take them to Adam."

They stepped out into the open, with their spears held in such a manner as to convey a warning, and the women stopped. Sternly, the older man asked, "Who are you, and what is your business here!?"

Startled, Adah jumped behind Naomi. "I am Naomi—the wife of Cain, from the land of Nod."

The men looked at each other, trying to remember where they had heard those names.

"I am the oldest daughter of Adam and Eve. Tell me, are they still living? Have you ever heard of me?"

The men seemed uncertain as to a correct plan of action, but after a few moments hesitation, Dedan ordered the women to follow them. They entered an area of modest dwellings, but dwellings that were nicer than any the women had ever before seen.

People were most curious at the sight of these unknown women and within moments the news spread. The men led them to the largest dwelling and the older man went inside while Javan kept watch. While inside, he explained the situation to Eve and me and we were most curious. Walking to the opening of our home and focusing on the two, especially the older one, I was in a state of disbelief and very uncertain of my eyes. To myself I whispered, "Naomi?"

While I continued to stand at the doorway, trying to decide if it was all a dream, Eve pushed me aside and raced toward our daughter with nary a shred of doubt in her mind. I was slow to follow, still uncertain if that woman was our first-born daughter. Her hair was graying and her face lined. As I observed them standing together, Eve, older by far, looked to be the woman's younger sister. I thought to myself, "You poor girl! Has your life been so hard as to completely rob you of all youth?" Tears welled up in my eyes and I ran to join the joyful gathering. I waited my turn as Eve put on quite a lengthy demonstration as to the proper reaction concerning the return of a long-lost loved one, with hugs and kisses aplenty. She finally allowed me to have a turn and I held my daughter at arm's length and looked into her face . . . trying to remember that day when she and Cain set out on their own. Her eyes, filled with tears of joy, removed all doubt from my mind—it was Naomi. I hugged her and held on for nearly as long as her mother. Eve eventually forced me aside and took up where she had left off. Others waited to offer a greeting—very few who knew her any other way than by old stories: only Rachel, Enosh, Peleg and a few others. There was genuine warmth as they embraced their sister and asked about children and such.

While Eve was occupied, I turned to the younger woman, who appeared quite uncomfortable. I said to her, "Please forgive our rudeness, young lady. What is your name?"

It seemed, at first, a struggle for her to speak, but she finally forced out the name "Adah." I reasoned that all the commotion was a bit overwhelming and suggested that we step away from the gathering so as to speak. I asked, "Are you Naomi's daughter?"

She stared at me for a time, searching my face as though she had seen it before, but was not quite able to identify me. Then, softly she said, "You are my . . . grandfather."

I smiled and replied, "Then you are Naomi's daughter. Well, welcome to this family and the land of Eden, my grandchild." I reached out to her and at first she was hesitant, as though not accustomed to such things. Not wanting to force the issue, but giving her ample time to accept my offer of affection, I continued to hold out my hands. Looking intently into my eyes for only a few more moments, she then nearly lunged into my arms and began to weep as she clung to me. I patted her on the back and consoled her, "There, there my child. You have surely had a long, difficult journey . . . some nourishment and a good night's rest will do wonders for you. Later on, we will talk of your life in Nod and countless other things that will add to a long discussion."

She finally backed away and looking straight at me, smiled and said, "You are just as I pictured, and the many good things that Mother spoke, concerning you, surely are true."

I was a bit uncomfortable to be so highly regarded, but smiled and thanked her. We walked back to join the others and Adah clutched my arm as though starved for a decent, honorable male role in her life. And by her actions I formed an image in my mind of life in Nod.

It was at this point that I exclaimed to all present: "Tonight we celebrate! Spread the word to every member of the family." We were all very familiar with hard work, but on occasion we made time for recreation, and at the moment the order was given people ran in all directions to spread the news. This day topped all others in my estimation and so we planned a feast which included baked goods topped with cream and honey, several kinds of vegetables seasoned by the little salt that was available to us, the choicest of fruit and juice from the same, to be followed by games and carefree, lively conversation. Of course it would take a while to accomplish the feat, but nearly everyone took part with enthusiasm; and since the event held such a special meaning for my wife and me, we were granted the privilege of not having to take part in the preparation.

As happy as was the occasion, something weighed on Naomi's mind and she told us that she had a warning. Judging by the troubled expression on her face, it appeared to be news of a grim nature, and she had my full attention. As soon as we separated ourselves from the others, the four of us sat down to talk about the matter. Naomi told of life as she had experienced it and several times she broke into tears and held onto Eve. We had not seen her cry since she was a child and the moment was especially precious for the two women. Adah had never seen her mother as anything other than rugged and composed, so once the sense of shock lifted, she also shed tears and placed hands of support on Naomi. As soon as this period of emotion had run its course, she began the return to her usual self. She wiped the tears from her eyes and apologized, "I am so sorry. Maybe fatigue has caused me to be so weak. I . . . I just . . ."

Eve took her by the hand and said, "Nonsense. I doubt that any other woman on this earth could have survived under the conditions that were part of your everyday life. So you just disregard this moment of what you describe as weakness. As for me, I will always remember . . . and cherish it!" They hugged and tears flowed once more.

I appreciated the long-overdue sentiment, but this "warning" that was mentioned earlier had caused some angst within my spirit, so I interrupted the moment: "Daughter, you were on the verge of grim news a while ago. Is it still that way?"

My tone evidently carried with it a lack of patience and Naomi, recognizing it, returned to her old self: "Yes. Cain will come after me and he will bring as many men as he thinks necessary."

"What makes you so certain of this? It sounds like too much effort for one who rarely exerted himself, outside of fighting with his brother . . . and sometimes farming."

Eve remarked, "I remember that he was a jealous boy who always had to win, no matter the cost. If he thinks that Naomi's absence is a slap in his face he might very well come here."

I paused and remembered some of those battles in which he and Abel engaged, then answered, "Yes . . . yes, I had forgotten. Perhaps she is correct in her thinking."

Naomi felt as though she had been left out of the discussion and retorted, "I was married to this . . . man, had children by him, and lived with him plenty long enough to know his ways! He will be here, and the quicker we prepare the better it will be for all of us!"

I squeezed her shoulder and apologized for disregarding her opinion. She then went on to tell us some of the details of these later days. After hearing her words I said, "You mentioned the one man who escaped from that valley. You said that it appeared he had injured his foot. If so, that will greatly slow his return. Assuming that he made it back to Nod, it will take a few days to organize a venture of the size you envision. So . . . since they will not be here for some time . . . the party will go on as planned! No one is to mention what we just discussed tonight; tomorrow will be soon enough. Let us just enjoy life for at least one night."

All three women looked at me as though that was a most reckless decision, but I held my ground and said there would be no further discussion.

Word concerning the party quickly spread to every member of the clan and soon there were men, women, and children from every corner of our land. Only a few were left to guard the livestock, but with the understanding that we would work in watches so all could take part in the occasion at some point.

The food was soon ready and both guests enjoyed the meal, eating more than many of the men. People flocked around them asking questions such as: "What is life like in Nod? Do you have many children? Are the animals the same as the ones in Eden? Does Cain really have a red face? How many days did it take to walk that far?" And on and on it went until Eve and I put forth the idea of playing some games. While attention was momentarily away from the two women, they slipped away. The rest of Eden laughed and sang silly songs and led the children in games designed for their enjoyment and after a while, I noticed that Naomi and Adah were no longer part of the festivities. Several of us began a search, not wanting them to miss any of the activity. We soon found them curled up on some straw that we stored in one of the nearby caves. They were in a deep sleep; totally oblivious to sound and touch. I say that because we called their names and even patted them on the shoulder, but there was no response. Well, it somehow seemed wrong to continue the party without the guests of honor, but we decided that they needed the sleep and we needed the entertainment. We could enjoy their company at a later time, so we went on with the fun well into the night.

Back to Business

The next day, most of the family slept until the sun was well off the horizon, and that was understandable. Naomi and Adah, still curled up in the same position, remained asleep until the midday meal when Eve decided to wake them.

Earlier, I spoke to Enosh, Peleg, and Seth as they were heading to the fields. We had fallen behind because of the unexpected, yet welcome diversion to our everyday life, but now was a time for planning.

"Men, I know you are in a hurry, but this is important and we must discuss some matters critical to our safety." They looked at each other with eyes full of curiosity knowing that I was usually the one pushing for more and more where work was concerned. I was not sure how to begin. There was no need to spread panic . . . I mean, there was a reasonable chance that the men of Nod would never make the long journey . . . then again, it was a chance we could not take. "Well . . . what do any of you remember about Cain?"

Enosh, after a few moments of silence answered, "I remember that he was the biggest and strongest in our family, and for a while it was my hope to be like him; later on, I wanted to slay him but you warned us about the curse that was on anyone who carried out such a deed. It has been so long . . . all other memories are dim."

Peleg offered, "I was a very young boy at the time and my only recollection concerning Cain was that something about him frightened me. I did not like him."

Seth said, "All I know are the stories that have been passed down to me . . . and to be honest, I sometimes wondered how much was true."

I said to them, "Those are honest assessments . . . Enosh, being the oldest would have a little more to remember. Let me try to refresh all of our memories and add some recent information also."

I reminded them of his evil concerning Abel and his rebellion against me and anything pertaining to God and family. The things that Naomi had related were brought into the discussion and we all agreed that he was surely more dangerous now than in earlier days.

After sharing enough about the past and preparing hearts for what might happen in the future I said, "Let us return to the fields and the livestock, but as you work . . . think about the measures we might take to defeat Cain and a force of many men armed for battle. We have never in our existence faced the possibility of having to battle . . . and probably kill . . . fellow humans. Let me warn you . . . if he follows through with this, there will be no old feelings of warmth, no negotiation, and no mercy. We must prepare as though a pride of lions with human cunning was about to attack our wives and children. In fact . . . from what I sense in my core being, we would stand a better chance against the wild animals."

The young men set out with their jaws clenched and their gazes fixed straight ahead; already deep in thought. Between the four of us, our imaginations stirred, there would be answers to our problems . . . of that I was certain.

In as far as work was concerned, it was probably a good thing that we were more in the line of overseers; else our labor would have set a terrible example with all that was on our minds. Throughout the course of the day I came up with a couple of ideas as did the others and by early evening we met to share our imaginations.

"Well, let us begin with the youngest. If we hear the thoughts of the oldest first, Seth may lack the confidence to voice what may prove to be quite useful." All agreed, and we turned to the young man and waited for his words.

Staring at the ground for a few moments, trying to decide how best to communicate that which consumed his thoughts for an entire day, he slowly began, "Since these men will be similar to lions in as far as strength and aggressiveness, maybe we could set a trap that would take advantage of over-aggressiveness and get them off their feet where their size and power would be negated."

We all leaned forward, looking at him with, at first, great anticipation, then impatience as he began to lose confidence.

Peleg growled, "Well! Let us hear it!"

I held up my hand to settle Peleg and to reassure Seth that we would not make sport of his notion.

"Well . . . we have only tried it twice, but it has worked both times. Remember the young male lions that attacked our herds over by the twin lakes? Right in the middle of a main trail we tied the ends of some vine ropes to netting laid between two young trees; then we wound the ropes around the upper branches of those trees and pulled them down to the ground where we tied them to tree roots. Men were stationed close to those roots, hidden from sight. When our goats stopped to get a drink the lions crept along the usual trail for an easy meal; but as they walked over the netting, the ropes were cut causing the young trees to spring back to their former position. The netting was pulled around the lions, lifting them into the air and trapping them, making for an easier, safer kill. Admittedly, a second time was not quite as successful as the lion nearly fought his way out of the netting, but we speared him just as he hit the ground."

There was dead silence as Enosh, Peleg, and I pictured this in our minds. We had already heard of its success from some of the other men and thought Seth might mention it, so after a few winks we remained still just to see Seth's reaction. After a time of continuing silence, he began to fidget, then blurted out, "Now look . . . I prayed about this for a good part of the day, and I believe God gave me this idea! But if you believe it to be foolish, then never ask for my view again!"

The three of us, for a moment, looked at each other in mock surprise, then broke into laughter, patting him on the back and complimenting him for a good idea.

I added only, "Location will be the hard part—finding the near-perfect place to spring such a trap. And timing will also be of utmost importance! By that I mean . . . along with knowing when to cut the ropes . . . which men will be willing to wait in hiding so close to our attackers? Now . . . did you and God come up with anything else?"

Seth frowned a little as though he wished for more to say: "Nothing other than to invest much time practicing with spear and hatchet over the ensuing days."

I squeezed him on the shoulder and said, "We will put those ideas to the test. Now . . . what next?"

Peleg, with only a moment's hesitation, offered, "You used to tell us about the time Abel dug the hole, filled it with thorn branches and nettles, then concealed it with long-stemmed grasses and palm leaves in order to inflict suffering on Cain. What if we dug a series of trenches across the main trails but instead of thorn branches we drove sharpened stakes into the ground, so that Cain's men would fall on them and at the very least be injured?"

I inwardly winced remembering the day that Cain fell into the pit, but not willing to voice anything resembling weakness I replied, "That sounds somewhat gruesome . . . but we will be fighting against a foe that, given a chance, will do worse than that to us and our families. So we must all, at the proper time, God forgive us, grit our teeth and go against conscience. Your idea is quite sound."

Enosh wholeheartedly agreed and added, "I have two thoughts: We could search the woods for hornets' nests, then wait for evening when the little beasts are not so active, wrap the nests in bags made from goat hides and pull them free from the tree branches. The bags will seal them until the moment that our enemy has to walk along the east creek bottom; then we can drop these little terrors down on them from the bluff above the creek. Now . . . I know that these men will probably not turn back because of this, but every irritation will weaken their resolve. Also, and I know, Father, that you will probably not approve, but Nashor and I have recently made improvements to the bow and arrow and if we could train our men in its use, who knows the success we might see!"

I had listened to him speculate on the use of this weapon before and was never swayed on its effectiveness, so after casting a look toward the sky and shaking my head I said, "You persist in speaking of the potential of this weapon and I am left with the same argument, that if it is only good at short range why not use the spear and axe? Even the sling is preferable because of its long-range possibilities, and though it will not result in many kills at least its user will have time to drop it and grab his spear before the enemy is upon him."

"But we have greatly improved the arrows, fixing a stone point to the tip and feathers to the butt end for truer flight. Nashor killed two wild dogs yesterday and the day before that I severely wounded a male lion and watched him stagger into the brush."

"Wonderful . . . a wounded lion to pounce upon the first person that enters that area!"

Exasperated he replied, "We tracked him into the brush and killed him later that day."

I hesitated for several moments, rubbed my forehead and finally granted some leeway: "If you and Nashor want to use these as weapons of war then do so; but I will not encourage its use to the others. And promise me that—after it has failed the test—you will have the good sense to make use of the more reliable weapons."

Enosh was momentarily discouraged, but never one to remain in such a state, he soon took heart in receiving my less-than-enthused blessing.

The three younger men then looked at me expectantly awaiting my plan of action. At that moment, I have to admit to a tremendous amount of pressure that weighed heavy on my heart. The thought of all that might well be at stake began to make itself very real.

"Well . . . first, I am sending a scouting party about a three-day journey to the east. They will remain there for as long as two . . . possibly three weeks watching diligently in that direction. If they see any sign of activity such as campfires, trail dogs, or humans, they will return at a run with warning. Also, beginning this very evening, we will commence with explaining our plans to the others; and implementing said plans at the first light of morning. The women and children will have to take a more active role in working the fields, with about one third of the men working beside them for reasons of protection and instruction. The two thirds will labor furiously with digging pits, making nets, extra weapons, training in warfare, and whatever else comes to our minds as we enter into this act of self-defense. And during the time of battle . . . if it becomes evident that we are not able to stand our ground . . . there is one final notion that has crossed my mind as a last measure. And it will stay with me until such time as needed."

They cast curious looks at each other but accepted my secrecy without question.

The next morning, our entire tribe was up at dawn to begin carrying out our directives. A scouting party of seven, lead by Nashor, loaded up with supplies and headed toward the east. Once they traveled three days there would be hills high enough to provide an excellent view of all main trails; to attempt to reach Eden by any other way would be pure folly with steep cliffs in some places and insect-infested swamp in another. Naomi agreed with me that Cain would never attempt to enter Eden by any dangerous routes, especially if he was personally involved in such a venture.

The rest of the men divided their time between the previously discussed activities. We saved the training in weaponry and hand-to-hand combat for the end of the day. That part of it was like a game to them, as though they really doubted a time of trouble was nearing. Enosh strongly warned them about complacency, even lunging forward and grabbing Ezra by the throat when he appeared to ignore the warning. All the men seemed very attentive after that.

Seth brought up the possibility that the women might be well served to also practice with spear and axe. With very little hesitation I wholly agreed that we must be prepared for the unexpected and gave the command for such training . . . beginning the next day. It was dark and rest was important at this juncture. There might be little time for it in the near future.

Seven days went by with no word from Nashor. Trenches were now finished, with stakes set in place and coverings made up of branches, weeds, and palm leaves. The vine netting was woven and in place, the trees pulled down and tied. Of course, we had to spread the word for all of Eden, people along with their livestock, to avoid those areas until further notice.

I walked around and checked the workmanship of the traps. The trenches were a little bit shallow, tree roots being a problem in the digging process. But we agreed that an injury might be just as good as a kill, forcing our enemy to deal with a suffering kinsman. The mesh squares in the netting were large to my notion, almost big enough for a man to fall through, but after testing it I could see that only a boy would be slender enough for that. And from Naomi's description of the average man in that tribe, it appeared unlikely that there were any who would be viewed as "slender." We decided to wait on the hornets, hoping that our scouts could give us enough warning that we could gather them at a more timely moment. Enosh had done some exploring and spotted several nests.

It looked as though we were about as prepared as was possible, so I went for a much-needed, calming stroll toward the west . . . toward the Garden.

The Sighting

It was rare for me to walk on the paths that led to the west. None of us ventured very far that way and after covering only a moderate distance, the paths then left to me were made by animals. The Garden was in that direction and memories from there served to remind me of personal failure. Nevertheless, I walked and walked, mindless it would seem, until darkness was nearly upon me; and though it was unsafe to be so far from home at such a time, it appeared that a mood or even an unseen force encouraged me to continue. At last from a nearby hilltop I viewed my former home. At that moment the same inner voice, if you will, stopped me there . . . and that brought relief to the common-sense side of me. I knew what guarded those borders. Watching from the hill into the near dark, I could see a bright, flaming light in the midst of all that vegetation.

> *Genesis 3:22-24 "The man has now become like one of Us, knowing good from evil. He must not be allowed to reach out his hand and take also from the tree of life and eat, and live forever." So God banished him from the Garden of Eden to work the ground from which he had been taken. After He drove the man out, He placed on the east side of the Garden of Eden cherubim and a flaming sword flashing back and forth to guard the way to the tree of life.*

This was as close as I had been since the day we were driven out and I wanted desperately to leave this area and run home, even in the dark; but the roars of nearby big cats forced me into clearer thinking. "Climb a tree and spend the night in it!" was the thought that seemed to shout through my mind; then finding one that was about average in size, I did just that.

This night was terribly long, especially with no large limbs to comfortably support my body, and not much of anywhere to rest my head. Ravenous creatures soon paced back and forth at the base of the tree. They sensed my presence and caught my scent. Loud roars near the beginning of evening before I sought refuge, now gave way to expectant purrs and low growls. It was as though they were speaking to one another: "He is up there . . . such an easy meal just one strong leap away; but the branches protect him for now. If only he had dropped that spear during the climb, we might chance going up after him . . . but the limbs are not large enough to support us. Oh, how sweet it would be to kill and eat one who has murdered so many of our brethren! Here is one of our younger members; maybe the limbs would bear him up long enough to drive the man from his perch."

By now I could barely see by what little light the moon provided; but they could see me clearly, and that was certain. One of the smaller lions accepted the challenge and started up the tree, slipping here and there as he struggled to find a sturdy limb from which he might leap. Thankfully, I had not chosen a large tree in which to spend the night . . . and just as thankfully had managed to keep a grasp on my spear. He eventually maneuvered onto a fairly solid limb about a spear's length away. As agile and coordinated as he was, it was still difficult for him to take action and maintain balance, but the killer instinct pushed him to give it a go and he lashed out at me with those padded but deadly weapons. The moon, mercifully, now provided enough light for me to see and I jabbed my spear into that slashing right paw. That hurt and surprised him, to the point that he fell from the only limb that could safely support his weight and movements. He grabbed at every limb and leaf on the way to the ground which softened the impact. Loud roars now erupted with the frustration. I was near to smiling but felt a little uncomfortable in my core being, not wanting God to think me overconfident while still in such a precarious situation.

Once again, a feeling of thankfulness came into my heart because I had passed on climbing the large tree next to this one. It would have provided them surer footing and probably have led to my death. Then it dawned on me: "They could climb the big tree and pounce from above!"

My prayers had not been particularly meaningful for too long a time. Life had been so tolerable during these latter days that there seemed few reasons to seek Divine guidance; nor was there much desire, of late, to even offer up a daily greeting to the One who created me. But it was now time to get back to the ways of old and I earnestly prayed that dumb animals would not reason together and discover a solution to their problem. Sleep, or the thought of sleep, was far removed from my mind as I watched the ground below and the over-hanging limb from the neighboring tree. My heart pounded as hard sitting still as it did during the climb and stayed at that rate for most of the night. On two occasions the lions walked over to the adjacent tree, but each time they returned to the base of the smaller to gaze longingly upward.

How wonderful to see those first rays of dawn, but comforting as that was it would be a long while before it was safe to touch the ground.

You know, earlier in the night I desperately needed to relieve myself but circumstances forced me to put it out of my mind for a time; but now, the time for waiting was fast coming to an end. I wanted to take care of matters on the solid footing of earth, but could see the outline of a large male lion crouched in the brush below, just salivating at the prospect that my balance would desert me at some point. So relief came while sitting in the tree . . . and with nerves stretched to the breaking point it took only a short while.

As the sun climbed higher into the morning sky my large friend finally rose from his position and gave a low growl that seemed to say: "Maybe next time." Then he yawned and sauntered on down the trail, hopefully for a long, uneventful rest.

I watched him until he was far off and then began a cautious descent. A death grip on the spear, my feet eventually did touch the ground; but I kept my left hand on the lowest limb for a time, taking no chance that a hard-earned success would turn into a foolish defeat.

Another prayer offered (with eyes open) and I was on my way with the intention of going home, but once again that unseen force was at work, driving me toward the Garden; a direction not of my choosing. I am not sure why I resisted so, because this was the part of my plan left unspoken to my sons at our last meeting. This was the plan of last resort, and I did not want to face it at this time. I wanted to wait until circumstances were dire and there was no other choice before making this trip. But evidently, there was something I needed to know, so on I walked.

Swampland with reeds and tall grass surrounded much of the trail before me; then, there it was—the lush and lovely place where I dwelt for a time. Feelings were mixed as part of me fondly recalled, "What a wonderful place!" But there was also, "How could I let this slip away from us?"

Standing there admiring the view, I suddenly saw a sight that made my night in the tree look like a game. Cherubim . . . warrior angels . . . were massing at the Garden's border. They were half again my height . . . fiercer looking than any man, with great, muscular wings. They were under the strictest of orders, ones that had been dispensed a very long time ago; and though the only defensive action taken in all that time was far from heroic—keeping certain animals out—there would be not a single instance of negligence counted among them. A rumbling voice came to me, whether just to my mind or to my ears I am not certain, but it said, "Far enough, Adam! I had knowledge of your plans and wanted you to make a wise decision concerning such plans. Examine this area and make sound judgment for the good of all Eden; then go to your home and make not a habit of walking this far west."

Those words carried a warning, but left some room for daring; and after a bit of thought it seemed to me that, in an emergency, my plan might prove viable.

I stood still for a short while, trying to make sense of the situation, but one more look at those anxious guardians led me to cease further planning. While walking away, I surveyed the surrounding area and locked a few things into my memory.

My body was already worn out from a stressful night and now, this extra little adventure added to that. Suffice it to say that the pace toward home was slow, but at least there were no attacks of any kind.

Early evening found me in the grateful arms of my wife, and despite her many questions, and the groans from my stomach, and the food that beckoned before me, answers had to wait as the need of sleep dominated all else.

The next day many concerns were raised as to my whereabouts, but I kept it very simple: "Some lions chased me up a tree and I had to spend the night there."

Eve gasped and went on and on about the need to be more careful and to stay with a group. I nodded in full agreement while winking at those standing nearby.

The March Continues

"What has delayed Cainan, my trusted son and heir to much that is mine?! He surely saw Lamech double back and chased after him. By now he has crushed that toothless puppy!"

Onan answered, "How you ever found any tracks in the cleft of that cliffside and in the area of those rocks above is beyond me, but it certainly looks as though he hid there and moved in the direction of Nod."

Enoch added, "Lamech was a fast runner, despite his injuries; so he may have run all the way back to Nod where he could then use his powers of persuasion to convince some of the women to hide him."

Cain acted as though he heard not a word of that. "Hmm . . . in a contest of this type Cainan would follow tirelessly like a pack of dogs until he overtook Lamech, and well before he could ever reach Nod. Of course, that task completed, I could see my son less than enthused about hurrying to catch up to us. But mark my words: he will appear before the first thrust of our spears."

Several of the men were curious concerning the number of days until the first sight of Eden, but Cain was uncertain, having no memory of the current surroundings; then, they saw some smoke on the distant horizon at the top of a high ridge. The likeness of a man's face stood out just a little short of the top of that ridge, and the sight of it jogged Cain's memory. He was able to estimate another three days to their goal—maybe less if they ran part of the distance. "That smoke tells me that Adam's men may be watching for us . . . we must hurry so as to give them as little time as possible to prepare!"

As one man the entire force gave out with growls and shouts, exhorting one another on to the glory of battle!

Lamech, after some grueling days and nights pushing his body to extremes he would have earlier thought impossible, finally caught sight of some members of his clan. His fatigue had brought with it some carelessness and as he cleared a small stand of trees into a stretch of open ground he saw the stragglers nearing a small rise. He dropped to the ground behind some weeds and one man, Nabal, turned thinking that he had heard something. Alone he walked back down the trail to check for danger. He reached a point near the tall grass that hid Lamech, and there he stood stone still, watching and listening. Lamech had his hand on a rock about the size and general shape of a man's foot, ready to strike his kinsman in the head if necessary. He knew that anything less than a quick, solid strike would allow for a cry of warning to the others. Tired as he was, the thought to be mentally prepared to, once again, run a very long way entered his mind . . . and how he dreaded that possibility. He slowly, silently got to his feet, but stayed low in a crouched position, clenching the rock in his right hand. Nabal was a strong man, equal with Lamech in every physical way, so this would not be an easy task. Then, for a moment, Nabal turned slightly, giving his brother an opening for a quick kill. Lamech rose off his haunches slightly, ready to spring. "Just a moment longer," he thought. Then, right before the instant of no return, Nabal's attention was captured by the shouts of the others, to hurry. They had nearly disappeared over the ridge and he ran to catch up with them.

Lamech breathed a sigh of relief and soon began to reckon a way around his kinsmen. "My body needs rest . . . where will the energy for such an undertaking be found? A little wild fruit, some greens, and a crust of dried bread fall short in supplying enough strength for non-stop travel. But I must reach Eden ahead of them to warn those people . . . and help them fight, if permitted."

The Scouting Party

"Nashor! We have been waiting here for . . . I have lost count of the days!"

"Ten, Hazor. Ten days. And we will wait a little longer if necessary. We must be sure, and we must follow orders. All of Eden depends on our determination and patience . . . and the sharpness of our eyes."

"Then test the sharpness of your eyes in the distant valley. Unless my mind is playing games with my vision, those are men coming through that slit of a pass above the canyon!"

Nashor bounded over to the high ledge that gave the best view of distant trails. He watched for a time, at first to make sure Hazor's sighting was true, then a little longer to get some idea as to the number of men. And, to hopefully, catch a glimpse of the evil man he had heard his elders mention around campfires. "I cannot tell from this distance the color of anyone's forehead, but there looks to be well over a hundred men! We will not wait for a more precise count. Douse the fires! They may not have seen the smoke. We make for Eden immediately, and as though our . . . Well, our lives and the lives of many others depend on a swift return. Push yourselves near to the point of collapse! We can rest a bit, after the warning has been delivered."

The fires were doused, remnants of food packed away, and weapons gathered and gripped. Towards Eden they ran, occasionally slowing their pace to a trot, but there was no stopping to rest until the full black of night.

The night arrived and though they were familiar with the path, Nashor wisely stopped them to rest. They were, to a man, gasping for air and clutching their sides. "Drink your fill of water, and eat what is left of our food; because at first light we will resume this pace and will not stop until we are home! No fires tonight, so let us huddle together for protection. We are in an open area devoid of vegetation, so that should make it more difficult for anything, man or beast, to catch us unaware. We will take turns sleeping, half of us awake at all times."

Lamech's Good Fortune

"Climb! Climb for all you are worth!" shouted Cain as he led the way up the steep bluff. It was a tough go for weary men as loose soil permeated with small stones caused many to lose their footing, and others further downhill to be hit by rolling rocks. Finally, they reached the top—every last man in the unit—and after scrambling and clawing their way over the edge to level ground, every man, except for Cain, collapsed and remained that way for a time.

"Look at you! All of you are young men, but not a one able to keep up with my pace. Hey! Get away from that water! No one will drink any water until I give permission to do so! I suppose you . . . little children, will have to rest for a bit . . . maybe eat something to regain your strength! All in good time . . . after I give the order."

Rest began to ease some of their misery, but their tongues were sticking to the roof of their mouths and their weakened bodies cried out for food as well as water. But no one dared open his mouth to voice a complaint, knowing that Cain would ridicule them and withhold nourishment all the longer.

"How can he continue to do without?" was the question uttered by many.

Finally, though he made it look as though it pained him to do so, he gave permission to drink and eat.

Satan smiled at the toughness displayed by his adopted son. And like Cain, he was certain that Cainan would show up soon, adding to an already formidable fighting force; then, a doubt arose in his spirit. He thought, "Maybe I should find him and strike some enthusiasm into his heart. Surely he is within a day of rejoining us."

Confident that Cain's forces were prepared, he took flight to begin the search for Cainan, and to gloat over the dead body of Lamech that he was so sure to find.

Only by the grace of God did Lamech go unnoticed as Satan passed by him. He had found a gap in between two boulders and was lightly sleeping. The slightest movement or sound would have alerted the powerful, angelic being. Fortunately, Lamech had found favor in the eyes of a more powerful Being.

Something startled Lamech and within a moment, fully alert, he jumped to his feet. His heart raced at the thought that while he slept the others might have continued their march. Near panic set in, but when he peeked out from between the boulders and saw only a little activity in the encampment, he quickly calmed. He knew they would not arrive at Eden tonight, so he would have a time of darkness to sneak past them. This stretch of land that they were now on, and as far as the eye could see, was a narrow plateau with steep sides. Hopefully it would widen at some point making for a better chance to slip by unnoticed.

Cain was soon finished with this lull and when he was finished, everyone was finished. "Get up! Get up you lazy dogs! We will reach the next ridge top before nightfall or the hide will be whipped to shreds on more than a few, so move!" Every man who had been stretched out flat on the ground managed to summon the strength necessary to get to his hands and knees, then after a few more moments in that position, and upon hearing a growl from their task-master, they reached their feet. Darkness was near but there would be no rest for a while longer. Cain gave the order to march and though in need of sleep, they moved on toward that next ridge.

Satan quickly covered the path back to Tamara's grave, where he puzzled over the gravesite seeing that her stones had been neatly restored. He looked the area over and sensed signs of a struggle at the steep slope above the valley. He thought to himself, "Surely the body of Lamech lies at the bottom . . . at least, the remains of it. But where is Cainan?

He would not have returned to Nod and risked such shame, and I could not have missed him along the way, not a being of his size. I will go to the bottom and find answers."

An instant later he was at the base of the cliff searching for clues. There was a large piece of animal skin hanging on one of the limbs that protruded from the cliff wall. It was the type of skin used in Nod for clothing, but looked to be too big a piece for Lamech. A further search turned up the hank of hair that was pulled from Lamech's head. Satan, convinced of the death, rejoiced with a spirited jig. "Ha! Ha! That is Lamech's!" He hopped around, first on one foot then the other, leaped high into the air, clenched and shook his fists, grinning all the while. "My pets have done well to leave me a sign for confirmation . . . and peace of mind!"

Suddenly, the little dance of elation stopped as quickly as it started, and he became his usual, brooding self going into deep, suspicious thought: "How did the grave get rebuilt? Would Lamech be so foolish as to take the time to rebuild it beforehand . . . with death dogging his footsteps? Maybe he was unaware of the danger or maybe he thought he had more time. And that piece of animal hide is too large to be his. Maybe he ripped it off Cainan during the struggle. Hmmm . . . at this point I have more questions than answers. But there is no more to be gained here, so I will travel toward Nod. Perhaps he is injured."

So, Satan, continuing the search, moved in the direction of Nod.

———————◆•◆•◆———————

Finally, the force from Nod reached the next ridge and the plateau they were on did widen considerably, bringing the stealthy Lamech a feeling of confidence as he surveyed the area from the shadows.

The black of night fell quickly, but Cain forbade the lighting of fires, so they bunched together with those on the outside acting as guards for the entire unit. They had little trouble staying awake as vulnerable as they were. When one group on the outside felt that they had done their share of duty they would raise a fuss until they were relieved by those who had been safely sleeping; thus they took turns this way until dawn.

Cain, to the aggravation of all, remained on the inside the whole time claiming that he was too essential to risk injury.

Lamech could not have asked for a better situation, with the men clustered together in the dark instead of spread out with the light of fires working against him. Still, it was a bit unnerving to walk alone in the gloom listening to the roars and shrieks of wild animals, causing him to look over his shoulder every few steps.

He thought to himself, "If only I can manage to survive this night and reach Eden. If they are as Naomi remembered, life there will be more than tolerable . . . if only they will accept me."

Some yelps and whines in the nearby brush focused his mind back on reality and he guessed that it was a pack of wild dogs. A little before this, Lamech made the decision to stay near the trees instead of walking in the open, and it proved a wise move. The pack caught his scent and seeing he was alone they were especially emboldened. They chased after him and he raced to the nearest tree; with adrenaline flowing he grabbed a lower limb and climbed with all the agility of a boy. He had barely reached the second limb when the pack surrounded the tree, yelping and leaping into the air barely missing with those snapping, powerful jaws. The young man hurried the upward climb, energized by a situation with no options. Several of the brutes even tried to climb the tree, but of course, their paws not made for that, they fell back to the ground where the others trampled and bit them, seemingly for their failure.

Lamech was fairly certain that dogs were unable to climb, but in this life and death situation all manner of doubts entered his thinking. They tarried there for a time, yelping, growling, and howling, finally leaving to search elsewhere for food. The young man was shaking with fear, not only because of the dogs, but of the possibility that his kinsmen would investigate the commotion and capture him.

"Oh . . . I may have been better off had those dogs stayed a little longer. Maybe I should get down out of this tree and put some more distance between myself and the camp. Then again, it appears as though the pack has returned to the brush . . . but are they waiting nearby? Well . . . I will continue . . . cautiously." Reaching the ground and remaining close to the trees, he walked a sling's throw further toward

Eden, just over the crest of the next ridge, at which point he climbed into another tree for safety and rest.

Cain's camp did hear the disturbance, but did not venture over that way, squeezing their spears a little tighter and huddling a little closer, even the ones tucked safely in the middle were now, voluntarily, on guard.

Satan flew all the way to Nod, searching, but found no sign of Cainan. He watchfully retraced his path all the way back to Cain's camp, frustrated at the absence of the young warrior. But he put his frustration aside momentarily as he felt something in the air nearby, a spirit of violence outside the camp and maybe something more. It was a similar feeling to the one he had in the valley some time ago. He moved to some trees which were in the area of the attack and listened into the night air. "Hmm . . . some creature was in this tree." Using his powers of intuition and his sense of smell he snorted, "Wild dogs . . . if only one of the big cats had been here, there would have been a kill." He stood there for the longest time, just listening. Finally, sensing nothing more, he returned to the camp to incite the men to forthcoming violence.

A Day of Decisions

Lamech had gone a spell with little in the way of a truly peaceful rest, so even though the tree he climbed was hardly a bed of straw he managed to sleep. He soon awoke upon hearing the song of an ambitious bird telling him that the sun's early rays were hidden by foliage, and it was time to be on his way. He surveyed the area below and then carefully touched ground. His walk was slow at first as he looked first this way, then that, rightly believing that one man alone could not be too cautious. As the sun's light began to chase away the shadows of night, and the deep shade of leafy limbs, he gained in confidence.

Further down the path was an open stretch which was easier walking, though a little unsettling with its lack of cover; but he gritted his teeth, stayed low, and kept on the move, soon reaching a stand of timber.

His senses, always keen, were made even more so by the trials of these last days, and just as he pushed his way through the scrub brush at the edge of the trees his hearing picked up a voice behind him. He quickly hid behind the trunk of a large sycamore and watched. There was Cain, that red forehead beaming, with another of his physically imposing brutes at his left hand. It was Anak—nearly as large a specimen as Cainan and just as greedy for power; an unsightly individual with a sinister smile made up of twisted teeth, a large crooked nose, an overhanging forehead, scraggly black facial hair, and a way about him that made his missing brother appear trustworthy. Several of the men had ganged up on him in the past, beating him senseless on two occasions, but just as soon as healing took place he quickly resumed mocking, stealing, picking fights with those less skilled in battle, and spreading lies in the hope of seeing others whipped and tortured by his grandfather. Cain had a certain fondness for Anak, but even he did not often turn his back on the younger man.

There was now no time to be cautious, so Lamech ran through the trees, and as he ran there appeared what looked to be a seldom used foot path. He continued a near-sprint on this trail and was quite confident of his body's ability to maintain the fast pace. The sun was just a little short of straight overhead when he finally had to rest. He was, at least on this day, in excellent physical condition, but there was a limit and he reached it. Gasping for air with his head down and hands on his knees, a human footprint caught his attention. Dropping to the ground he examined the print and thought, "At last! I am nearing Eden's people. And here are more scattered prints . . . and in the distance a field that has recently been harvested. I will reach them before nightfall!" Once again, he took up the swift pace, driven by an unnatural stamina and a strange desire to aid an unfamiliar people—who might kill him before he had the chance to speak.

After countless strides, the run slowed to a jog; then with energy reserves near their end, the jog became a walk. A little longer and his body demanded a pause every few steps—and that would have to do until the intake of some nourishment, and at least a little rest. The sun soon stood about a hand's span from the horizon. He was staggering and faint; finally admitting to himself that despite his earlier confidence, time was slipping away. He so desperately wanted to have some interaction with Eden before darkness; even if they ran him through with a spear . . . if he could only remain conscious long enough to warn them. At last, as he stumbled along and fell through one last thicket, he heard voices and saw three men, but exhaustion had its way and he just stood there unable to speak.

The men, armed with spears and hatchets, glared as this haggard stranger emerged from a clump of brush. Alarmed, they raised their weapons and readied for a kill. Lamech offered no resistance, nothing but a blank stare; then . . . somehow, he found the strength to hold up his palms as if to say, "I am not here to battle against you."

They waited anxiously for him to take some sort of action and he obliged them, collapsing to the ground, face-first. The men warily approached, much as they would a wounded lion. As they stood over him, one of them took the butt of his spear and jabbed his motionless body, then quickly jumped back in case of trickery. Lamech stirred slightly and groaned, mumbling to them to prepare for attack. Those few words did little to win their hearts, but believing there might be something to gain they gave aid to this outsider. Caleb had a pouch of water and with some reluctance, elected to share it.

Lamech, at first, had no sense of what was put to his lips, but soon, call it reflex or instinct, he attempted to guzzle the water while grabbing at the pouch. Irritated, they jerked it away from him, but those few swallows were enough to clear his mind to a degree, and he reached for Caleb's arm to offer a grave warning. The quick move startled Caleb and he delivered a slap across the face and jumped to the side. Again, Lamech held up his hands as a sign of peace and with a weakening, raspy voice said, "Forgive my intrusion . . . into your land . . . but you must listen to me . . . a force of men are . . . making their way to Eden as we . . . speak." Never had a few spoken words taken such a toll on a man, and this time he lapsed into unconsciousness.

The men stood there undecided as to what their next move should be. Judah said, "He is not one of us . . . the safest action would be to finish him here and now."

Caleb suggested, "Since we are not far from Grandfather's camp, let us carry him there and see if Naomi or Adah remember him. If nothing else, he may give forth important information, that is . . . with enough persuasion."

Judah and Jared cast a glance at his expression and saw his meaning from the twinkle in his eyes. All three broke into a smile followed by laughter as a picture ran through their minds of entertainment—the type rarely seen in Eden.

Using vines they tied Lamech to a tree limb and carried him to the nearby encampment.

I was there, along with Naomi when they laid him by our fire.

"This stranger to our land stumbled into our presence as we readied for war. We were not sure what to do with him so we came here," offered Caleb.

I asked Naomi if she recognized the man.

"Yes. It is Lamech . . . one of those who pursued us when we first escaped from Nod. He was not one of Cain's favorites, but he certainly pursued us with a diligence." She looked down at the ground for a few moments and reasoned further, "Of course, if he had rebelled in the slightest, his life would have been forfeit . . . still, he should not be trusted . . . not yet."

"Nashor and Hazor have already warned us of the approaching danger, so whatever this man could add . . . then again, any bit of information could be of help. Naomi, to the best of your knowledge, what manner of fellow is this . . . Lamech?"

She took some time, carefully searching her memory in order to give an accurate account and shortly related a few details: "Tamarah used to watch over him when he was a boy—more often than did I—and she praised his good nature. She was fond of him. I remember that of all the young males in Nod, there were only three who ever asked any questions or showed the slightest interest in the Godly teachings that you passed down to me. Lamech was one of the three. But one day, after Cain spoke harshly to him, warning of my 'foolish talk,' Lamech went the way of all the men, and we had little to do with one another after that. But when our paths did cross, he was not as disrespectful as the others, and I sometimes had the feeling that he wished circumstances were different. But I repeat . . . this is not the time to take a risk!"

I agreed with her, but my heart was somewhat softened toward the young man. "Put him into the cave just behind my dwelling, where we keep some of our food. And have one man standing guard until further notice! I will check later to see if this . . . Lamech, has awakened."

Darkness was nearly upon us when Nashor, who heard about the stranger, wanted to talk with me concerning him. He approached and said, "Those men could not possibly be here until tomorrow evening or the next morning. This man must have been a day ahead of them—a scout perhaps—unless he ran the entire distance at a sprint. But no one could do that."

I remarked, "It appeared that he collapsed from exhaustion . . . maybe you underestimate him."

"No! The scouting party, of which I was in charge, ran and jogged much of the way on very short rest and arrived here a little past mid-day. We were on the mountain top while they were still far down in the valley. I want to talk with him and sort out truth from falsity. Let me cuff him about the face a few times in order to rouse him from this . . . *exhaustion*; perhaps he is only pretending."

Normally, I would go with my instinct, which seemed to be saying that he could be trusted, but with so much at stake . . . "Let us both go to him and put him through a time of testing."

We made our way toward the cave and saw Enosh along with several others carrying some hides. I asked, "What are your plans for those?"

"Have you forgotten? We are going to the forest to gather the hornets' nests. The darkness will calm their behavior and make the task easier to carry out; then, after we have them bundled up, we will wait on the bluff above the creek bottom. Some of Nod's finest will surely pass through there and when they do . . . we will be waiting."

"That sounds good! But in order to avoid being caught unaware have several men, in shifts, watching at all times. That will allow everyone to get some rest. Do not neglect rest . . . you will truly need it."

My warning seemed to throw a few drops of cold water on their enthusiasm, but they were looking at this as if it was a game. But soon, very soon . . . when they saw their fellow human beings wounded and possibly dying, never again would they look at war as a game.

Nashor hurried on ahead of me, probably in the hope of arriving first and feeling freer to use the means of his choice to get answers. I quickened my pace so that we reached the cave at about the same time. The guard was dutifully carrying out my orders at the cave's opening.

"Has he yet stirred, or is he still feigning exhaustion?" asked Nashor, quite cynically.

Jared was now on duty, a very reliable young man, and he alertly answered, "He is sitting up and has tried to talk, but I warned him to remain silent or suffer punishment!"

I stepped into the conversation at this point: "Let me speak with him first and attempt to, initially, use reason rather than violence. If he appears to be lying, or refuses to tell us anything, then Jared and Nashor . . . he will be in your hands." Judging by the look of eagerness on their faces, I would say that they were hoping for Lamech's exhaustion to leave him totally mute.

"Young man, tell me your name?"

He immediately answered, "Lamech. And who are you?"

"You will answer questions for now; later on, you may be permitted to ask some." That met with a certain amount of grumbling from my two companions. "How is it that you are here so far ahead of your kinsmen?"

"I purposely separated myself from them because of my hatred for Cain, and when I saw that they were nearing your land I ran as hard and far as possible."

"Why would you do that? Are they not your kinsmen?"

"They are my kinsmen, but that means very little in the land of Nod. Few of us know which man is our father, and many of the women look upon children as a curse. Naomi and a few of the older daughters are the only examples of kindness that I have known." His demeanor then changed in a moment from contempt for his people to what looked to be concern for mine. He grabbed my arm and looking me straight in the eyes implored, "If you will let me, I can be of great aid to you." His eyes then softened as he searched my face and he asked, "Are you . . . Adam?"

"I am Adam. You have knowledge of me?"

"During my childhood, Naomi spoke often of you. She described your outward appearance—that is how I recognized you—and she told of your boldness in protecting your family, and how hard you worked to gather food for everyone. She also told of your closeness to a being known as God and that you had conversations with Him. I longed to hear more, but Cain kept us apart and told me that Naomi and Tamarah were silly old women with many tales to tell, and that I needed to spend more of my time in the company of men so that I could learn their ways and become like them. That was a proud moment for me . . . to have the leader of our tribe seemingly show some interest in me. It took a very long time, but I began to be bothered by the behavior of the men . . . well, not just the men, but everyone; and Cain's ways troubled me greatly."

As the young man spoke, I again grew somewhat embarrassed with the thought that Naomi may have held me in too high of regard and that I surely could not live up to such praise. And when he spoke of closeness to God, my conscience nudged me, and my mind thought back to the days when there was a more genuine closeness. As he continued, my heart wanted to believe every word the young man spoke, but I had been around people long enough to know that some very spirited stories are told under times of great pressure. I lifted his grip from my arm and said, "Lamech, allow me some time to consider your words and perhaps to speak with this being called God—our Creator—concerning your presence here . . . before I place my trust in you."

He seemed a bit frustrated that I did not quickly accept his offer of help, but waiting was his only option at this point, so he was resigned to his present situation. As I turned away he spoke fervently: "They will be here soon! Many of them are physically imposing compared to what I have seen of this tribe. A few of them, near-giants—larger than Cain! You must be prepared to do some things unexpected."

I wanted to tell him that we were quite prepared for battle, but thought better of it; no sense to divulge information to one who might prove untrustworthy.

Immediately Jared and Nashor, speaking at once, tried to tell me what I should do with Lamech, but they became silent when they realized that their warnings were unheeded. They departed when they saw me sit beside the clear, cool spring that flowed between two large rocks which were near our village. They knew that was my location of choice whenever I needed a time of deep thought.

I remained isolated for a while, and in the darkness that was just short of pitch-black there was such a feeling of peace, listening to the water that bubbled over the rocks and casting my gaze toward the stars. There was no better place to escape the discontent of my family members.

Now, bowing my head, I earnestly sought and spoke toward God; and questioned Him about the young man, and the upcoming battle. One thought quickly came to me: that, too often of late, I did not receive because I did not ask. But on this night after several inquiries there was no counsel . . . no sensing of God's presence. I had no memory of any other time in my life when I felt so alone—like a child lost in the wilderness. And there was a hollow feeling inside, and a far-away voice seemed to say, "Why should you expect God to interact in your life, since His fellowship and counsel are sought only when you are in trouble?"

So, it appeared I was on my own, at least for the time being. I pulled away from my haven, then walked up to Jared and told him to continue guarding Lamech; but I also told him there was to be no violence against the young man without good reason. Jared seemed a bit disappointed but accepted my words without dispute.

Day of Battle

All through the night Satan went from ear to ear, sometimes hovering just above the sleeping warriors and sometimes kneeling by their side, whispering words of incitement; mostly to inflame their naturally hot tempers so that they would be at their killing best. Of course, if those uncontrolled tempers led them to spill some of their own blood, that would also be gratifying. Before the night had given way to dawn, he managed to speak to every man once, and twice to some, with Cain being the beneficiary of a third visit laced with all kinds of motivational and instructive ploys. Cain, not terribly gifted with a strong memory, would have done just as well with the speech that all the others were given: "Be strong; be brave; show no mercy to men, women, or children! Take the land of Eden and make it your own!"

Cain awoke while it was still dark, stirred by the sound of a voice he had heard many times in his life, but always without a face to accompany it. He stood for several moments gazing into the dark and could see the occasional flicker from distant camp fires. He wished for just a single ray of the sun's light so as to begin the glorious task of warfare, but after seeing no trace of dawn on the east horizon, he returned to rest.

———◆◆◆———

Operating without the Divine guidance so desperately needed, I told the people to keep their fires small and do not sit next to the flames, thus giving the enemy a clear target in case of a night attack. I highly doubted that Cain would take such a chance in territory that had become unfamiliar to him in his long absence, but a word of caution was passed throughout our scattered family.

Unease had become my constant companion, especially since the arrival of Lamech. His appearance gave signal of the reality of battle—that it was on its way and there was no escaping it. Never had any in Eden faced the possibility of death in this manner. We had, on rare occasions, lost family members to the attacks of wild animals, some to various illnesses, but no lives had yet been lost to outbursts of temper or murder—not since Abel. My mind carried me back, as it had on more than a few occasions, to that happy day when Eve birthed our first child.

The faintest smile crossed my lips and I shook my head in wonder at the happiness we shared; to actually have had a part in creating a life. But how, through our family's history, that pleasantness had taken such bitter turns; never more than with the death of Abel . . . and now, tonight. I thought to myself, "What would the morrow bring? The death of one child is so hard to bear, but to face the death of many . . . And who knows . . . if Cain's tribe is victorious, will he annihilate the whole of us?"

Once again I fell to my face and prayed earnestly for the comfort and guidance that only God could provide. As sweat and tears streamed down my face and dropped to the soil, a quiet, but commanding voice came to my ears: "Adam, it is good to hear your voice. You have, of late, not remained in the habit of seeking My advice, or friendship. You are concerned . . . and well you should be. Cain's forces are powerful and ruthless . . . and they are often incited by the very one who played such a major part in your downfall. And just like you, they are unaware of his influence. But unlike you, they would do no differently if they were aware of his leadings—at least, not the vast majority.

I will aid you in this battle, provided that you listen . . . not so much with your ears but with your inner self. Certainly rely on the wisdom you possess, but in times of dire distress when all reasonable decisions appear to be failing, listen to the quiet voice that speaks to your subconscious. If you are able to maintain your faith, even under the most difficult of circumstances, you will defeat this enemy. But if you weaken and lose courage, or rely too much on your own understanding, or the advice of men, you will be defeated. I need not point out what that will mean.

I leave you now, with a decision I have made which should provide your heart and mind with some peace: as it has been in much of this land's past, Satan and none of his demon followers will be permitted entrance into Eden. Also, Lamech has the spirit of Naomi and he can be trusted."

With that said, all was quiet, and I sensed God's presence had withdrawn for now. I thought to myself, "Whew! I now am able to stand a little taller with such weight lifted from my shoulders; not that all will be easy from here on, but hope wells up in my heart. If hope had been delayed much longer, courage and leadership might well have deserted me at a most crucial point. Well . . . time to get some rest in order to better serve my family. There will be no sleep, but just reclining will be of some benefit."

As I lay there with a multitude of thoughts entering my mind, I almost laughed at the concept of Lamech's release tomorrow, and the subsequent reaction of certain warriors. But, there will be no time to give heed to their complaints.

Surprisingly, I did sleep, and awoke in time to see some rays of light in the east. I jumped to my feet, heart pounding in my chest, and ran to wake the others. Nearly all were awake and preparing for the fight. Spears, axes, slings, and even rocks for throwing, were in plentiful supply throughout the camps. Just at the moment I prepared to encourage some of the younger fighting men and offer some words of comfort to the women and children, a shout of alarm was passed down through the ranks from a distant scout. He told us that the enemy was sighted inside our eastern boundary close to the bluffs where Enosh waited with the first line of defense—the smallest of our weapons.

Satan had called upon his angel subjects to aid in the destruction of Eden and they were most eager as it had been a long while since their master called upon them for anything significant. As they smugly marched alongside Cain and his troops, relishing the idea of witnessing, maybe even taking part in, the destruction of the ones who were the cause of their fall, they talked of the coming glory.

"Surely God has lifted the hedge that has protected them for so long," said Satan. "I have viewed Adam of late, from a distance of course, and sensed that something has changed in the man. Perhaps a prouder look on his face or a swagger in his walk or his chest out too far—he is not seeking God as he once did. I perceived, from the life forces of some of the big cats, that recently they nearly made a meal of their long-time tormentor. If they were that near to success, we must make the most of our opportunity because another time like it may be long in coming . . . and though I possess the quality of patience, I do not desire its use."

Baal took the opportunity to improve his standing and offered, "No other being in all creation has your insight! Hope now flows where there was doubt and dread. This may be the day we destroy Eden's civilization—God's precious people."

Molech also spoke saying, "Maybe we will have another chance at the archangel, Michael . . . if we prove our strength this day."

"Other than Adam's death, nothing could please me more," said Satan. "If possible, I will guide Cain in capturing his father; then I will be most certain of watching a slow, torturous death." He smiled as he entertained mental pictures of the many violent events he had arranged and witnessed . . . and he had a vivid memory.

They made their way through the last of the steep, rocky passes, avoiding that foul-smelling, mosquito-infested swamp that awaited any who dared approach Eden by another route. Those living in Eden had no desire to graze or farm in this direction and it made for added protection near the eastern border. Satan flew ahead followed closely by his rebellious followers, and with heads and hopes high they prepared to enter Eden.

Making the final turn through the last of the rocky ravines and stepping into the creek that flowed at the base of the overhanging bluffs,

Cain and his men paused to look on with envy at the lush vegetation of this land, when compared with their own.

Satan and his band were smiling . . . smiling with the thought that feelings of envy would drive these men to reach deep inside themselves and fight all the harder. Then . . . in an instant those smiles vanished. Bump. Bump. What was happening? Satan and Baal, who were in the lead, flew face-first into what seemed to be some sort of invisible wall. Those who were following murmured back and forth to each other as to the reason for the sudden halt. Baal, in disbelief, slowly reached out and rubbed his palm back and forth over the smooth, hard surface of the obstacle that totally barred their advance. By now, questions were fired from the rear to the front concerning the delay. Satan had no answer for a time, their questions not really registering in his mind. He was perplexed and thought to himself that this was not truly happening. Surely there was now no hedge, no barrier of any kind, to stop him from flying into all the places of the earth.

Maybe the ability to fly was not as sharp as at other times; perhaps they had not exercised the action in too long a time and were just fatigued. Satan was particularly skilled at penetrating and passing into and through obstacles, but despite all his great strength and skill he could not gain the slightest entry into this obstruction. The men marched right through, leaving the fallen ones to watch in disbelief and utmost frustration. Satan slammed into the barrier, again and again, kicking and beating against it!

Never one to submissively watch an opportunity slip away, he grabbed a huge boulder and threw it with all his might; but it passed right through to add to his seething rage. He stopped for another moment to gather his wits, to devise a way around this unexpected setback.

"There must be a way! Let us fly to the heights, maybe we can go over this!" And they flew high. As high as they had been since their banishment—upward, higher and higher, until they rammed into a similar obstruction that seemed to permeate the heavens. Nowhere to be found was there an opening; so Satan, still undaunted, gave the order to follow him. Back to the earth they flew, descending just as fast as they ascended, frantically desiring to take part in the upcoming battle.

They reached the ground and Satan ordered, "Dig! Dig I tell you! If we cannot go over, we will go under!" And they dug and dug with all the power that was in them, truly exerting themselves for the first time since the great battle in Heaven. Their hands became as stone claws throwing dust, dirt, and rock high into the air. Deeper and deeper they dug into the earth, but no matter how deep, the barrier still blocked their way into Eden. Then the digging stopped. Satan stared up from the freshly dug chasm, shaking his head in disbelief; finally, beyond apoplectic, he flew out of the abyss. Reaching the top he gave out with a scream of rage which, to the human ears in Eden, sounded like nothing they had ever heard. It began with a deep rumbling such as one might hear from an avalanche followed by what seemed the roaring of a thousand hungry lions at close range. Such a noise at this time was quite unsettling to members of both tribes, each expecting to be attacked at any moment by some very powerful, unseen enemy.

I tried to calm everyone's fears, but my legs were shaking and my insides had churned to the point that I felt ill. But, evidently, my facial expression held steady, and nerves gradually returned to a level that allowed for clearer thinking.

Cain and his men, shaken by the unknown rumblings and roars, looked in all directions, unable to pinpoint a source or direction from which the sounds came. Cain trembled with fear and his muscles lost some of their strength. He did not understand it, but Satan's absence from his side took away that something extra he needed to fight and lead the troops into battle. So along with all the others, he watched over his shoulder, and looked up into the trees, and approached bushes with apprehension; every move an uncertainty. But after a time, and hearing nothing more and seeing nothing of which to be terrified, they regained some of their confidence. So, with confidence regained Cain growled out orders: "March! March on! No force from this land can defeat us . . . and no rumblings without a face or body, no matter how loud, will cause us to become weak!"

On they marched, staying right in the middle of the creek and under the rocky crags where Enosh and company awaited with all the enthusiasm of boys on their first hike without an adult's watchful eye.

Hornet's nests were not easy to come by, but they had spotted five over the last few days and managed to find all of them in the dark of the night. As stated earlier, darkness caused the little creatures to be a bit more sluggish and allowed the men to cut down the nests and wrap them in bags made of goatskin. Now, each one raised the bundle over his head, and heard the agitated buzzings of angry little warriors inside—and there were second thoughts. As they readied to open the bag and throw in one motion, might the hornets also attack those on the top of the bluff . . . if by chance the delivery did not go smoothly?

Seeing some worried faces, Enosh spoke calmly and as a leader: "Be men of courage. Our prayers have been offered, so trust in God."

And when the marchers down below had passed under the bluff to about the halfway point in their line, Enosh gave the order, "Now!" Four of the men timed their release very nicely and the nests sailed over the edge of the cliff on their way to the objective. One man mis-timed his throw a little, the nest glancing off the cliff's edge, rolling down a slight embankment that was just before the steep slope. This allowed a few of the ill-tempered little beasts to find their way back to the source of their short-lived capture. There were some stings to be sure, but not enough to chase Enosh and company from their vantage point.

On the fortunate side for those at the hill's top, the roll down the bluff exceedingly provoked an already angry brood and the vast majority attacked the first flesh-covered life form they saw—and that was the good men from Nod. The air seemed saturated with flying insects, and the incessant buzz from whirring wings struck fear and dread into those once arrogant. They swatted and ran, some crying out as women in labor. The hornets were relentless, stinging not just once, but again and again, deftly avoiding all attempts to swat them, slap them, and even axe them—from two or three desperate individuals. Finally, the creek became deep enough to provide some escape, though the insects remained vigilant and continued to sting as heads surfaced for air.

Many of the creek's deeper pools were not quite deep enough for the large men of Nod, and as they dove, trying to get under the water, their backsides remained slightly exposed—a target that did not go unnoticed by supposedly mindless creatures.

Enosh thought to himself that if only he could strike now, the enemy would be so weakened with pain, and yet blinded with fury and frustration, they would be unable to fight with a clear head, wasting energy by lashing out with no success. He and those with him were so amused by the scene below they practically forgot their own pain. But . . . though the sight was an amusing one, now was no time to forget that this was war and very soon all merriment would be far from their thoughts. So they rushed back to assist their brothers with the trenches and snares.

At the bottom of the hill, after what seemed to have been the better part of a day, the hornets' ire gradually subsided and they flew away from their victory to begin other nests.

Cain rose up from the deep pocket of water that granted him some welcome relief from his tormentors. His nose and one of his eyes was swollen, and similar injuries were widespread among the rest, with some so swollen from stings they could barely (depending on what area was most exposed) see, breathe through their nose, or sit down. Cain, with no sympathy whatsoever, yelled, "Get on your feet! You can still kill with blurred vision, and you can breathe through your mouths, and we will not be sitting any more this day!" So onward they trudged, their pride shaken and their desire to fight temporarily subdued.

Enosh and company made their way back to report all of this to me and to join the rest of us for battle. At another time there might be laughter concerning the hornets, but right now, battle and survival was at the forefront of our concerns.

I immediately strode to the place where Lamech had been detained and ordered him freed. Jared's facial expression told me he did not approve, but mine told him to remain silent. Taking Lamech by the shoulder I looked him in the eyes and said, "You have my trust as one who will fight by my side. Perhaps there are things you can tell me which will aid us in the coming battle; but if you would rather not take up arms against your countrymen, I can understand that."

Looking straight into my eyes he replied, "There are no feelings of unity or brotherhood for my tribe. We were taught, in Nod, to use any means possible to gain the advantage over others; usually by size and strength, though on rare occasions, he who was most shrewd won a victory, but for the most part size, power, and ruthlessness rule our people. So if any allegiance dwells inside of me, you have it . . . no one else.

His words were more than reassuring and I felt no doubt in any part of my being. At this point, with nearly all of our people present, I led them in a short but heartfelt prayer, and then urgently addressed them: "We have enough time for some last remarks to all of you. Please listen . . . my countrymen . . . and heed my direction! Naomi and Eve will take the women, children . . . and dogs to the western ridge immediately. The dogs may prove to be very useful in guarding our precious ones, especially with Naomi's fine companion, Keber, setting the example. There they will remain until further notice with Naomi in charge, ready to use their weapons only as a final resort.

As for you men . . . you will be divided into four groups: those who live near the lake will be under my charge; Seth will take those who live in the meadows; Enosh, over those by the forest; Peleg and Nashor, over those who live near the fields. Cain's men, because of the lay of the land, will surely have to come through the area that has been fixed with traps. Enosh and I will combine forces and lay in wait on the east. Peleg and Nashor will be on the west and we will try to keep the men from Nod between us forcing them into the area of the trenches. Seth, you and your men will be in charge of working the net-snares to make sure that all goes as it was designed . . . and be very cautious with your every step in that place of ensnarement. And if any of our enemy fall into the pits and survive the fall, let them not avoid death a second time.

Let me add this: In just a little while we will all be facing the very real possibility of injury and even death. I know that some of you relish the thought of battle . . . I only hope that today ends all such desires. But do understand—I know Cain . . . and we either defeat these people or hand our women over to a lifetime of slavery . . . and our males, both young and old, to certain death.

These words of mine are the harshest ever to come before your hearing, but this is a time of kill or be killed! Also, understand: do not give your life in futility. By that, I mean if you are clearly outmatched or you have been injured to the point that you no longer are able to properly defend yourself, draw back toward the western ridge and wait there for further instruction. Take no unnecessary chances and do not mistake wisdom for cowardice. Once again, when all appears lost, draw back to the western ridge as a refuge of sorts! My fondest desire is to lose none of you. To those on the ridge, if you see my face before the battle's end it means we will use a plan of last resort: to move further toward the west and employ a different strategy. But *pray* for victory in our present setting!"

Facial expressions were not as before; looks of overconfidence and excitement had turned to concern and grim determination.

"They are coming!" was the shout from some of the scouts as they scampered for the perceived safety of the assembly. Gasping for air more by reason of excitement than exertion, they exclaimed, "We saw them just beyond the twin oaks at our eastern creek's bend . . . they are large and fearsome in appearance! We look as children when compared to them!"

The very few still confident, now began to have doubts.

I asked, "What was their pace? Running? Walking?"

He who brought the report thought for a moment and said, "They were walking, not fast . . . and many with a limp."

I winked at the assembly and said, "We can thank Enosh and his winged warriors for that." Smiles returned to their faces for the moment and with the men in a calmer frame of mind I offered, "Do not let their outward appearance cause you to shudder! Take heart! Remain out of their sight at first to give the traps a better chance for success, then strike! Strike the first blow at every opportunity and let them have the doubts! Now . . . each man to his place!"

Sounds of quiet encouragement came from their lips and were passed back and forth as my words seemed to have the desired effect; spirits were restored. Surprisingly, for men whose experience was limited in such matters, our movements were coordinated. I expected to see at least a few cases of awkwardness as men tripped over each other in the excitement of the action, but no; and in less time than it took to milk a goat, everyone was in place. And to a man, we were still—many of us having learned the art of stealth from hunting predators. No words were spoken, only occasional glances exchanged as though to say, "What will this day bring?" or "Why do they delay? or "They should be coming through the trees at any moment now."

The day was unusually warm and with circumstances adding to the heat, sweat beaded up on every brow. We waited and waited, patience nearly at its end for the younger ones. Their eyes implored the older ones to offer some comfort, and the older ones used outstretched hands and clenched fists as a way to say, "Be patient. Grip those weapons and hold steady."

Finally! The first sight of our enemy . . . and it was Cain at the forefront, that blood-red forehead shining bright in the sun, with all that sweat adding an unnatural gleam to the mark, making him seem even more fearsome. I have to admit that, even I was taken aback as I gazed upon the immense being not so far in front of us. Had he grown even more in his absence from Eden, or had it been so long since I last saw him that I had forgotten? When last we crossed paths, my mind entertained thoughts of being able to defeat him in battle, but doubt now took the place of confidence.

I could read the minds of our brave men as they looked at each other, their own confidence slipping: "It is true! He has the red mark put there by God! Will God still hold to the promise He gave about avenging Cain's death seven times over? Maybe there is a way to subdue him without his death, but how? Look! Many of those who follow are larger still! That west ridge may draw us sooner than hoped."

———•◦◦•———

The men from Nod soon broke into full view with Cain in the lead and Anak at his right hand. Cain held up his hand as a signal to stop. He surveyed the area, intently looking for signs of his enemy. We attempted to remove all traces of daily life in order to cause some uncertainty as to our whereabouts, doing our best to maintain any slight advantage.

Cain said, "They are near. This flat area looks to be a place of encampment; one that would serve us well. Maybe we should set up camp first and then seek our foes."

The expressions of my men ran the gamut from: "Now what will we do? Will we have to attack them as they set up camp? Has Adam made a mistake in tactics? Dare we trust him further?"

I have to admit, Cain's hesitancy caused me a few more anxious moments, and the thought of passing the word to attack on my signal came into my thinking. It was certain that none of us would watch and wait while the fearsome, dreaded foe set up camp. But fortunately, Cain reverted back to the arrogant ways for which he was known, bringing a great sense of relief to my mind . . . at least, as much relief as one can possess at a time like this.

"No. They are near—of this we can be sure. We will not give them another instant to run and hide. There are some tracks and trails heading through the middle of this area, so we will quicken the pace and attack." He displayed a rare, but gruesome grin, with nearly half of his teeth missing. In his mind was a picture of victory and annihilation of all who had been a constant irritation in his memory.

"Set a fast pace and let us overtake them while the sun is high in the sky. By evening, Adam will not have a male still breathing . . . but leave him to me! You will know him . . . he will be the old man who moves like a turtle. Follow me!" Shouts of premature triumph echoed throughout Cain's army.

Under my breath I said to myself, "Hmmph. 'Old man who moves like a turtle.' If only I can remain alive long enough to face him—even with the Divine vengeance that is sure to come to me with his death."

Led by Cain, they charged forward, right into the place of snares and pits. We held our positions and watched, inwardly smiling to see creatures so driven by foolhardiness. At first their formation was two by two, but as they entered the trees they began to spread out, which was good for us. Suddenly, screams of surprise arose from those on the right as four of their members stepped into a snare. Seth cut the vine rope and a sturdy young tree, green and ready to stand straight again, snapped into the air, taking the four bewildered young men upward before they had time to think. The wide mesh of the netting worked well as legs dangled through the open areas and vines dug into the groins of the two on the bottom. The weight of the two brothers who were on top pushed down causing intense pain for those beneath. At nearly the same instant, three more of Cain's troops shot up into the air accompanied by screams of agony and a pleading for an axe or knife to slice through the vines. By now, Cain and company were in total confusion as they saw men suspended in air by a contraption never seen in their corner of the world. So these hard-chargers now took on an attitude of caution, and steps were slow and measured. With each step they first looked up into the air then at the ground, uncertain as to which direction the danger would come.

More screams were heard as two men stepped into a trench. It was at this point that conscience played a part concerning my men. The two who had fallen into the trench, impaled on the stakes, did not die quietly or quickly. Seth and those with him saw them fall and heard their death cries, causing some discomfort in their souls. Fortunately, words of "kill or be killed" returned to their minds hardening them for the approaching struggles.

Those of Cain's men still suspended in the air, managed to wriggle and cut their way from the netting. They hit the ground in pain only to face sudden death from our spears. It was, especially at first, difficult for my men to kill—something deep within making it so. And nearly to a man, that first encounter, that first thrust of a spear, took everything they had to carry it out; but not so with Cain's men—they thrilled over every lunge and thrust—and how they rejoiced when blood was drawn.

Seth's troops performed well and with Cain's men back on their heels the remainder of my tribe attacked. We hit hard and fast and did our best to win this war in such a way so as to never need to repeat these actions; but as well as things went initially, events seemed to take a turn against us. Some of the snares did not trip as expected, and the men from Nod began to test the ground ahead with their spears, avoiding the trenches. Their size and strength and skill with a spear began to make a showing. But then . . . something happened which I thought would take much of the fight from them. During the heat of battle, Cain became careless and in his haste to deliver a death blow to Caleb, stepped into one of the trenches, plunging headfirst into the deepest of them. Several of us witnessed this and we were near to overcome by our good fortune. And my mind traveled back to that day, so long ago, that he fell into Abel's trap; that same headlong plunge. But now . . . who would be blamed for his death. I asked God to hold me accountable.

On and on the fighting went that hot, miserable day. Despite our early victories and Cain's demise, Enoch, the first-born son of Nod, along with the hulking Anak, seemed quite able to rally their men. It was almost as though the two were receiving instructions and encouragement from someone very experienced in warfare. How could these ruthless, ignorant young brutes who knew nothing but selfishness and greed take such a position of leadership and see any triumph? Their men had no allegiance toward them; none trusted Anak. Enoch might possibly have been held in a slightly higher regard. Maybe it was just the burning desire to seize Cain's place of leadership that pushed them to fight so skillfully and vigorously.

———◆•◆•◆———

From a vantage point high and far away, Satan watched the conflict with glee and did his utmost to send his guidance through the air. "If only Anak will continue to listen, relying not on his own thoughts."

The Plan of Last Resort

A t the outset of this conflict, truly wondering whether we could hold our own against Nod, I told my people not to mistake wisdom for cowardice, but early on it seemed as though we had things well in hand and that my advice was unnecessary. But the men of Nod began to recover and after observing a number of the man-to-man battles, it should have been obvious to me that momentum had shifted. But it was just too difficult to admit to myself that I was staring at the very real possibility of defeat after a victory seemed within our grasp. So with pride guiding my decision-making I watched as Hazor was struck down, then Caleb was wounded, as was Nashor. Finally, I ordered them and several others to the west ridge, though it grieved them to retreat.

Steadily, the fact that I had not listened to God's earlier instruction crept into my mind. His earlier counsel was overshadowed by a desire to win this war by my own skill; but, at present, it was plain that whatever skill had been mine was now diminished. All too quickly, pride drove me to forget the very instructions I gave to the men at the beginning, with the result being loss of life and limb for those in my care. "Fall back! Fall back to the ridge!" I shouted. The word was passed from man to man.

Enosh was against this: "Victory will yet be ours! We will defeat them!"

"I will not watch another man die because of my flawed strategies! Retreat to the west ridge!"

Lamech was at my side and had fought valiantly, but he knew the decision was correct. He offered, "These men of Nod are ignorant in many ways, but they know how to fight; through pain and injury they will fight until they are dead. And they are hard to kill. The first plunge of a spear seldom brings their last breath. And whenever they manage to get those incredibly strong hands on one of yours, the advantage is theirs."

Enosh still resisted and implored, "No! We can do this! My bow and arrow has caused much in the way of injury. And our spears have found their mark many times today. Let us fight a while longer and see if we will yet prevail!"

"Enosh . . . my son . . . you have the heart of a lion, and great faith, but those arrows of yours cause mostly injury. And like vicious animals, the men of Nod fight even harder when wounded. Death comes only after a spear is driven into their hearts—and, as Lamech said, it is not a simple matter to thrust through the massive flesh and bone of these devils. We will retreat to the ridge for now . . . but in all likelihood there will be another opportunity to fight this day." Enosh lowered his gaze in disappointment for a moment, but not a man to remain dispirited he was fast encouraged by the thought of battle at a later time.

The sons of Nod saw our retreat and their heads were as high as their opinion of themselves.

Upon my instruction we ran for the west ridge and though it looked cowardly it was the action to take at this time. We reached the ridge with its women and children and I ordered: "To the west! Toward the Garden! Quickly!"

I led the way, knowing that few, if any, could see the peril that awaited those who ventured too close to that Garden. It was not a small thing to approach this area of Eden where God had strictly forbidden us to enter; to draw near to it alone was more than I would normally risk, and now there were many involved.

As we jogged to the west, our pursuers gained ground on us, and though it was deeply troubling, I ordered that the dogs be released to attack. It would serve only to delay our enemy, but it might be just enough to make the difference. Many of the men, rather than lose their four-legged friends, desired to make a stand of sorts; willing to risk their own lives to give us needed time. But, difficult as it was to face, it was far better for dogs to die than my flesh and blood. Naomi, sadly and reluctantly, instructed Keber; others did the same with their old friends, and off they charged toward the enemy, barking and snarling, anxious for this chance to serve. As for Keber, he would have the opportunity to inflict some pain on those who had caused him pain in the past.

There was an atmosphere of melancholy over our people as we trudged onward, extreme fatigue also setting in added to the misery. In the distance, we heard the sounds of men screaming and dogs yelping and we knew that the tactic saw at least a minor victory. As to how much time we gained from it . . .

Finally, there it was! That place of beauty of which only Eve and I had intimate knowledge and fond memories. Most of the others had never even seen it from a distance because of my frequent warnings and because of a spirit of fear that seemed to emanate from this part of Eden. But on this day, fear was mixed with anticipation, making the unapproachable seem a possibility.

From our view on top of the bluff which overlooked the Garden, we were able to look into the distance behind us and see our pursuers, steadily marching. They would be upon us well before the setting of the sun. So with time now in short supply, I ordered: "Listen to me! Everyone is to run, if at all possible, to the trees at the edge of the Garden. But under no circumstances is anyone to set foot inside those trees!"

So we ran. When the children and the wounded faltered, those who were whole supported and carried them, allowing us to regain some lost ground on the foe. We reached those trees, gasping for air, desperately needing rest, but having not the time for more than a few deep breaths and some instruction.

I looked at the entrance to the Garden and encouraged everyone to pray silently for some manner of deliverance. My personal prayer was for God to allow us a temporary escape into the lush foliage. After a few moments, with my head no longer bowed and eyes now open, I once again saw that most fearsome of sights! The Cherubim—angels who guarded the way into this place—were massed and ready to strike.

Had we taken one more stride these God-appointed sentinels would have finished what Cain's men started.

So it was evident that God would not rescind His commands despite our very perilous situation. Rather than being angry, though, I reasoned within my mind: "I know that . . . down through the generations, and at various times, God has spared the people of Eden from misfortune; and I am certain that He would have little in the way of special feelings toward the Godless men of Nod . . . Surely, after all these prayers, He will not leave us to face death at their hands."

I opened up my mind in an attempt to receive guidance from the LORD, and something came to me. I took a deep breath and edged near the opening in the trees. Using my spear I made a line in the dirt, just short of the entrance. As I made the mark I could see the angels storming up and down that line, so close they could have reached out and snatched me at any moment. At first, my eyes saw the angels as they really were, large and fierce, but soon, in my mind, they began to take on the look of my most dreaded fear: serpents—gigantic, hissing snakes, ready to strike me down. My blood ran cold. But I set my jaw, forced myself to look away from them, and tended to business until the mark was in place.

That being accomplished I then gave orders—just loud enough for Eden to hear: "Men . . . listen to me. Step toward the Garden's entrance, but do not step on that mark. Again, do not step on or past the line. Trust my words, we must make it look as though we all entered. Once you have stepped forward to the mark . . . backtrack, retracing your steps; then scatter throughout the cattails. Women and children . . . backtrack now, into the cattails and hide yourselves. And remain silent at all cost! Men, once again, as soon as they are hidden, step to the mark then backtrack to the cattails."

Everyone did as charged, and we had no more than gotten out of sight when the warriors of Nod appeared at the top of the bluff. They stopped just long enough at the crest to get an idea as to our whereabouts. Seeing nothing, they hurried toward the Garden, maybe a bit surprised that they had not yet overtaken us. Cain was the only one who would have had any knowledge of this place, hearing the many stories his mother and I told, and he only saw it once from a distance when he was just a boy; but he was not now present, so his tribe was in total ignorance. Onward they came, arrogant and ready to kill even the women and children if it appeared too much trouble to enslave them.

Those next moments were not ones to be wished on anyone. If our enemy looked closely at the tracks and saw that we did not enter in, they would be suspicious and investigate the area. There would then be no choice except a fight to the death.

It is so much more difficult to be patient than to take immediate action, but to remain still and wait is the plan and we will stay with it, God willing. So after what seemed the equivalent to a hard, full day of work in the heat, we finally heard the sound of their footsteps charging along at a brisk pace. They stomped right past our hiding place and with their backs soon to us the desire to strike a surprise attack was in every man's thoughts . . . but we held our position. Anak was slightly in the lead, with Enoch close at hand, and they stepped up to, but not on, the mark. Enoch held up his hand as a sign to stop; then he dropped to one knee, examining the footprints which seemed to stop right at the opening. He said to Anak, "There is something strange here . . . notice that footprints are numerous up to here, but there is no sign of them past this point."

Anak studied the setting and offered a possibility: "There are some tree limbs in full leaf lying on the ground. Perhaps they were used to cover the tracks. I have seen that trick used on two or three occasions . . . with success."

By now the troops were extremely anxious to continue the chase, displaying it by banging foreheads, thumping their chests, and yelling words of encouragement back and forth. So intense was their desire— like wild dogs ready to begin the hunt for prey—jumping and pacing, unable to remain still, in action or word. Anak, with his head cocked to one side, appeared to be listening to something . . . or someone . . . but with the noise of the impatient troops and their incessant, eager challenges to each other and their leaders, Anak became flustered. Seeing that the big man was disconcerted Enoch shouted to him: "I am not certain as to the best plan of action, but I could take the first three rows of men into this area and give chase! You keep one row here, for now, in case of the unexpected. You can join us after events become more predictable. I will tell you, though, at this moment there is an uneasiness inside of me . . . but the men are hungry to kill and I will not hold them longer!"

Wait Enoch! I will take the three rows of men and you will stay here. There will be no argument."

Choosing not to engage in a battle for authority at this time, Enoch deferred to his arrogant kinsman.

Now, seemingly the undisputed leader, Anak raised his fist to the screaming mob and shouted, "To the chase! Seek and slay all from Eden!"

Animal-like sounds came from them as some held their heads back and unleashed a screeching noise that began at the back of the throat and exited out the nose; and some gave out deep, guttural growls as fearsome as prowling lions. All quite unnerving to our women and children, but they managed to remain still—possibly too scared to move. I, on the other hand, broke into a smile, as though we were about to play a child's game. Lamech and Enosh saw the expression on my face and their mouths dropped open. They looked at each other, their eyes sending a message that told me their thoughts: "The heat and strain of this day has injured his mind. What a terrible time for command to be thrust upon us!"

I held up palms assuring them that all was not as bleak as they imagined. And knowing they did not see what I saw added to the sparkle from my eyes.

As Anak rushed forward a stampede followed him, running and yelling with all their might, spears and axes held aloft. They thought nothing on earth would stop them, and after they entered by several strides and no harm befell them the look of confidence on my face was replaced by bewilderment.

The angels stepped aside and let them enter. "Could it be?" I thought. "Will God allow them entrance after barring us from the same?" But I soon saw the plan of action: After the first two groups had totally committed themselves to entrance with the third close behind, the angels formed a half-circle, blocking any further advance. Then at last, those unseen became visible, and the men so eager to fight were as though they had run into a stone cliff. Heels dug in and necks were jerked backward at the unearthly sight. So sudden was their stop that those who were trailing behind ran into and over their brothers. Not yet seeing the reason for stoppage, the usual curse words spewed from their mouths, but after following the line of sight from terrified eyes, all were soon locked in place by fear. Now that Anak's men had passed the point of no return the Cherubim closed the half circle and steadily began to move in on the once-fearless warriors who now huddled together like frightened children. And just as it was with me, they saw them first, as they were—frightening enough—but their eyes soon saw what was most dreaded in each man's mind. One saw huge serpent-like creatures; another saw roaring, male lions; another saw the vicious, two-legged lizards from the swamp; still another saw a blazing fire ready to consume him. Whatever was looked upon as torturous and frightening—the things of night dreams—became real to them; all this added to the severity of the punishment.

Irad grabbed Sidon by the arm and shouted, "We are dead men either way, but let us run and at least have some hope!" Off they scurried through the only opening left to them, towards the middle of the Garden. Two of the Cherubim broke away from the formation to follow.

That small opening quickly closed to all the others and they fell on their faces. The guardians had waited long to be put to any kind of test and they would now fulfill their sworn duty. What they were about to do would be a witness to all men who might ever again venture to this site. With the remnants of Nod, and much of Eden watching, the angels tore into flesh and blood. No animal on earth could have slaughtered with such speed and efficiency. The men were torn apart so quickly the feeling of pain—if they felt anything at all—was momentary. The grisly sight before us left even the men from Nod feeling a bit queasy. Then, just to ingrain the lesson a little deeper into our hearts, beams of light, bright as the sun, shot forth from the angels' outstretched hands, disintegrating the remains strewn on the ground, leaving the Garden as it was . . . before the trespass.

The men left in Enoch's care fell to their knees, moaning and crying, begging their commander to lead them out of that awful place. To my great amazement, though he was shaking with fear, he told them: "Irad and Sidon broke free of the others. We will wait for a while . . . to see if they return."

———————◆•◦•◆———————

From an observation point high in the sky the demons watched much of the battle. They cheered wildly whenever a man from Eden was injured or killed, and they remained silent at the death of those from Nod—though they were not totally dissatisfied at the death of any human.

At Cain's demise Satan openly displayed frustration and he deemed the battle all but lost because of Cain's "incompetence and awkwardness." Though he saw some success sending commands through the air to Cain, sadly that would no longer be an option. But then, Anak took charge, and Satan, with renewed interest, poured his skill as a military tactician out through time and space, into the open, ambitious mind of another son. And it worked quite well and saw great achievement, until the episode at the Garden. Satan could see the angels at the entrance and tried to warn Anak, but distractions proved too much for the young fool.

Seeing that his guidance went unheeded, Satan knew that something had gone awry. Once more, in a final act of desperation, he and his followers tried to take part in the battle, ramming into the invisible barrier again and again, wanting so very much to fight against the Cherubim. This time, it did not take as long to see their futility and one by one, beginning with Satan, they flew away to deal with this shattering disappointment, each in his own way.

———————◆•◦•◆———————

Genesis 3:24 After He drove the man out, He placed on the east side of the Garden of Eden cherubim and a flaming sword flashing back and forth to guard the way to the tree of life.

The two terrified men ran through the foliage, stumbling and falling over every vine and unseen limb, running with no plan in mind except to escape what was behind them. Soon, a flashing light from the only open area attracted their attention and they made directly for it. Their pace slowed a little as they drew closer to the source of the light. It was a weapon of some kind, bright and flaming; unlike anything they had ever seen. Swiftly it moved, covering the area all around the tree first; next, the branches and the trunk; then back to the area around the tree, completing the circuit in a flash. The two now came to a complete halt captivated by the sight.

"The weapon glows with beams of sunlight, and flames of fire are through it and around it," said Irad.

"Tubal-Cain has tried to melt rock and create a similar thing, but he has not seen success," replied an awestruck Sidon.

"Why does it protect the tree?"

"It is as though it has a mind and moves as a living creature. And it does appear to guard the tree! But why?"

"Let us draw closer, Sidon."

"No, wait! Let us study it from this distance. I have yet to see anything in this place to stir feelings of assurance within my being."

Irad chose to listen to the sound advice of his brother and together they sought answers by logic. But the longer they looked, admiring the tree and everything about it, the stronger their desire to investigate became.

"Irad, look at the size and shape of the tree, unlike any in Nod. It is perfect in form and seems to have an abundance of fruit of some sort. And that hint of fragrance in the air . . . perhaps we could nudge in a little closer to gain a bit more information."

The men drew steadily closer, attracted beyond normal curiosity; finally stopping about ten steps short of the far-reaching limbs.

Irad carefully watched the sword as it made its rounds, trying to discover a pattern so that he might find an opportunity to touch the beautiful, dark, red fruit that filled the branches. "Sidon, watch! When the weapon reaches the uppermost limbs it tarries there briefly . . . just long enough for me to seize some of the fruit."

"No! You will not have time! And if you did manage to come away with even one, would that which guards the tree permit you to escape? Think about what you are planning!"

Irad gave the matter some thought, but he was not in the habit of denying himself, and temptation in this case was more than he could resist. He waited and watched for the sword to reach the upper limbs where it tarried as before; and just as his legs began a forward bound Sidon leaped in front of him and took hold of one of the red gems hanging within easy reach. Filled with anger, Irad was near to spearing his brother, but he was brought back to his senses by the look on Sidon's face. His expression was like one in intense pain. He hand had grasped the fruit and was now locked onto it, unable to break free. No sound came from him, but his face contorted, and his body at first shook, then went rigid. Irad gave a thought to pulling his brother free, but before he could act on the impulse the sword broke its pattern and raced down to the intruder. In a matter of moments it passed over Sidon's body, slicing into the outer layer of skin and shaving every strand of hair as it went from the scalp to the toes, leaving not so much as an eyelash. On the next pass, the sword burned his skin stopping the flow of blood, but instead of blackening the hide it was made a bright white, looking as though he went through a purification of sorts. Then, Sidon's face went expressionless, his eyes stared straight ahead but saw nothing and his rigid body was lifted from the ground into a horizontal position. Slowly, feet-first, he was pulled into an area of the tree where the leaves and branches were so thick that the only human witness lost sight of the body. Irad's legs were locked in place and his eyes were fixed through all of this. He was unable to run and unable to look away. He just stood there, helplessly watching as Sidon's face regained awareness near the end; and with a last look that begged for help he disappeared into the dense foliage. Irad, sickened that he had no help to give, finally regained the ability to move, and he began stepping backward as he saw the sword move toward him.

One of the two angels who followed was about to destroy the lone survivor, but his companion stopped him, saying, "We are not to take the life of this one. A witness is necessary in order to make certain that no man comes here again . . . ever."

As the sword menacingly continued on its path toward Irad he turned and ran faster than ever before, not daring to cast a glance over his shoulder and never knowing that the sword stopped and returned to the tree.

He had made several decisions that day—some wise, and some unwise—but the two decisions to run were far and away the wisest; and he raced on toward the Cherubim caring not a whit about the trouble he had faced earlier at the entrance. He only knew that despite the first nightmare, there was something about the danger behind that terrified him even more. So he continued with the frantic pace and the exit quickly came into view along with Enoch and his fellow soldiers. If only he could escape this place of death before his legs and heart faltered. The Cherubim had been instructed to allow him safe passage and they obeyed as ordered, stepping aside as he mindlessly sprinted through their midst and out of the Garden.

His legs gave out a few strides before reaching Enoch causing him to fall face-first; but so great was his fright he clawed the ground and managed to get to his knees, crying hysterically and babbling something about a tree that consumed Sidon. Enoch reached down and pulled him to his feet. Irad grabbed Enoch by the shoulder (a bold move, but allowed this one instance) and tried to relate the story, but was too exhausted. His eyes rolled partially back into his head and he collapsed right there. The troops nearest the fallen man looked at each other in disbelief and said that he was delirious or crazed. Enoch looked them in the eye and said, "After all we have witnessed here, how could you doubt his words?"

At any time in the past Enoch would have taken the remaining troops and left the man on the ground, but for some reason he ordered two men to aid the poor wretch and follow as they made their retreat. Maybe he wanted to hear more as to what Irad saw, or maybe . . . with Cain out of the way, he was a different man. Either way, Enoch led the army of Nod back up the bluff fully intent on returning to their homeland—and for once, there was not a word of dissent. And the two men assisting Irad did not fall behind even an iota as they charged up that hill, energy flowing to every muscle in their body, especially the leg muscles.

I gave the order for everyone to get to their feet and follow after our adversaries, just to be certain they truly were on their way back to Nod. Some of the men, in their eagerness, wanted to make haste and re-engage them in battle, but by the time we reached the hilltop they were far ahead of us and there was no need to further exhaust ourselves. And really, that was a blessing as I had little desire to continue the fight.

While we walked along there was joy in our hearts as we gave thought to our great victory, but we were too weary to do any cheering; then we came upon the bodies of our animal friends and our joy was dampened. Naomi's eyes scanned the area for Keber but did not see him. With darkness closing in, it was decided to go home first and wait until tomorrow to care for the dogs.

Despite the darkness and their fatigue, most of the men wanted to follow Nod's army at least to Eden's eastern edge where there was that high ridge that would offer a good look into the distance. They would remain there for the night standing guard and checking for distant torches and campfires. That seemed to me a wise move and they went with my blessing, but I told them that a few needed to remain at our main campsite to help me start some fires, in order to keep wild animals away from the bodies of our fallen members. Lamech and Enosh gladly volunteered, and Seth led the rest of the men to the east.

I ordered the women and children to get to their homes for food and rest . . . and most of them obeyed wholeheartedly; but Eve, Naomi, Adah, and Rachel wanted to assist me and I did not refuse their offer. So with the help of the two young men and the four women, we soon had flames blazing away in a number of well-placed areas. And with the fires now burning bright the women searched for more firewood. I thanked the young men and suggested they travel east to keep watch with their brethren. I told them that all was now well and they assured me that in the morning they would be ready to take care of burials.

After the women supplied several batches of limbs and smaller logs they went back into the brush one last time just to be certain of having enough wood. I fed the closer fires first then carried some wood to one of the more distant blazes. On my way toward it, I saw Rachel stumble out of the edge of some timber not far from the perilous trenches. She was beyond tired and I called to her, "Rachel, sit down and rest until my return! Those trenches are no place for a tired person! Just rest . . . and do not deny yourself a well-earned sleep."

Rachel, too tired to shout, weakly replied, "Yes father. I will wait for you." And she waved her hand to indicate that all was well, then plopped down on the ground in a sitting position. I smiled to myself and continued on my way to feed the next blaze.

As she sat there enjoying the light and warmth of the nearest fire and the evening's peace, her chin began to drop to her chest. She took no notice of the shadowy figure that emerged from out of the deepest trench. For a large creature it moved along quietly, until it was only a few paces behind her. Finally, there was the snap of a twig and Rachel heard it, but was not concerned, as she was certain that all danger was past. She supposed it was probably one of the women with a load of wood. The figure stopped momentarily waiting for her chin to, once again, touch her chest. It soon did and slowly the figure took another step, and then another. Just one more step and it would be in the perfect position . . . but a dead twig snapped again and with all that weight standing on it the noise was loud enough that she whirled her head around in time to see the frightening face of Cain. She gave out a high-pitched scream but it was cut short as he grabbed her from behind and placed his grimy, gorilla-like hand over her mouth. I was busy with the fire and thought the sound came from some type of animal.

Though she struggled Cain held her tightly, enjoying the touch of her flesh. And in a whisper he rambled on with words that meant nothing to her, "When I fell into that hole, head and shoulders first, somehow landing between the stakes, I knew there was a reason. So I stayed there throughout the battle, confident of victory, but in the event of a defeat, I reasoned to catch Eden at a weak point . . . in the darkness. Ah, if only I could kill Adam . . . then silently find my way through the paths of Eden and back to my homeland where I could regroup and rebuild the forces of Nod. Even if it took two more generations . . . I could come back here and finish that which was started. But as I sat in that trench with dead men on each side, wondering how much longer my patience could possibly hold out . . . I heard your voice. I heard your voice and my heart leaped in my chest. After all this time . . ."

As he spoke those last words his mind drifted into thoughts of what life would be like having Rachel for his very own and his grip loosened . . . and loosened enough that Rachel bit into his fingers with all her might. Cain instinctively pulled his hand from her mouth—just long enough for her to scream again. He then slapped her hard across the face, silencing the scream and knocking her to the ground, unconscious.

This time, I heard well enough to know it was a woman's scream and ran toward the place where Rachel last sat near the fire. As the fire's glow came into sight, I saw the shape of a large man carrying something over his shoulder. "What could this be?" I thought. "After all we have been through this day, surely it is just my tired mind?" I shook my head to clear any dullness from my sight, but the vision was real. It was Cain carrying Rachel. I ran toward him, blocking his path from any further advance, somewhat startling him; to the point he threw her to the ground and readied his spear. With a low, animal-like growl he prepared to do battle, not recognizing me at first. Then his eyes took on a look of recognition and his stance relaxed. He tilted his head back, a slight smirk parting his lips as he looked down at me.

"Well . . . after all this time will I now have this pleasure? You know, Adam, I may have to take another look at this God of yours. He has kept me from death in the trench, dropped Rachel right into my hands, put this red mark on my forehead to protect me . . . and now look. I will have the pleasure of slaying the one whose memory has tormented me for generations and driven me to battle this day."

"You needed not my memory to drive you to kill. You kill because you derive pleasure from it, and you gain power from it. Pleasure and power . . . the only two things that ever drove you. And if you do manage to kill me, how will you ever slip past the men of Eden who are between you and the land of Nod?"

"Do I hear doubt in your words? You said 'if.' That is not the man I remember. He would never have entertained the possibility of defeat in battle. No, Adam, I will carry Rachel along paths that I remembered from my boyhood and I *will* "slip past the men of Eden." And if by chance any of them meet me along the way . . . they will wish they never had."

"You are still the same arrogant, boasting, murderer that was forced from this land so long ago. Well, let us see if your fighting ability has kept up with your boastful mouth."

There truly was some doubt in my mind as to whether I could defeat the first son. He had gained much in the way of muscle after he left to dwell in Nod, and it would take all my skill to have any chance against him, beginning with the skill of provoking an opponent into a mistake. With a look of hatred flashing out of his eyes he rushed at me with a quickness that was not present in earlier days. I jumped to the side and as he flew by I hit him in the back of the head with the butt of my spear. He sprawled face-first and was slightly stunned, so I leaped on his back and placed my spear under his chin, pulling back with all my strength, certain that his airway was shut off and victory was mine; but he threw me off as I would a child.

This time, I was stunned, not by a blow but by the experience of fighting against a being who possessed such power. We both jumped to our feet and he coughed and spit a few times while I regained my breath. My next move was to edge closer to the fire believing that to find an opening I would need every bit of available light. After spitting one last time he calmly remarked, "That was a good move for one so old. I will not make that same mistake again."

Rachel regained consciousness and I shouted, "Rachel, run to the woods and find the others; then hide until morning."

Cain growled, "You stay there or I will make you sorry you were born!" Frightened, she hesitated for a moment, then, regaining her senses decided she would take her chances in the brush, leaving Cain to spew out all manner of threats.

I bluffed a charge in his direction causing him to re-focus on battle. His face took on a slightly different expression, still of hatred, but now mixed with determination. In his younger days with a chance to gain a prize such as Rachel, rage and pride would have driven him to rush

225

his opponent time after time, but evidently, in the art of battle and temperament he had made improvements. He crouched low this time, positioning his spear so that he had more control. We faced each other, circling slowly, each of us looking for an opportunity. At one point he was very near the fire and I thought about throwing my spear at him to possibly knock him into the blazing, red-hot timbers, but if I missed . . . all would be lost. We were closer now, and along with other doubts I had a clear view of his spear. It looked like the lower limb of a fair-sized oak. Even if he missed with the point, the sheer weight of it would break bones with a glancing blow. And Cain seemed to recognize my fading confidence and that faint smile appeared on his face once again. I had to take a risk, something unexpected, so at another point when he was very near the fire I charged forward and reared back as though to throw my spear. It caught him by surprise and he stumbled backward, dropping his weapon and falling into the edge of the flames, then rolling out with a quickness unusual for a man of that size. While he was on the ground I ran forward and jammed my spear downward toward the soft flesh of his mid-section. He caught my spear just as the point touched his flesh, stopping its downward plunge an instant short of serious injury. Despite my strongest efforts, he pulled the spear out of my hands leaving me at a grave disadvantage. He then broke it over his knee and threw the two pieces into the fire. To my surprise, he left his spear where it lay and began a slow, purposeful walk toward me.

I said, "Well, my first son . . . are you not one who still has a fit after every set-back?" There was irritation in his eyes, but I saw it more at the moment he heard the term "first son." The other words did not appear to have much effect.

"I know not how to answer that, Adam . . . you see, I have not known defeat since the last time we fought, when I was but a boy. Since those days I have grown physically, and learned much in the art of battle . . . and survival. To remain the leader in my country a man has to be strong, quick-thinking, and skillful in combat."

"The former and latter I can imagine, but the middle trait is one that brings doubt to my memory."

Cain's eye brows came together for a bit while he pondered those words, their meaning becoming clear to him in less time that I would have thought. His expression immediately changed from one in deep thought to fury. The insult had the desired effect in that he lunged at me with outstretched arms which allowed me to use his weight against him by grabbing his wrist and throwing him to the ground. Of course, the man was so heavy I could not throw him far, even with my vast experience in the field of wrestling; so he was not injured with the fall. He got to his feet as speedily as did I and, once again, managed to gain control of his temper.

"Well done again . . . Adam. But that was your last victory, and you did not gain much by it. This time all the skill in Eden will not benefit you to the least degree."

I now sensed that he was correct in his assessment because fatigue was having its way with me . . . and it was a type of tired that does not go away with a few deep breaths and moment or two of inactivity. So I chose not to expend my strength casting further insults toward him. I had barely enough left on his next charge to step aside and drop under a swinging fist. That created just enough time to run toward the fire and make a grab for his spear; and though it might not be considered right or fair this was no game with rules to follow; much more was at stake here than just my life. Reaching the spear a few steps ahead of Cain I bent down and grasped it, surprised at its weight and how difficult it was for my smaller hands to get a tight hold on it. As I turned to wield it, the slight delay brought on by my lack of familiarity allowed Cain to be on me quick as a cat; and he displayed not a sign of fatigue. Again he pulled a spear away from my hands and again, instead of using it, threw it behind him. He meant to kill me with his bare hands and all I could do was look at the ground for a rock or stick, anything to slow his momentum; but there was nothing and he soon had me cornered at the fire. He swung that huge right hand at my head, catching just the crown as I dipped under, but it was enough to knock me to the ground where he landed on top of me driving what little wind was left out of my chest. He placed those hands around my neck and began to squeeze. I bit and clawed and squirmed, but it all proved to be of no effect, and soon, even by the light of the fire, darkness began to settle around me.

Cain, knowing death and victory were near, seemed somewhat saddened rather than jubilant. But despite this momentary spirit of weakness—as he would define it—he would carry out the action to completion. He looked straight into my eyes and softly said, "Goodbye . . . my father." That was the only time anything resembling remorse ever came from his lips.

As awareness slipped away from my being, an unfamiliar sound came to . . . what was left of my hearing. It could best be described as a pfft, followed by a thud. Cain's grip loosened, and after a few moments his hands left my neck completely, and he struggled to his feet. Light began to return to my eyes, and though it was a struggle at first I was soon able to take a deep breath. Pulling myself up to one elbow, gasping and coughing, I stared at the man who nearly took my life. Why did he spare me? His brow furrowed, there was a look of fear and bewilderment on his face. His eyes were focused on his chest where an area of the skin protruded. He placed his fingers on the mysterious bulge and squeezed. Blood and a small stone point broke through the skin, and Cain now became panicked, conscious of a burning pain all through his thick chest. He had no idea as to how this *thing* lodged itself in his body, but he instinctively understood that, this time, there was cause for alarm. But how? He looked around and, at first, saw no one. Then he heard footsteps running, and there was Enosh, carrying a strange looking piece of curved wood. Surely that was not the reason for his pain? He dropped to his knees and in his torment shouted, "I have the red mark on my head! No man, or animal can kill me!" He clutched at the object on his chest and pulled, but succeeded only in causing more pain. He fell on his side, writhing and kicking, trying to reach the middle of his back where the object entered, but he could not. Finally, with one last surge of strength, he managed to get to his knees, where he glared at the two of us in total disgust; then, as a last act grabbed at the ground, took a handful of dirt and looked longingly at it, watching it sift through his fingers as he remembered working the fertile fields of Eden in his youth. When the last bit dropped from his hand he fell on his face and breathed his last. By the glow of the fire we gazed in amazement as the marked forehead steadily faded, and then disappeared. I was not certain as to what, if anything, this might mean. But seeing that mark disappear reminded me that God's hand was in all this, and I knew that through this entire encounter of defending myself against Cain's relentless assaults, my mind was too overwhelmed to seek God's guidance. So now . . . with Cain's death coming at the hands of Enosh, I fell to my knees and prayed: "Gracious God, do not hold this against Enosh! Allow the punishment to fall on me—no matter how severe." I waited, but heard nothing . . . and felt nothing . . . nothing in the way of pain or comfort. Then a voice came to me, "I guided the arrow's path, therefore no punishment will be forthcoming." At that, I fell from my knees to my face and voiced my gratitude.

After a bit, though every muscle in my body was quivering with weakness, a helping hand from Enosh made it possible for me to get to my feet. Enosh, seeing that no harm had come to him from Cain's death, excitedly said, "Father, I did it! My bow and arrow did what nothing else could do!"

I took on a serious expression and said, "Where is your spear?"

His enthusiasm dampened, he looked at the ground and softly said, "I stepped into a grove of trees to relieve myself and . . . well . . . I left it leaning against one of the trees."

Somehow, I managed to keep that stern expression and continued, "What are you doing here? Were you not supposed to be with the other men . . . guarding our eastern border?"

"Lamech was troubled in spirit and suggested that I return to our camp to make certain no harm had come to you."

"I see. Lamech must believe himself to be something of a seer. Now . . . what would you have done if your arrow had missed?"

Enosh, seeing a twinkle in my eye said, "I had a plan in mind to run down here and push Cain away from you; to challenge him myself knowing that he was near to exhaustion from the great battle you had waged."

We looked at each other for a moment and burst into laughter. Oh, it felt so good to laugh again!

Enosh put his hand on my shoulder and said, "Are you now willing to admit that the bow and arrow has potential?"

I chose not to tell him of God's intervention in the matter, the young man was so enthused with his invention and had suffered my skepticism and the ridicule of others. "I will admit that it has *potential*, Enosh. Continue to work with it until it is perfected . . . I know you will." A look of gratitude shone out from his eyes—to finally receive my blessing on a project that, initially, met with such resistance.

Then he asked about his wife, Rachel, and it dawned on me that the women were still in the woods. I looked at Enosh and said, "Let us, somehow, get the body over to the trench."

He wrinkled his nose and retorted, "I say we leave him here and let the birds of the air and the wild animals feast upon him!"

"No. Your mother still holds a love for him and it would be better that she not see him like this. My guess is that they fell asleep, making it hard for Rachel to find them, but they may appear at any moment." So each of us grabbed a leg and pulled him to the place where he hid throughout much of the battle. And had the ground leading to the trench not been slightly downhill, it might have made a challenging task impossible; but we proved ourselves up to it on this occasion.

With Cain's body now at the edge of the trench, we stopped to regain our breath. As we struggled for air and wiped the sweat from our brows the distant sound of footsteps on dry leaves and limbs came to our hearing. "Quickly!" I said. "We must get him out of sight!"

We shoved with all our might and once the massive upper body began to fall the lower portion easily went with it. And this time, judging by the sound, the stakes did what they were designed to do. He would not rise again.

Enosh asked, "Should you offer a prayer for him? He was your first-born."

Without hesitation I said, "No. I have no inclination to do so and he would despise the gesture. And since there was not a single instance of repentance at any point in his life, it would be a waste of time, spiritually speaking."

After saying this, Naomi burst out of the trees, spear in hand, ready to do battle. Eve was close behind followed by Rachel and Adah. We greeted them and they came running toward us, all quite worried.

The four of them speaking at once, asked all the usual questions along with providing us many hugs and loving touches. Finally, I quieted them and pretended to be irritated asking, "Where have you been? Surely you did not fall asleep at such a time when my life was in great danger?"

Eve recognized and did not appreciate my playfulness at this time, and pointing her finger in my face let her feelings be known: "I want you to understand, Adam, that while you men were fighting, we women watched from that ridge with no outlet for our frustrations and fears. What would be the end of it all? If our men were killed would we have to watch as our children were taken from us or murdered before our eyes? And what would be our fate? Were we willing to become slaves or should we fight to the death or . . ."

At this point I put my hand over her mouth to silence her and softly said, "It is finished. The victory is ours. God was merciful to us." I hugged her tightly and added, "Now, get some sleep and Enosh and I will tend the fires until morning."

Enosh and Rachel walked together, a short distance away, reliving the events of the day and evening. Eve and Adah walked to our dwelling to rest, while Naomi decided to stay and assist with the fires. The three of us were too tired for sleep, so along with tending the fires and keeping watch over our fallen warriors we spoke of many things: olden times, Enosh's bow and arrow, all the things we needed to do to get life back to the way it should be.

The Future—Near and Far

L ater in the day we buried our dead, gave thanks for their service, and prayed over them. Next, we threw the men from Nod into the trenches and filled them in, not really desiring that they have a burial, but believing it the safe thing to do lest some of our own make a slip and suffer needlessly. After that, we searched for our dogs and buried them. Three were still alive, injured but they recovered. Keber was not among any of them and our hopes were high, but we soon found his remains not far from our campsite. He had crawled a good distance before death took him. Of course, Naomi was greatly saddened, but some time after this, one of the three survivors had pups which bore a strong resemblance to Keber. Naomi claimed them and taught them how to guard our livestock and families against the ever-present danger of predators.

Naomi lived out the remainder of her days with Eve and me. She was a very wise woman and a tireless worker. Several of the men wanted her for a wife but she had no desire to ever be married again.

Lamech and Adah were married, and I performed the ceremony. They stayed with us many weeks learning more of our ways . . . and God's ways. After a time, they thought it best to return to Nod, not wanting to mix Cain's line with our own, and desiring to take our teachings with them in the hope of changing the minds and hearts of Nod's people.

Over the course of my remaining days we saw them on three occasions. During the last visit they told us that it took much in the way of patience, but nearly a third of their countrymen had become so impressed with Eden's customs that they also made some changes—even Enoch. The vast majority, though, held firmly to their old habits, refusing any change, thus guaranteeing that Cain's rebellious ways would not be lost. (Generations later, at the time when Noah built the ark, the Great Flood wiped out Cain's line . . . or so it was thought; but actually, Noah's son, Ham, married a woman born in Nod, though no one knew it at the time.)

Thorns grew up all around the Garden, so thick that no army of men, were they so inclined, could have hacked their way through it. (The Great Flood later destroyed it.)

Eve was taken from me when she was about 500 years of age (God explained to me the concept of months, years, decades, centuries, and such) and since I was ill at the same time it stood to reason that my life would soon be finished. But for whatever reason, the Heavenly Father elected to keep me on the earth for another 430 years. I swear to you, the reader, that those days without my best friend were so lonely. Each day brought to my mind the memory of that first day—the day when I first saw her—and we were the only people. But my experience and knowledge in all earthly and spiritual concerns proved quite valuable to Eden, so I understood God's way of thinking in the matter—though I often asked to be reunited with my wife. Thankfully, Naomi was present to ease the loneliness.

Finally, after living a number of years with gray hair, aching bones, and an ever-increasingly bent body, my request to exit this earth was granted. Oh, what a day! Angels escorted me into the presence of God and I heard His voice, powerful but not threatening, say: "Welcome good and faithful servant." I wholeheartedly fell on my smiling face, so grateful to have existed so as to experience that moment! An angel pulled me to my feet and motioned toward a line of people, Eve at the beginning, and I kissed her lips and held her for a very long time. Abel patiently waited through the husband and wife reunion and I gave him a manly hug and a pat on the back. The two of them stood beside me, Eve on my right and Abel on my left, as I shook hands with many of my children, grand-children, and so on. And somewhat to my surprise, there were also some people from the land of Nod. Judging by earthly time, this must have taken a full day, but we were not tired and we had no wish to hurry through warm words and loving exchanges.

So for the most part, my existence in Eternity has been nothing but peace and comfort, though from time to time I have been troubled by the thoughts of my failure in the Garden. But writing this story has already eased my pain considerably; and very soon, I believe, all remembrance of my shortcomings will be in the very distant past.

In closing, many years after my departure from the earth a very wise man, King Solomon, wrote in *Ecclesiastes 1:9 What has been will be again, what has been done will be done again; there is nothing new under the sun.* Ah . . . but there was a time when all things were new!

The End

CPSIA information can be obtained at www.ICGtesting.com
Printed in the USA
LVOW132346120613

338284LV00002B/3/P